MINU

Nicholas Blake, Laureate Cecil ... was born in County Laois, Ireland ... in 1904. After his mother died in 1906, he was brought up in London by his father, spending summer holidays with relatives in Wexford. He was educated at Sherborne School and Wadham College, Oxford, from which he graduated in 1927. Blake initially worked as a teacher to supplement his income from his poetry writing and he published his first Nigel Strangeways novel, *A Question of Proof*, in 1935. Blake went on to write a further nineteen crime novels, all but four of which featured Nigel Strangeways, as well as numerous poetry collections and translations.

During the Second World War he worked as a publications editor in the Ministry of Information, which he used as the basis for the Ministry of Morale in *Minute for Murder*, and after the war he joined the publishers Chatto & Windus as an editor and director. He was appointed Poet Laureate in 1968 and died in 1972 at the home of his friend, the writer Kingsley Amis.

ALSO BY NICHOLAS BLAKE

NICHOLAS BLAKE

Minute for Murder

VINTAGE BOOKS
London

Published by Vintage 2012

2 4 6 8 10 9 7 5 3 1

Copyright © Nicholas Blake 1947

First published in Great Britain in 1947 by Collins Clear-type Press

Vintage
Random House, 20 Vauxhall Bridge Road,
London SW1V 2SA

www.vintage-books.co.uk

Addresses for companies within The Random House Group Limited
can be found at: www.randomhouse.co.uk/offices.htm

The Random House Group Limited Reg. No. 954009

A CIP catalogue record for this book
is available from the British Library

ISBN 9780099565574

The Random House Group Limited supports The Forest Stewardship
Council (FSC®), the leading international forest certification
organisation. Our books carrying the FSC label are printed on FSC®
certified paper. FSC is the only forest certification scheme endorsed
by the leading environmental organisations, including Greenpeace.
Our paper procurement policy can be found at:
www.randomhouse.co.uk/environment

Printed and bound in Great Britain by Clays Ltd, St Ives plc

CONTENTS

CHAPTER I

THE CLEANER rose from her knees, collecting bucket, brush and duster, and creaked towards the door. There, as usual, she turned, beamed, said, " Ta-ta, Mr. Strangeways, be good," before clanking off to do the Deputy Director. Mrs. Smith had been above herself ever since, two years ago, a popular actor had given a radio talk about a Mrs. Smith, a charwoman with gouty knees and a lion heart, who cleaned her Government office while the bombs whistled round her ears, and represented all the indomitable charwomanhood of Great Britain going about its task with a heartbreak in its collective bosom and a racy Cockney joke on its lips. Mrs. Smith had taken the tribute as a personal one, treating her Government gentlemen thereafter with an easy camaraderie for the higher grades and a certain hauteur for the lower.

Nigel Strangeways, as usual, blew the dust off his desk, and emptied yesterday's cigarette stubs out of the window. It was nine in the morning. He liked to start work early, before the telephone and his colleagues could interrupt. Until ten o'clock the Ministry of Morale would be silent, but for the clankings of the Mrs. Smiths and the furtive scurryings of a few conscientious junior officers not yet affected by the slackening of morale which had set in since V.E. Day. Nigel drew out a sheet of draft photo-captions, composed by Brian Ingle.

Swift and inexorable as a sheaf of arrows flung from the hand of Nemesis, he read, *these Spitfires are pranging German rail traffic concentrations in the Gelsenkirchen area.*

He altered " pranging " to " attacking." He scribbled

in the margin, " Arrows are not flung by hand." He glanced at the photograph to which the caption was keyed and added, " They are Typhoons." Good old Brian, he thought : incurably inaccurate ; invincibly romantic ; never at a loss for the wrong word, the muddled metaphor —what should we do without him ? Poor old Brian, after five years of it still bringing to the labours of caption-writing the same luscious and uncritical enthusiasm which before the war had made him the ace novel reviewer of the *Sunday Clarion*. Clever of Jimmy to pick him for the job. But Jimmy *was* clever at picking his staff. That's what made him a first-rate Director. " No," he had said firmly at the start, " I don't want advertising men for my Division. I want people who believe in what they are saying. We shan't sell this war to the public with our tongues in our cheeks." And how right he was. When Brian Ingle told the public that a squadron of Spitfires (or Typhoons) were a sheaf of arrows flung from the hand of Nemesis, the public believed him, the appropriate response was registered once again : a just war. Nigel took his indiarubber and rubbed out " Arrows are not flung by hand."

The door opened. A Messenger shambled in, his arms heaped with files and letters. As usual, he looked help-lessly about him, then moved with the compulsive gait of a sleep-walker to Nigel's desk, placed a selection from his burden in the Out-tray and remarked dismally that it was a beautiful morning for the time of year. As usual, Nigel moved the pile of documents from the Out-tray to the In-tray. Yes, it was a beautiful morning, he agreed, glancing at the rent in the opaque material which the Office of Works had pasted over the window frame when the glass was shattered by a flying bomb.

" We've not seen the half of it yet," said the Messenger darkly.

" The half of what ? "

" You mark my words, sir. When peace comes, as you might say real peace, there'll be chay-oh in this country. Proper chay-oh."

Nigel translated rapidly to " chaos."

" What makes you think that ? " he asked.

" Stands to reason. Millions of young men trained to kill—proper artful too ; look at these here Commandos and such, unarmed combat my eye, plug 'em in the tripes with a tommy-gun more like—well, they comes back, and what do they find ? "

" Chay-oh," replied Nigel involuntarily. " That is to say——"

" You said it. Missus gone off with a chap, couple of extra nippers in the house, some embuskay sitting on his fanny in your job—what do you do ? Stands to reason. Start shooting. Violence begets violence—see Aldous bleedin' 'Uxley. Millions of 'em. Now after my war," continued the Messenger, indicating the 1914-18 medal ribbons on his dark-blue uniform, " it was different. All killed off we was. What come back, we'd 'ad enough : anything for a quiet life. Cowed, that's what we were. You may think it a 'arsh saying of mine, sir, but this war hasn't killed off enough, not on your bleedin' puff it ain't. Now take this 'ere demob scheme."

After ten minutes of social analysis, the Messenger nodded morosely to Nigel and ambled out, dropping in the doorway a large envelope marked with a red " Most Secret " tab, two files and a pink letter addressed to James Lake, Esq., C.B.E., and giving off an unofficial perfume. Calling back the oblivious Messenger, Nigel restored the large envelope and the files into his arms. The letter he decided to deliver himself : it would give him an excuse for a chat with Our Blonde.

Our Blonde, as the Director's personal secretary, Nita Prince, was called throughout the length and breadth of the Visual Propaganda Division, represented visual propaganda at its full range and dizziest peak. She combined, as Merrion Squires, the art-work Specialist, put it, the crude appeal of the poster, the mystery of the isotype, the glamour of the glossy studio portrait, the golden mediocrity of Brian Ingle's captions. In the tradition of the Visual Propaganda Division, she concealed high efficiency beneath a studied vagueness, amateurishness, insouciance. When Nigel entered, she was pecking helplessly at an In-tray brimming with documents, her bright hair tumbling over her face.

" Hallo, Nita."

She straightened up from bending over the desk, a tall, smooth-limbed creature, and gave Nigel the full benefit of her morning make-up.

" Oh, it's you," she said. " Look at this In-tray. I sometimes wonder why we go on at all."

" We go on because the British people, having unsheathed the sword, will not lightly sheathe it until, shoulder by shoulder with our gallant allies, we have slashed off the last hydra-head of the totalitarian aggressor."

" If you ask me, we don't sheathe it because a sword is a damned sight more difficult to sheathe than to unsheathe—you watch 'em trying to do it on the stage. What've you got there ? "

Nigel held up the pink, perfumed envelope.

" Another love-letter for the boss. Old Kirby dropped it in my room."

Nita Prince's ravishing face gave no hint of emotion, not even that faintest smirk of self-satisfaction which reveals the woman confident in her own power against all competitors. She was reaching out for the letter when the telephone on her desk rang.

" Hallo. This is V.P.D. Yes ? . . . No, the Director is in conference, I'm afraid. I'm his secretary. Can I help you ? . . . Oh, Mr. Snaith. Good-morning." Nita Prince rolled up her eyes in a look of mute long-suffering at Nigel, and holding the receiver away from her ear, fished in her bag for a cigarette. Nigel lit it. The telephone crackled and gobbled.

"Well," said Nita, when it was silent for a moment, " we're getting on as fast as we can with your folder. We should be able to show you pulls in a fortnight's time." The telephone came back with an atmospheric storm. "Yes, we quite appreciate the urgency. It's too bad your having to wait so long," replied Nita, in a voice like molten honey, " but there was a difficulty over a canned photograph : the Censor has not yet released it . . . What ? . . . No, the Naval Censor. *Your* Censor, Mr. Snaith "—Nita put out her tongue at the invisible Mr. Snaith, who was momentarily silenced. The atmospherics started again.

" Oh, that's another matter. You should really speak to the head of the Editorial Unit about that."

Nigel made for the door.

" An incompetent bungler ? Oh, come, Mr. Snaith ! Perhaps you'd like to have a word with him now ; he happens to be in the room . . . No ? . . . Well, I'm afraid the Director is very busy to-day. Let me see "—without referring to her engagement book, Nita reeled off a list of the Director's commitments. " To-day doesn't seem possible. And to-morrow . . . oh, you can't manage to-morrow ? Well, perhaps we'd better leave it then. You can rely on us to fulfil our dates . . . Yes, it's going very nicely. The wholesalers have ordered just over 700,000 copies already, and it's being translated into six, no eight foreign languages, I believe. . . . Yes, we'll keep you informed. Good-bye, Mr. Snaith."

" The human calculating machine," said Nigel. Then, obscurely feeling the remark to be a shade off-colour, " I just don't know how you keep all those statistics at your finger-tips."

" Oh, I forget nothing. Born that way."

" What's Snaith fussing about now ? "

" That new job in the Pacific series. Silly old hen. These Public Relations Officers ought to be blotted out. And Snaith's the worst of the whole bunch. A flea in your ear on the telephone, and a pinch on the bottom when he pays a personal visit."

" If I was a naval rating in the Pacific," said Nigel dreamily, " I shouldn't want a folder full of pictures of bamboo huts and potted Melanesian history, and how to be tactful with the natives ; I should want a folder full of huge great pictures of whopping great pin-up girls. Like yourself."

" You'd better discuss your change of policy with Jimmy, then," replied Nita, smiling faintly. " And I wish you'd go away. Haven't you any work to do ? Let's have that letter first."

Nigel flipped it on to her desk. At the door, he turned round. Nita was staring at the letter, where it lay, with a frozen look, as though it were some venomous tropical spider suddenly appeared on her desk. She quite noticeably refrained from touching it. Her fingers were locked rigidly in her lap.

" It won't bite," said Nigel from the door.

Nita Prince started. " Oh, damn you, Nigel ! Do get out or come in properly. I can't bear people standing in doorways. . . . Sorry, I'm fussed this morning. That pestilent Snaith."

Oh, no, thought Nigel, you've been dealing with Snaiths for nearly six years and not turned a hair. It's the letter. And as you haven't opened the letter, it's the hand-writing on the envelope. Someone has written to Jimmy who shouldn't be writing to Jimmy. Someone out of your past life, perhaps ? Well, let it go. It's not my business.

But Nigel's inveterate curiosity about other people's

lives would not let it go. It was the first time he had
seen the ravishing and all-conquering Miss Prince
thoroughly shaken. Even during the summer of the
previous year, when flying bombs passed as frequently
as a suburban train service over the Ministry of Morale,
and the top storey of the building jerked and swayed
with their explosions, she had remained at her desk,
taking down minutes, soothing ruffled telephone-callers,
enclosed in her usual aura of invulnerability. " Any
sensitive bomb," Merrion Squires had remarked, " would
think twice before making a date with Our Blonde." But
Squires, as he was the first to admit, did not believe in
blondes, on principle.

Sitting in his own room again, mechanically glancing
through a MS. entitled *The War Story of our Four-
Legged Friends,* which had been sent to the Minister by
an optimistic animal-lover with the request that it
should be published at the Government's expense, fully
illustrated (" I have some perfectly sweet snaps of my
own doggie, Mopkins, who has been on Active Service
throughout the blitzes, always barking to warn me when
the sirens went "), Nigel reflected how little he really
knew about his colleagues. From 1940 till a few months
ago, they had all been working their heads off—anything
from ten to fourteen hours a day—all, that is to say, but
Edgar Billson, one of the permanent Civil Servants on
the staff, who knew his rights and departed, bowler hat,
umbrella and brief-case (empty) sharp at five every
evening. But, slogging away like that, year after year,
though your fellow-sloggers became as familiar as the
face of your watch, their private lives, like the works of
the watch when it is in perfect running order, were not
disclosed. One knew that Merrion Squires disbelieved in
blondes ; that Brian Ingle had a weak heart ; that Edgar
Billson lived at Pinner ; that Jimmy Lake was married
to a nice quiet girl who gave him his head. But, now that

the worst was over, such scraps of information were not enough for Nigel's inquiring turn of mind.

For instance, was Nita Prince Jimmy's lover ? The Division, for the most part, assumed that she was. But Nigel had been much too busy to find out, and too tired to care. And had Brian Ingle, who treated her like the Holy Grail, any conception of the human being she really was ? Had Nigel himself, for that matter ? And why did Harker Fortescue, normally an uncompromising, rough-tongued man, fail to discipline Merrion Squires, who so often spoke to him disrespectfully in the presence of junior officers ? And was Edgar Billson as pompous at home as in the Ministry ?

I shall start a new file, said Nigel to himself : a Most Secret file ; a dossier on the Division. I shall see how much, during the few remaining months I have to stay in Government service, I can find out about my colleagues. And I shall put it all down in my Most Secret file. And, the day I go, I shall burn it. It will get my hand into practice again. The hour may yet strike when I shall be dabbling once more in crime. Though God forbid !

To him, at this auspicious moment, entered Brian Ingle. A smallish, fattish, fairish man, he gave the impression of always going through life at a trot. He trotted up to Nigel's desk and all but wagged his tail.

" Oh, yes, your captions," said Nigel. Ingle's brown eyes began to sparkle with a dotty kind of enthusiasm. " I've suggested one or two alterations. Those aircraft are surely Typhoons ? And——"

" Of course, of course," interrupted Brian Ingle breath-lessly. " But you like them ? On the whole ? Up to standard, you think ? Not just a leetle too, ah, rhetorical ? "

" No, they'll do very well. With the alterations I've suggested," added Nigel firmly.

Brian Ingle, he knew by experience, was in love with his own words. All of them. For ever and ever. He was quite capable of putting them back at final proof stage. It was quite a game between him and Nigel : Nigel had, in fact, invented an elaborate procedure for counter-checking final proofs, largely in order to block this manœuvre of Ingle's.

"What amazes me is how you keep it up."

Ingle perched himself on the edge of Nigel's desk.

" Keep it up ? "

" Yes. The German War over, and you turn out captions about it still with all the sacred fire of 1940."

" You're pulling my leg, aren't you ? "

" No. What I mean is, no one's going to be interested in this *D-Day to V-Day* production. The subject is dead. The public are sick of stories, photographs, exhibitions, films about the war. We're only going on with the production because the Service Departments can't fight down their lust for publicity—a lust we ourselves, I admit, were first responsible for provoking in them ; or rather, they can't bear the thought of another few hundred tons of paper not being wasted in the good old Service way, and —where was I ? "

" You'd better not let Jimmy hear you talking like that." Brian giggled. " But seriously, if you mean why do I go on putting my best into this show, when there's nothing but paper in the house—I say, rather an appropriate metaphor that ! . . . Well, I suppose the answer is that I enjoy writing. Writing anything."

Ingle had come out with this last revelation after one of those long, silent pauses for incubation, or self-examination, which contrasted so oddly with his normal brisk and breathless manner. Nigel's heart warmed to the little chap. He decided to become outrageously personal.

" And because, having moved heaven and earth to get into the Armed Forces, and been turned down every

time on your medical, you thought the next best thing
you could do was to work yourself to death here ? "

Brian Ingle was petrified for a moment with the
Englishman's embarrassment at such intimacies. Then he
unexpectedly thawed.

" Oh, nonsense. That applies to all of us, anyway.
No, the fact is I have all the creative writer's equipment,
except creativeness. Curiosity, exuberance, spiritual
stamina—the whole paraphernalia. But I can't invent.
So I became a crit—a book-reviewer. So now I write
flaming captions : the photographs supply the invention,
the ideas ; I just embroider on them."

It would have been Nigel's turn to be embarrassed, if
he had been capable of such a reaction. His habit of
regarding human behaviour with absolute detachment,
never colouring it with his own emotions and prejudices,
prevented this, however.

" You ought to get married," he pursued.

Another of Ingle's pregnant and interminable silences
followed. He seemed to be studying the suggestion, an
abstracted look in his brown eyes, from every possible
angle. Or perhaps he was merely embarrassed again.

" ' Remember thy Creator in the days of thy youth ' ? "
he replied at last. " Perhaps you're right. Trouble is, I
have rather a high standard that way. Unlike my novel-
reviewing, the high-brow boys would say," he added with
a wry twitch of the mouth.

He seemed to be on the point of further disclosures
when the door blew open as though a bomb had exploded
in the passage, and Pamela Finlay, Nigel's assistant,
rushed in.

" Morning, all ! Sorry I'm late, Strangeways. Been at
the dentist. Pheugh !—what a fug ! "

She strode past Nigel, papers fluttering off the desks
behind her, so that the long narrow room resembled a
permanent way in the wake of an express, and flung open

the double window. Standing at the window, she inhaled vigorously and sketched a few deep-breathing exercises. Brian Ingle was trotting about the room, picking up papers.

" I really think I must buy one of those sticks with points on the end that park-tidiers have," Nigel remarked mildly. " I should quite like to be a tidier of parks."

" Here are your Vallombrosa leaves, Miss West-Wind," said Brian coyly.

" Vallom——? Oh, the high-brows at it again. Shelley, huh ? T'chah ! Well, to work ! "

Miss Finlay tore off her coat in a frenzied manner, as though it was the shirt of Nessus, plumped down at her desk, and glared at the papers on it.

" Brian and I were discussing marriage," said Nigel. " In our high-brow way."

" The stroke's not on," said Miss Finlay decisively. " Not on ? "

" Not on. That is, if you're referring to Ingle's prospects. She wouldn't have him. And I may say, Ingle, if you knew what's good for you, you'd thank your stars she won't. It beats me how men——"

But Brian Ingle, colouring deeply, had snatched up his captions and photographs from Nigel's desk and scuttled from the room.

" The tactlessness of women makes my blood run cold," said Nigel presently.

" Oh, bosh ! Why can't you men ever look facts in the face ? "

Pamela Finlay plunged at the internal telephone, and proceeded to conduct one of her celebrated dual-conversation turns.

" Three five nine three . . . Everyone knows that Our Blonde . . . Hallo, Three five nine three ? Bloggs ? Mr. Strangeways' assistant speaking. Where are those proofs ? The Far East series, number four . . . is a human

B

limpet, and it's not Ingle she's fastened to . . . But you promised them yesterday. . . . However much *he* may be stuck on *her* . . . Come clean, Bloggs! Have the proof-readers started on it yet? . . . What he needs is the mother type . . . Oh, they've nearly finished? I've heard that one before . . . not the courtesan. Anyway, Our Blonde is faithful after her fashion. . . . I know you're busy; so are we: the dead-line for the printers is the 15th. Mr. Strangeways must have those proofs by mid-day sharp. If necessary, I shall come and fetch them in person."

The threat evidently sufficed. Miss Finlay slammed down the receiver while it still cackled unconditional surrender, and resumed the other branch of her conversation.

". . . After her *fashion*. Which means one man at a time. And that's all it does mean. She was supposed to be engaged to Charles Kennington when he was working here. And the moment *he* left, she was off with Jimmy. I admit she's given him a long run. Maybe he's got under her skin. But it doesn't stop her treating all the rest of you males to that enigmatic, come-hither-if-you-dare look, now and then. And you all fall for it. Poor little Ingle. T'chah! The fact is, she can't help it. Give her that."

" Well, well, well," commented Nigel.

" Go on, say it."

" Say what? "

" Say I'm jealous. Of course I, am. Any healthy woman would be. The whole of this floor buzzing with eligible males, and all of 'em buzzing round Nita. Shocking maldistribution of the basic commodities."

Miss Finlay's boisterous laugh rattled the partition walls, already much shaken by the blast of V-bombs. The usual minatory knocking sounded from the Deputy Director's room next door.

" Including Fortescue ? " asked Nigel.

" Oh, he's a deep one, is old Hark'ee."

" What I was thinking is—how little we all know about each other. Of course, the place has always been full of gossip. But it never meant much : there was no malice in it, no deep curiosity really. We've been working too hard to have strong personal feelings. Or at any rate, we've repressed them, in the interests of making an efficient Division, and helping to win the war ; and because blitzes breed a certain tolerance for one's fellow-blitzees. But now everything has slacked off, don't you think all those repressed personal feelings are going to rise to the surface ? In fact, haven't they begun to, lately ? "

" You mean, the Division has been getting bloody-minded ? "

" Some of us, wouldn't you say ? "

" Let me think."

Miss Finlay was one who commonly suited the action to the word. She knitted her brow, buried her large, fresh-complexioned face in her hands, ran her fingers through her frizzy mop of hair.

" I'm trying to remember—of course, it was the Thursday before last. It was my turn for lunch-time duty at the Divisional Call Point. Well, I'd just sat down at the telephone with my knitting, when the D.D. poked his nose through the door and said I could scat ; he'd be in his room all lunch-time and would answer any calls. I thought it a bit odd. Hark'ee doesn't usually go out of his way to pamper the lower grades. Well, I nipped back in here, and I footled about a bit ; and then, just as I was going over to the canteen, I heard a sort of shindy blowing up in the D.D.'s room. Him and—you'd never imagine who. Give you two guesses."

" General Eisenhower."

Pamela Finlay let out one of her bawls of laughter.

" Don't be an ape ! It was that twerp, Billson."

" Hark'ee slanging Billson ? Nothing odd about that. We all do. Have to keep the Permanents in their place."

" No, what was funny was that Billson seemed to be making the running. You know how correct he is. Deferential attitude to senior officers and all that. Well, he didn't sound at all deferential. Of course, I couldn't hear much of what they said, through this wall. But the tone of the voices sounded like blue murder. Billson's especially. I ought to have a blister on my ear still, the way I pressed it to the wall. I did hear Billson say, ' This is the last chance I'll give you.' And a bit later Hark'ee, very coldly, ' You're in a cleft stick, Billson, and you know it,' and then something about ' Go to the dogs, for all I care.' I got the impression that Billson was threatening the D.D. and the D.D. sort of bouncing him off good and hard."

" What fun ! Anything else ? "

" Just the name ' Prince.' It seemed to crop up quite often."

" Oh, lord ! Back to Nita again."

" Yup. And that was all. Except, when I was just toddling off to the canteen, Billson shot out of the D.D.'s room and swept past me with such a look on his face as you never saw."

" What sort of look ? "

" Absolutely furious. No, furious isn't quite the word." Pamela Finlay tousled her hair, as though searching in it for the *mot juste*. " Desperate. Like a sheep at bay," she brought out triumphantly. " So what do you make of all that ? "

" Simple. Billson discovers the D.D. is having an affair with Nita. Attempts to blackmail him. The D.D. retorts smartly that Billson is in a cleft stick, as he (the D.D.) knows for a fact that he (Billson) has a family of no less than eight illegitimate children by Nita."

The room quaked with the blast of Miss Finlay's laughter. Angry knocking again sounded from the next room. The telephone rang.

"For you," said Miss Finlay.

The voice of Harker Fortescue's secretary said :

"The Deputy Director presents his compliments, and requests that Mr. Strangeways should buy a silencer and fix it on his assistant. Also, he wants to see you after coffee. Message ends."

Not long afterwards, the rumbling of trolley wheels at the far end of the passage was heard, and a voice dismally wailing, "Coffee ! Coffee ! "

Miss Finlay gathered up two cups and hurled herself out of the door.

Nigel sipped the beverage known in the Ministry of Morale as coffee. It did not improve with the years—an almost colourless liquid, which might have been brewed from a compound of acorns, dish-cloths and wormwood. Miss Finlay, who cherished a mild, motherly affection for him, was in the habit of slipping two or three lumps of sugar from a private store into his cup ; but they did little to palliate the bitter draught.

"What I was thinking of," said Nigel dreamily, "was higher up."

Miss Finlay knitted her brow in an agony of concentration, like a child trying to do a difficult sum in mental arithmetic.

"Yes, higher up still," Nigel pursued. "Jimmy himself is showing signs of wear and tear, don't you think ? "

"I wouldn't know. Don't move at such dizzy levels myself."

"Of course, after six years one might expect it. But I don't get the impression that it's just ordinary war-weariness."

Nigel fell silent. He was thinking. Jimmy's got amazing

stamina ; he kept us all going through the worst of it.
He put the machine together and supplied the lubricant
—his tact is quite incredible—never puts a foot wrong
in dealing with his staff—and what a heterogeneous,
awkward lot of chaps we are ! But lately I feel he's been
losing his grip—not losing it, perhaps, but having to
drive himself to keep it. Distrait at times. Has to wrench
his mind back to the business on hand. Not quite so
quick and confident when there's a decision to be made.
A bit irritable, and that's the strangest thing of all in a
man who's always been so even-tempered. Well, maybe
it's just reaction after the strain. The war's nearly over :
we shall be disbanded in six months' time with any luck ;
and then he can go back to his old job and take things
easy. He's a good chap. I've got really fond of him.

Five minutes later, Nigel went next door to the Deputy
Director. Harker Fortescue, as usual, was telephoning.
He flipped a cigarette at Nigel, who plumped down in the
luxurious leather arm-chair intended for the use of only
the most distinguished visitors, and patiently waited.
He studied, more attentively than usual after Miss
Finlay's queer little story, the bald head, the dyspeptic-
ally-hollowed face, the cold and fishy eye of his immediate
superior. The façade was familiar ; it told him nothing
new to-day. He had realised long ago that it *was* a façade.
Beneath the carefully cultivated, managerial manner, the
brusqueness, the impersonal drawl of the voice, at this
moment all concentrated upon the discomfiture of whoever it might be at the other end of the line, there was
undoubtedly, however much some of the staff might take
leave to doubt it, a human being.

Nigel had discovered this human being in the course
of the bad years, when he and Fortescue toiled together,
night after night, in a dour attempt to keep abreast of
the ever-growing work commissioned from the Division
by other Ministries.

Sooner or later, often after midnight, they would repair to the canteen, staggering with weariness, and Nigel would consume a trayful of spam, pickles, bread, buns and blancmange, while Fortescue toyed with a glass of milk. It was during these collations of the small hours that Fortescue revealed his secret passion. For years and years, with the zest and maniac pertinacity of a small boy autograph-hunting, he had collected—not autographs, not stamps, not china, not furniture, not matchbox lids, nor rare moths ; but what he called " my feelthy peectures." These were not filthy pictures in the accredited sense of the term. They were snapshots of the great, the famous or the notorious, caught in ill-considered or mercifully oblivious poses—pictures taken for the most part before the advent of that universal leveller, the " candid camera." His search for such treasures had taken him all over the world : he attended auction sales and combed old junk shops to buy photograph albums. He possessed an ancient film-still showing Tolstoy brusquely rejecting a bouquet offered by his simpering wife : he possessed a snapshot of Landru being arrested ; another of Dame Melba taken from behind in the act of driving her opponent's croquet ball into a shrubbery ; another of an Archbishop, celebrated for his powerful sermons on asceticism, about to stuff his mouth with a huge forkful of caviare. He claimed—and Nigel was not altogether prepared to contest it—that the *clou* of his collection was a snapshot, taken by some icy-nerved aide-de-camp, of Hitler chewing the carpet.

All Harker Fortescue's holidays from the photographic agency, which he ran in peacetime, had been devoted to this eccentric hobby. It was a hobby, thought Nigel now, wonderfully characteristic of the boyishness, the twisted sardonic humour, the streak of fantasy which underlay the Deputy Director's working façade.

" Yes, I appreciate that," Harker Fortescue was saying.

" But it isn't quite the point. If you want to present a complete picture of tank construction, it's essential (*a*) that you do not attempt to gloss over the mistakes made in 1939-41, and (*b*) that you give full value to the contributions of the fighting soldier. That is basic "—(basic was a great word of Fortescue's managerial personality). . . . " What's that ? . . . I can only say we've been doing this work for six years and we reckon we know something about it." The Deputy Director's drawl grew more pronounced : his cold eye was fixed, hypnotically glittering, upon the invisible caller. " Of course, if you want a different kind of production, Mr. Walters, if you just want propaganda for your Minister, you can always go direct to the Print Office ; I believe they undertake that sort of thing. We don't touch it here, we've a reputation to keep up ; the public has got into the habit of expecting to hear the truth from us, within security limits of course, and our policy of giving them the truth pays good long-term dividends, I can assure you."

The Deputy Director swivelled his chair from east to south-east, a sure sign that the crisis was passing. Nigel thought, not for the first time, that in such telephone conversations Hark'ee resembled a sheep-dog, tirelessly coaxing, rounding, driving an obtuse, woollyminded flock the way he wanted it to go, and occasionally snapping at an errant hoof. He was, indeed, the perfect second-string for Jimmy, with his remarkable grasp of detail and his cold pertinacity. Jimmy supplied the originality of approach, the broad outline of policy, the tact. Hark'ee contributed the logic, the ground work and the toughness.

Harker Fortescue gently replaced the receiver. Stroking his bald head, he turned to Nigel.

" That's fixed *him*. You'd better get on with it. Prepare an Acceptance Sheet for the job. They'll send a synopsis by Monday next. Put Billson on to a preliminary survey of the photographic material. And try and keep the Art Work Unit up to your schedule this time—they're getting slack. You'll have to deal with Walters from now on, but I've broken him in for you."

Fortescue continued to fire off instructions, which Nigel, apparently asleep in the arm-chair, memorised. Fortescue had long ago given up the effort to make Nigel take notes : indeed, he derived a certain subtle amusement from asking Nigel to repeat, after an arduous conference, some prolix and boring contribution made to it by one of the committee—which Nigel would proceed to do with the unflattering accuracy of a dictaphone.

"Now let's have a look at the Project Chart," said the Deputy Director. This was a formidable document, stretching half the length of the wall, and resembling the composite fever-chart of a five-hundred-bed hospital as seen by one of the patients *in extremis*.

"Must we ? " murmured Nigel.

"What I can never get you to realise," said Fortescue, " is that someone must keep his fingers on all the strings, otherwise we get bottlenecks. It's *your* job, as head of the Editorial Unit. I'm not going to do your work for you."

"Since you mention bottlenecks," returned Nigel mildly, " I must point out that that lamentable object .on your wall, useful though it may be to *you* as a warning against delirium tremens, is inaccurate." He strolled over to the chart and stubbed his finger against a purple ink line. "This project received approval at Ministerial level on the 17th—you've only brought it up to Controller level. Slipping, Fortescue, eh ? "

The Deputy Director's mouth twitched amusedly.

"Bring me my purple ink, chump," he said to his secretary. "*And* a pen. *And* a ruler."

Before he could protract the purple line, however, the door opened and Jimmy Lake came in. Tossing a letter

on to Fortescue's desk, he gazed out of the window, hands
in pockets, his back to them.

" Am I supposed to read this ? "

" M'ph," replied the Director, without turning round.

Fortescue read through the letter with his usual
deliberation. At last he said :

" Ker-rikey ! What a story ! Stultz ! Ker-*rikey* !
You remember Charles Kennington, Nigel ? This is
from him."

" But he's dead.

" Not dead," said Jimmy Lake, still staring out of the
window. " Let Nigel read it."

The letter was on pink, perfumed sheets ; the hand-
writing—large, flowing and ornate—the same as that on
the pink envelope which had given Nita Prince such a
turn earlier in the morning. Nigel began to read.

" My dear,

" What quite impossible notepaper. The Germans
really have *wonderfully* bad taste. Looted, of course. I
mean I looted the paper from the Germans. I do *adore*
the word ' loot,' don't you ?—so forthright and masculine,
and altogether *satisfying*. Well, I've been in the Father-
land for quite a time. Such an un-solid people—when
they're not bawling, they're boo-hooing. Boo-hooing like
mad, just now. I've been doing one of my female impersonation turns, the upshot of which, after some very
vulgar and *Boys-Own-Paperish* adventures in and around
Hamburg, was that we caught Stultz. Yes, I tapped him
on the shoulder with my own lily-white hand. *Not* a
sympathetic type. Not *at all* my idea of the beautiful
blonde Nordic he-man. In fact, I quite took against
him from the start. I am told he did some most dis-
obliging things in the concentration camps, but I can't
bear atrocity stories, so let us pass on. As I say, I tapped
this unappealing Stultz on the shoulder, and I must

have tapped him a *tiny* bit *hard*, for what did he do but disgorge his little pellet of This-Way-to-Valhalla—yes, spat it out, but literally *spat* it out, so startled he was. Which was a merciful dispensation for your little Charles, as I could not sustain the spectacle of someone dying of poison at my feet, though they do say cyanide is quick, as such things go. I am sorry to harrow you with sordid and *grating* details, I'm sure your life is quite full enough of them already. What I took up the pen to relate is that I shall be home as quick as quick. I've given this letter to a *devastatingly* charming Sergeant, who is just off on leave, and he'll smuggle it out and post it in England. Little Charles will be following *hotfoot*. Expect to get back on the 20th. Ring me at Claridges then. I can't wait to hear all your news. Love to Alice. And Nita, if she is still with you. And all the boys and girls.

> " Yours affectionately,
> " BERTHA BODENHEIM
> " (alias CHARLES KENNINGTON)."

" And is he back ? " asked Nigel, after perusing this remarkable letter.

" Yes, I've just rung him up," said the Director, still staring out of the window. " He's coming along here to-morrow morning."

" We must have a party for him," Harker Fortescue said. " Was it a put-up job when he was posted ' Missing. Believed killed ' ? "

" Presumably." Jimmy turned round at last. His musing expression broke into a smile. " That letter ! Oh, my aunt, that letter ! " He began to laugh, silently shaking with laughter as his way was. He flung himself into the leather arm-chair, tears of laughter rolling down his face.

CHAPTER II

" TA-TA, MR. STRANGEWAYS. Be good," said Mrs. Smith, clanking out with her bucket and mop.

Nigel opened the window and emptied his ash-tray on to the ledge which ran the length of the building at the level of the sixth floor. Below him, in the park, the tired and discoloured plane-trees were thrashing with a gusty wind that seemed to have been blowing all summer, flinging dust from the rubble of bombed houses in the Londoner's eyes, exasperating the nerves rubbed raw by war-time danger and discomfort.

It was on this ledge, the previous summer, that Merrion Squires had established his eyrie. When the flying-bomb attacks started, a special system of warning was set up in the Ministry. A prolonged note on the buzzer indicated that a clutch of the missiles was approaching this area of London. If any of them was then plotted to be heading for the Ministry, a series of short buzzes sounded. At this signal, the staff occupying the upper floors—particularly those on the south side of the building—had been instructed to make for the emergency staircase on the north side, and go three or four flights down. A few days of this procedure, with the short alarm buzzes sounding at irregular intervals throughout the day, and the Division piling themselves down the stairway once or twice every hour, played hell with the work. The bolder spirits took to remaining in their rooms unless the roar of the flying bomb came too near to be ignored.

At this stage Merrion Squires had set up as an independent spotter.

28

" I do like to be able to see what the doodlebugs are doing," he said.

Accordingly, when a general alarm sounded, he crawled out of his window and sat on the ledge, armed with binoculars and a police whistle. From this point of vantage he would rake the sky : if he judged a flying bomb to be approaching on a course which would take it directly over, or into, the Ministry, he blew his whistle. The Division soon found him to be a reliable prognosticator, and his whistle unofficially replaced the alarm buzzes as a signal to scamper for the staircase. Much working time was thus saved, and everyone was happy, Merrion Squires not least ; everyone, that is, except the Establishments Division. This Division, which concerned itself with personnel and maintenance problems, took an unfavourable view of Squires' activity. They paid official roof-spotters to give official warnings. Merrion Squires, on the other hand, they begged to point out, was receiving salary as a temporary Civil Servant (grade : Specialist) in the Art Work Unit of the Visual Propaganda Division ; they begged to inform him, therefore, that should he continue with his supererogatory task, they might find it necessary to deduct from his salary an amount equivalent to the period (or periods) thus daily consumed by him in cessation from his official work in the capacity set out above.

Merrion had instantly launched a spirited counter-attack. In a masterly minute to Establishments Division, he computed the total of man-hours saved per diem over an average week by his personal warning system, added to it—somewhat audaciously—the amount of man-hours lost by the official system over the first week of the attacks, and requested overtime payment to himself in respect of the total. Establishments Division, staggered by this unorthodox approach, had never quite succeeded in getting on to the offensive again. Indeed, a year later,

minutes were still passing desultorily between the
antagonists, although an absolute deadlock had long
before been reached, and neither side had discovered a
formula by which the impasse could be resolved.

Looking out over the park, Nigel could see the mark
of the bomb which had put an end to Merrion's ledge-
spotting. Not more than 150 yards away, there was a
patch of splintered and withered trees. Here one of the
last flying bombs to come over London had exploded.
They had all heard the distant, gathering roar ; heard
Merrion's whistle, sounding more urgently than ever
before ; dashed for the staircase and tumbled down it
pell-mell. Then a quivering silence. The bomb had cut
out. Then a winged swishing, as if Satan was falling out
of heaven. Then a paralysing blast ; another instant of
silence, followed by the tinkle of glass, lazily cascading.

When they got back to the sixth floor, they found
Merrion Squires lying insensible and covered with blood
in his room. His door had been blown off its hinges into
the passage ; the wall was riddled with daggers of glass ;
the floor looked like a refuse-tip ; and Merrion's whistle
was still firmly clutched in his hand.

On resuming consciousness, his first shaky words had
been, " Establishments Division shall hear of this."

It transpired that he had still been sitting on the ledge
when the bomb struck, and its blast had blown him back
into his room.

" Why on earth didn't you take cover, you silly
gubbins ? " Jimmy Lake asked.

" *What* cover ? " replied Merrion, in his indolent Irish
drawl.

Afterwards, he confided to Nigel that he had been too
frightened to move.

" There was I, your little cherub sitting up aloft. And
there was that murderous great thing sailing straight
down at me. And first I thought I'd wait a second or

two longer to see if it wouldn't turn away : and then I
thought, well, me boy, it's too late to get back into yer
room now—and anyway what's the use ? It had me
hypnotised. And," he added, " if Ingle sends me in one
more caption to mark up, about our gallant fighters of
the home front staring death in the face, I'll kill him.
I mean it, Nigel, I'll do in the little cliché-monger. Me
nerves won't stand it."

Nigel closed the window and went back to his desk,
ruminating on the bizarre exposures of war. A bomb
tore away the side of a house and revealed a vertical
series of lavatory bowls hanging on the edge of an abyss.
It tore away the façade of a human being, and you got
a view of the psychological plumbing : but only for a
moment ; the wall was soon up again, the interior tidied.
Tidied, but the structure warped, perhaps dangerously
and invisibly weakened. Or sometimes, for all one knew,
strengthened. If you found you had stood up to the
ordeal, the discovery gave self-confidence. That, no
doubt, as one could learn from primitive tribes, is what
ordeals are for.

From Merrion Squires, Nigel's mind strayed to that
other and more improbable hero, Charles Kennington.
It was pleasant to reflect how many of his sort the war
had thrown up. The long-haired, sensitive types, who
had voted at the Oxford Union that under no circumstances would they die for King and Country, and a few
years later had gone up into the air with the professionals
of the R.A.F. and helped to win the Battle of Britain,
fighting with the same skill and abandon as once they
had speechified. The conscientious objectors, who refused
to kill but performed prodigies of valour during the
blitzes as members of Rescue Squads and Fire Brigades.
The clever little dons, who vanished one day from their
universities and were next heard of having dropped by
parachute into occupied territory, organising the Resist-

ance, dynamiting bridges, standing up to a firing-party in a squalid backyard. The anonymous-looking scientists, who walked up to unexploded bombs and coldly took them to pieces, as though they were demonstrating an experiment in a laboratory, and generally were not blown to pieces. All the eccentrics, the amateurs, the people who did not believe in war and went into a cold fury when it interfered with their private lives, and were then extremely dangerous to anything that got in their light, whether it was a German or a piece of red tape. The people who proved so much the more disconcerting to the enemy because they did not wear their toughness on their sleeve, and because their minds would keep jumping the rails so earnestly laid down for them by Teutonic students of the English character. It was the streak of fantasy in it that gave this character its charm, and also gave it the unpredictability so formidable to a logical foe, Nigel reflected.

Charles Kennington was a fair representative. A young man of engaging though effeminate appearance, he had been a society photographer before the war. His clientèle, whom he bullied and insulted in a way they all agreed was devastatingly chic, would simply not have believed that, when he disappeared from their ken for a fortnight every summer, it was to attend a Territorial Army camp.

In September, 1939, he disappeared for quite a bit longer, to turn up again in his old haunts, after Dunkirk, with his arm in a sling, and a Military Cross on his tunic. He had, in fact, been more severely wounded and more outstandingly brave than either of these decorations indicated. Jimmy Lake, who was his brother-in-law, approached the War Office and got him seconded to the Ministry of Morale as one of the Military Censors. It was then that Nigel had first met him, for Kennington dealt with the censorship of photographic material and was therefore in constant touch with Nigel's Division. Charles

Kennington had, indeed, contributed a good deal to the
character of the Division, Nigel realised now—its flavour
of gaiety, insouciance, unorthodoxy. From the start, he
had been a problem to the Permanent Civil Servants in
the Ministry, through his habit of dating minutes by the
liturgical calendar of the Church of England. Edgar
Billson, who was Senior Officer in the Photographs
Library, and managed its financial affairs, was particularly harassed by this idiosyncrasy. On receiving a
minute headed "Third Day before the Feast of St.
Petronella, Virgin and Martyr," he had made a *démarche*
in person, only to be met by the shocked remonstrance
from Charles Kennington, "But, my dear, are you not a
Christian?"

A year later Kennington had a Medical Board and
returned to active service. Jimmy Lake heard from him
at long intervals, until the day when he was posted as
"Missing, Believed Killed," during the fighting on the
Rhine. And now he had popped up again, having by his
own account captured Stultz, the number three Nazi
leader whom the Allies had been hunting for two months.
It was all very satisfactorily in the English tradition,
thought Nigel: all very satisfactory, except for Nita
Prince, who had evidently not been too well pleased by
a message from the dead.

The door opened. "What's this?" asked Merrion
Squires disgustedly. "Thinking again?"

"Yes, I was thinking," said Nigel, removing his feet
from the chair on which they rested, and pushing it
towards his visitor. "I was thinking about Charles
Kennington as a matter of fact. And yourself."

"Sweet of you. What's the connection? I never met
him. Before my time."

"Eccentricity. Queerness. The fantasy-strain in the
English character."

"If you're suggesting that I'm either an Englishman

or a queer——" Merrion Squires exploded angrily, his long clown's face resting on the back of the chair, which he sat astride like a child playing at horses.

" Oh, no. You're just a West Britisher with an artistic temperament."

This double-barrelled insult failed to get the usual response from Squires.

" I say, talking of temperament, what's up with Our Blonde ? "

" *You* tell *me*, then."

" Did y'ever see that girl in a flutter before ? Y' didn't. Because she's not the sort that flutters. She just stays, all serene, like a damned great carnivorous orchid with its mouth wide open, and you all queue up to fly into it."

" I don't think much of your botany."

" Damn my botany ! " snapped Merrion. " I know about women, I tell you. Well, I had to go and see Jimmy yesterday evening, and just as I was outside the door, I heard her say, ' It's too late to back out now. You can't do it. Everyone knows, or guesses. There's no use trying to pretend you're not in love with me.' At that point I barged in. Our Director and Our Blonde were in the state of having been contiguous. Jimmy was cool enough, I must say. You know, staring out of the window, hands in pockets. ' Well, Merrion, what do you want ? '—the usual act. But Nita "—a note of relish crept into Squires' voice—" Nita was in a taking. Positively flushed, positively trembling, just as if she was a real woman. So Jimmy and I got down to work. And Nita started on her typewriter. Believe it or not, my boy, she had to tear up two drafts of what she was typing. Did y'ever know that girl make a mistake before ? Y' didn't. Well, then ? "

" I suppose she's a bit fussed about Charles Kennington coming back," said Nigel slowly. " They say she was engaged to him while he was here."

Merrion Squires snapped his fingers dramatically.
" Y've got it! I didn't know about that. She's afraid
Kennington will find out about her and Jimmy. That's
why she said it was no use his pretending not to be in
love with her : Kennington'd be bound to hear about it
sooner or later, since it's an open secret here. Well, if
this doesn't beat the band ! "

" And why are you so hellishly pleased, may I ask ? "

Merrion Squires gave Nigel one of his glancing looks,
half impish, half furtive.

" Oh, I like to see orchids being ruffled. Nothing
personal, y'know. Just an abstract love of justice. Now
that explains something else," he pursued. " When we'd
finished our work, Jimmy showed me Kennington's letter,
and told me he expected him along this morning ; asked
me to pop in at coffee-time if I'd like to meet him : half
the Division going to be there apparently : see the
conquering hero come stuff : wonder if Jimmy's hired
a brass band—mightn't go down well with Establishments. Well, the Blonde gave him a look and said she
thought Kennington would hate a fuss to be made of him,
and she herself proposed to take a half-day off. And
Jimmy—you know how suave and patient his voice
sounds when he's up against tough opposition—Jimmy
just said he couldn't let her off this morning, he's got a
conference at midday she must steno, and anyway didn't
she want to see Exhibit Number One."

" What's that ? "

" This fella Kennington is apparently bringing along a
phial of poison he took off the Nazi fella. Just to titivate
our ghoulish curiosity. But, don't you see, Nita is afraid
of Kennington seeing her with Jimmy at all, even in a
crowd : afraid their faces will give them away."

" What an unwholesome imagination you have, to be
sure," said Nigel. " I've never heard such a farrago of
guesswork. Why on earth should Nita be so upset ?

Kennington was supposed to be dead. She'd a perfect right to take up with——"

" Oh, you're hopeless. The fact is that Nita *is* upset—she's more than upset, she's frantic. And if you have a better theory——"

What better theory Nigel might have produced was forestalled by a knock at the door. They both groaned. Edgar Billson was the only person in the Division who ever knocked on a door before entering.

Edgar Billson crossed the room, as usual, in an unwelcoming silence, the toes in the elastic-sided boots pointing outwards, his eyes fixed upon the floor as if he could not recognise Nigel's existence till he had come within the official orbit of his desk. Having made the regulation approach, he looked up.

" Good-morning, Strangeways."

" Good-morning."

" I have a complaint to make. But perhaps you are busy ? " Billson's watery eyes swam half-way towards Merrion Squires, then turned back.

" I'm sorry to hear that. Do sit down, won't you ? " Then, as his visitor looked stiffly around, markedly ignoring the chair on which Merrion Squires still sat astride, Nigel added, " Take Miss Finlay's."

" Your assistant is away to-day ? "

" No, she's not turned up yet."

" Certain sections of the staff are getting very slack," said Billson, placing Miss Finlay's chair at a regulation distance from Nigel's desk and sitting down.

" So I am told," said Nigel blandly. " Are you having a lot of trouble with your Section ? "

" To the contrary. The attendance figures in the Photographs Library are exemplary."

" I'm delighted to hear it."

" I noticed Miss Finlay leaving the building at 4.52 yesterday."

" Do you wish to lodge an official complaint about my assistant ? "

" No—er, that is, no. Not at this present moment." Edgar Billson shot his starched cuffs and glanced uneasily at Merrion Squires, who was staring fixedly at him over the back of his chair, with the ruminative look of a horse gazing over the half-door of a loose-box.

" No, it was about these Pink Forms of yours. I can't work them, if the Production Units persist in filling them in in such a slovenly manner."

" Wouldn't it be better to discuss this with the Deputy Director. The Pink Form was his invention."

" Mr. Fortescue has asked me to discuss the matter with you."

" What's the trouble, then ? "

Edgar Billson laid a sheaf of forms on Nigel's desk. He coughed. " The purpose of the Pink Form——"

"——Is to captivate the masculine eye. Natural selection," Squires broke in irresponsibly.

" Shut up, Merrion," said Nigel.

" The purpose of the Pink Form," continued Billson relentlessly, " is to facilitate and co-ordinate the ordering of photostats and rough prints by the Production Units at the preliminary stages of—h'rrm—production."

" Yes, I know that," Nigel said. It was one of Billson's most tiresome traits, this lecturing you on the elements of work which you knew backwards.

" If you will examine these examples, you will note that the appropriate procedure has not been followed. Dates are missing : entries are sometimes illegible : the quality of print required is not always stipulated."

" I see one date missing. Only one," returned Nigel, glancing rapidly over the forms.

" Furthermore, the ordering of rough prints and photostats appears to me far in excess of reasonable requirements. Why, for instance, should your Unit have requested six copies of print Q.W.5339? Three at the most would suffice."

" It's to expedite the work on one of our rush jobs. The Q.W. series, you may remember, is a file of canned photographs. We wish to use one of them. To do so, it's necessary to re-submit it to three Security Censors— Naval, Military and Air. Three separate copies to speed things up. The remaining three are for our own use."

Edgar Billson had been growing red in the face during this measured reply. He now broke out, with unusual violence.

" The trouble with you Temporaries is that you have no grasp of Civil Service traditions. Speed is not every-thing in our work, Strangeways."

" You surprise me," put in Merrion Squires.

" There is also the broader question of the public economy. I am answerable to the Treasury for all Sectional expenditure under the internal vote. I am not prepared to squander public funds in this irresponsible way, on your pretext of accelerating the work of the Division."

" You'd better talk to the Director about it, then, if you want to dispute his rulings on Divisional policy," replied Nigel calmly.

" I fail to understand you. To what ruling do you refer ? "

" The general ruling, given by him at a Progress Meeting in May, 1940, to all Heads of Sections, that under no circumstances must red tape or any other form of official obstructionism be allowed to interfere with the smooth and rapid work of the Division."

" Are you suggesting that——? "

" I'm suggesting that my Unit needs six copies of Q.W.5339. And that, whenever we need six copies of a photograph, we shall continue to order them. And that I am tired of being lectured by you on my official obliga-

tions. And that, if you ever again use the word ' irresponsible' in reference to my work, I shall ask the
Director to take disciplinary action against you." Nigel
paused a moment. " If you will leave these forms with
me, I'll look into them."

Edgar Billson gave him one vicious look, then rose,
and made for the door. His would-be dignified exit was
spoiled, however, by the whirlwind entrance of Pamela
Finlay, which knocked him back several feet into the
room.

" I must say you've got the jargon all right," said
Merrion, when Billson had finally retired. " I've never
known that little rabbit bare his teeth so aggressively,
though. Have you ? Any one would think the Q files
were his personal collection of pornographic studies, he's
so touchy about them. . . ."

Twenty minutes later the Director sent for Nigel.
Nigel found him sitting on the edge of his desk, his long
legs dangling, a large part of the floor in front of him
covered with photographs arranged in groups. Jimmy
Lake flipped a hand at Nigel, then resumed his trance-like
brooding over the photographs. They were the proposed
double-spreads for one of the Pacific series jobs. From
time to time the Director referred to one of Merrion
Squires' lay-out sheets, hoisted himself off his desk,
altered the relative positions of some of the pictures or
substituted different ones from a pile that lay on the
window-sill ; then returned to his contemplative pose. It
was like a slow-motion game of Patience, thought Nigel,
played with 12-inch by 10-inch prints instead of cards.
He offered this fancy to the Director.

" Yes," Jimmy Lake replied. " I find it very soothing
to the nerves."

There was another long silence. Nigel was quite
accustomed to these silences, though this morning the

Director seemed more than usually distrait. At last
Jimmy spoke.

" No, it won't do. It's dead." He pointed at one of
the groups. " That one. Tell me what's wrong with it."

It was rather like being asked by Menuhin to explain
a flaw in a passage of virtuoso playing by Szigeti, for
Merrion Squires' technical brilliance in lay-out was only
excelled by the Director's extraordinary flair for the
visual presentation of stories and ideas. However, Nigel
took a dip at it.

" *This* is the key picture," he said, pointing. " It
ought to be given more value. Make a three-quarters
spread of it, and use the others in a vertical strip on the
right-hand page."

The Director smiled faintly.

" Pooh ! " he said. " Why isn't Merrion here, ducky ? "

Nita Prince said, " I've rung him once."

" Ring him again, then."

Nigel noticed a crumpled ball of a handkerchief on
Nita's table, and there were shadows under her eyes.
Her voice, when she asked for the number, sounded a bit
out of control, as if she was very tired.

" Merrion Squires I want," said Jimmy patiently.
" That's Brian Ingle's extension you asked for."

" Sorry." Nita tried again. It was odd, thought Nigel.
Whatever one might say of her private life, the girl had
always kept her mind on her work in the office. And the
look she had given Jimmy was rather odd, too : a look
of—reproach ?   Determination ?   Sulkiness ?   Uncertainty ?—Nigel found himself unable to define it. It was,
at any rate, very different from her normal look of confidence, of discreet possessiveness, of a happy secret
shared—more naked, more vulnerable.

When Merrion arrived, they got down to the photographs again. The faulty spread was pointed out to him.

" No, it's poor, that one," he agreed. " I was waiting

for the Q. prints to turn up: there's a much better picture amongst them, I know."

The Director lifted his eyebrows interrogatively at Nigel.

" I'm having trouble with Billson over them." Nigel explained the situation, as non-committally as he could : he had no wish to get Billson into trouble.

" Ring up Billson, ducky," said the Director. " Tell him we must have the prints from the Q.W. series in twenty-four hours. Tell him I say so."

" He's always sitting on those Q files," said Merrion. " He'll hatch them out one day."

" You forget Billson a moment and concentrate on your job, my son. These lay-outs of yours "—Jimmy held them up distastefully—" they're second-rate." Second-rate was the most offensive term of criticism the Director ever used, and he used it very sparingly. Nigel was startled by the rasp that had suddenly come into his quiet voice. So, evidently, was Merrion.

" Maybe I've outlived my usefulness in the Division," he replied, only half-humorously.

" You'll be told when you have—don't worry," said Jimmy, looking at Merrion directly.

Another queer little unsheathing of the claws concealed in his velvet manner, thought Nigel.

" You must take them away—this one and this one— and try again. I've asked you to alter them before. Now I'm telling you to alter them."

" And I told you your suggestions for improving them were no good." Merrion's Irish temperament took criticism hard, and Jimmy normally treated it in a more tactful way. " I can't adapt my technique to the brain-waves of amateurs."

" Amateurs " was, if possible, an even more offensive term in the Division than " second-rate."

" I think you had better control your language," said

Jimmy in his deadliest, quiet tone. " You are one of a
number of experts working here. You are not omniscient.
You are not even cleverer than the rest. And you have
given more trouble recently than the whole lot. The
Deputy Director tells me——"

" Oh, must we have all this now ? " exclaimed Nita in
a trembling voice. " I'm sure Merrion——"

" I can do without *your* sympathy, my lollipop," said
Merrion furiously.

Nigel expected an outburst from the Director at this.
But Jimmy Lake turned away to the window, as if
detaching himself from the whole affair and leaving the
other two to fight it out between them. It had the effect,
whether intended or not, of deflating the scene. After
a moment, Nita said, trying to smile :

" Jimmy is practising being hard-hearted. But it
doesn't work. Does it, Jimmy ? "

Nigel was to remember afterwards the tone in which
she said it. A tone whose undertones were curiously
arresting, yet impossible to interpret. At any rate, Nigel
could not begin to interpret them now ; for the door was
flung open and a small, lively-looking man in officer's
uniform stood there, hands clasped dramatically over his
heart, surveying them with an expression of the most
theatrical astonishment.

" My *angels* ! " this apparition exclaimed, in a high,
light voice. " Jimmy ! More distinguished-looking than
ever ! And Nigel ! And another handsome young
gentleman ! And *Nita* ! You sumptuous girl ! "

He swooped down upon her like a pantomime fairy on
a wire, and demonstratively embraced her. Behind him
a small, sedate woman entered the room, rather shyly.
Jimmy Lake, who was watching with an amused expression the scene at Nita's desk, did not notice this new-
comer till she touched his elbow. Then he swung round.

" My dear girl ! What *are you* doing here ? "

There was something like consternation in his voice, thought Nigel. And no wonder : Alice Lake had never been encouraged to come to the office ; not with Nita Prince there.

" Charles brought me," she said. Her voice had the same high, light timbre as Charles Kennington's—a doll-like quality. Nigel realised he had quite forgotten they were twins. Seeing them together now for the first time, while Jimmy was introducing Merrion Squires to Charles, he had leisure to observe their likeness—the tone of voice, the triangular-shaped face with broad brow and pointed chin, the small delicate bones. Only Charles seemed to have taken all the vitality : his sister looked flat beside him, a shadow of himself, pleasantly smiling but silent and withdrawn.

" Yes, I brought her," bubbled Charles. " Alice and I are inseparable. Aren't we, love ? We intend never, never to part again." He beamed at his sister from where he sat, perched on Nita's desk, his arm lying lightly round Nita's shoulders.

Nigel thought there was a certain atmosphere of constraint, if not of embarrassment, in the room during the momentary silence that followed. The Director, hands in pockets, half-turned away from them, was standing by the window. If he felt some awkwardness in his wife's presence there, he was making no attempt to smooth it over with his usual light touch for awkward situations. Everyone else suddenly started talking all at once.

" So glad to meet you again," Merrion Squires said to Mrs. Lake. " I thought your last novel was excellent."

" You do look different in uniform," said Nita, turning her lustrous eyes up to Charles Kennington.

" Now, my dears," Charles babbled, " I must hear all your news. How long is it ?—it seems years since I saw any of you. I feel quite out of touch with the world of affairs, the world where men are ciphers, and women are

—women." He kissed Nita lightly on the brow. " Put me in the picture," he demanded.

Nita said, " Oh, we've just been slogging away, while you were getting killed and coming to life again and having a gorgeous time looting in Germany."

" Not killed, dear," said Charles severely. " The rest is correct, including the coming to life again. But I was never killed, I give you my word."

" What a lot of ribbons you have ! " said Nita, touching the breast of his military uniform. " There was only one there when I saw you last. Have you been very brave, darling ? "

" Quite intrepid, my pet. I have probably faced more forms in triplicate than any man in the British Army."

" You and Merrion must get together," said Jimmy Lake dryly. " He's another hero."

" A hero ! " Charles Kennington stretched his clasped hands dramatically towards Squires. " You must tell me *all* about it."

" He saved us all from a bomb," Jimmy said.

Charles Kennington shuddered delicately. " Don't speak to me of bombs. I could not dislike them more. Particularly Anglo-American bombs. They kept dropping them on me when I was in Germany."

" Very inaccurate bombing practice," said Jimmy.

" Well, no. Not exactly. You see, I was rather far in advance of the troops, some of the time."

" A spy ? Charles ! Is that why you were supposed to be dead ? " cried Nita.

She was making all the running. Nigel had never seen her so flushed and excited. Her mane of bright hair tumbled over Charles Kennington's hand as she talked to him. But there was something conscious in the way she played up to him ; as though, Nigel thought first, it was really directed towards somebody else—directed, perhaps, at Jimmy Lake. Then he thought, no, it's just the slight

over-acting of a clever woman who must appear all
sweetness to her long-lost fiancé, and is at the same time
conscious of her new lover—in a conspiracy with him,
perhaps, to defer the moment when Charles Kennington
must be told the truth.

Nita Prince, flushed, melting, a Danäe in a golden
shower, certainly held the stage now. Even Merrion
Squires kept glancing round at her as he talked with
Mrs. Lake in a far corner. Only Alice Lake seemed out
of the picture, as she sat there with eyes downcast upon
the hands loosely clasped in her lap.

"My dear old colleague, the Archdeacon!" entoned
Charles, as Harker Fortescue came in, with Brian Ingle
behind him. "How are the offertories keeping up?
Ember Days bearing fruit an hundredfold, I trust? And
Brian, lovely to see you. Well, this *is* like old times. But
stay!" He lifted a pastoral forefinger in the air. "One
of the clergy is missing, surely. Where is the Reverend
Billson? Not taken from our midst, I hope?"

"You *can't* want to see *him*, Charles," said Nita,
laughing.

"My love, in the sight of God we are all equal. Pray
send at once for our fellow-worker in the vineyard."

Nita applied herself to the telephone.

"We've got to congratulate you, Charles," said the
Deputy Director. "A first-class job. Saw about it in
the papers, of course, but they didn't mention you by
name. 'Young English Major Captures Number Three
Nazi.' Absolutely first-class."

"I shall treasure up your words, dear Archdeacon."

"I hope you're going to tell us all about it," said
Brian Ingle. "Were you—I mean, did you work alone
in Germany? It must be frightfully n-nerve-racking, a
job like that," he added wistfully. "I do admire people
n-no end who——"

"Just about as nerve-racking as sitting at a desk here

when the V-bombs were falling, I should think," replied
Charles with a very sweet and winning smile, his affectations put aside for a moment. Nigel noticed the same smile
appearing, like a reflection, on Alice Lake's face. Brian
Ingle flushed, unconsciously straightening his shoulders.

" Oh, that's n-nonsense, Charles," he said happily.

" I'll certainly tell you the tale. Not that it's madly
stimulating," said Charles Kennington, with a return to
his normal manner. " Social realism at its drabbest, my
dears. Hallo ! If it isn't Edgar ! And not a day older ! "'

Charles was the only person in the Ministry of Morale
who had ever called Mr. Billson by his Christian name.

Edgar Billson moved across the room, picking his way
with pigeon-toed gait amongst the photographs which
still littered the floor. Having reached Charles, he raised
his eyes for the first time, coughed, extended a large
white hand, and said :.

" Very pleased to see you again, Major. Permit me to
offer my congratulations on your daring coup. H'rrm.
Quite a gathering for you," he added on a faintly cen-
sorious note, as though it had just occurred to him that
the Treasury might not sanction the present expenditure
of Divisional time on social entertainment.

" Yes, too delicious, isn't it ? If only I had my camera !
What a charming, informal group you would all make.
Or I could arrange you—let me see—yes, like one of
those Victorian intellectual picnic groups. You know—
littered all over a mountainside. The Higher Thought
amongst the boulders. The gentlemen couched full
length upon sphagnum moss, gazing in every direction
at Progress ; the ladies being strenuous with luncheon
baskets and volumes of verse. And "—he clapped his
hands delightedly as the cry of " Coffee " wailed from the
end of the corridor—" and here comes the picnic !
Beautiful, nourishing coffee ! "

Nita went out with an array of cups on a tray. Merrion

Squires, who had been unwontedly silent—the centre of the stage for him or nothing, thought Nigel—said :

" Well, where's this blood-curdling exhibit we've been promised ? "

" To be sure. I'd quite forgotten. Delighted you share my naughty passion for sensationalism." Major Kennington fumbled in the large pockets of his tunic, bringing out in turn a ball of string, a manicure set, a Bible, a bag of toffee, some revolver bullets and a matchbox. " Ah, here we are." Opening the matchbox, he took out a thin cylindrical object, about the length of his thumbnail, rather like a lighter-fuel container on a miniature scale. He held it up gingerly between thumb and forefinger.

" The idea was to lodge it between your back teeth, when a state of emergency declared itself. Then, if one of the armed thugs of the Pluto-Democracies laid hands on you—well, just a little wriggle with the tongue, and a sharp crunch, and the gates of Valhalla opened to you."

The little group in the room had broken up, and re-formed around Charles Kennington.

" You mean, it's not soluble ? " asked Jimmy Lake.

" No. Different from our type. But be careful how you handle it. The case is madly fragile. And the contents —well ! " Charles rolled up his eyes.

" What ? Cyanide of potassium ? " Harker Fortescue asked.

" Pure hydrocyanic acid."

" Ker-rikey," said Harker.

At this moment Nita came in with her trayful of cups, and the group broke up again, Jimmy and Brian Ingle moving to help her. The others were passing the little container from hand to hand.

" Come and get it," said Nita. The tray was now on the Director's desk.

" Mind my photographs," said Jimmy. " Sorry, we

ought to have cleared them off the floor. Nita, would
you——"

"Certainly not," said Kennington. "I can never resist
photographs. Oh, goody, what a treat! What are they
for ?"

Jimmy Lake told him. "Merrion and I were just
quarrelling about those two spreads," he added with a
pleasant smile at his subordinate. Merrion acknowledged
it, a little stiffly.

They had all gravitated now towards the end of the
room where Jimmy's big desk was. Some held their cups
of coffee, others put them down on the desk beside them.

"Wait a minute, though. You must see Merrion's
cover-designs for this job. One of them is first-class." The
Director seemed intent on conciliating Merrion Squires.
He opened a drawer and took out the designs. Then he
was moving across to the bookcase on the left of Nita's
table, his hand lightly holding the girl's elbow. "Come
and help me put them up."

When they had propped the designs upright against the
books, he took her elbow again and moved aside with her
so that they could all get a clear view.

"Now, Charles, which do you like best ? Hark'ee and
I are at loggerheads about them."

It was the Director's normal practice, when alternative
cover-roughs had been prepared, thus to take the opinions
of his staff upon them. His staff, on the other hand, knew
that his own decision had been made already, and they
must be prepared to justify their choice with a wealth
of critical judgment if they wanted him to change his
mind. They all scrutinised the designs in silence for a
little, shifting about to get a good view of them. At last
Charles Kennington said :

"I think *that* one. The bloodthirsty type peering out
from amidst the bougainvilleas."

The Director glanced towards the Deputy Director,

whistling softly between his teeth. Charles had evidently chosen aright.

"Nah," said the Deputy Director. "It's too literary." He paused, to summon up a still more offensive word. "Too refined. Put it beside one of Clegg's covers and it'll disappear."

"Hark'ee's idea of a cover-design is a tooth-paste advertisement poster," Merrion Squires put in, not best pleased at the reference to his chief rival designer.

"I say you've got to hit them in the eye straight away, or you're sunk," declared the Deputy Director stubbornly.

The telephone bell on Nita's desk rang. She moved from Jimmy's side to pick up her coffee-cup from his desk before answering the call. "Damn that telephone!" she exclaimed. "Which is mine?"

"This one, isn't it?" said Brian Ingle, indicating one of the two coffee-cups nearest her hand.

"No, that's Mr. Lake's. This is mine." She took it up, went over to her desk and began to answer the call. Jimmy followed her, taking his own cup. Sitting on the edge of Nita's desk, his long legs dangling, he indicated the Deputy Director's choice with his free hand.

"Look at this design, Hark'ee. Take it easy, relax, and just *look* at it. It's pitiable, the way you fall for the obvious. This design is dead at birth, it's still-born, it's an abortion. Here have I been nearly six years trying to educate you in visual values, and you have the nerve to tell me that this—this crudely-coloured platitude—is a cover design. T'chah." Jimmy took a gulp of his coffee.

The Deputy Director's mouth twitched. "There's only one principle for a cover design for our public. They *must* be obvious, they *must* be crude. That one"—he jerked his finger towards the Director's choice and poised himself for a knock-out blow—"is a good design, I admit; a good design for the dust-jacket of a volume of Bloomsbury *belles-lettres*."

D

Alice Lake giggled. "'A bloodthirsty type peering out from amidst the bougainvilleas'? Poor old Bloomsbury!"

"The trouble with you, Harker," began Jimmy Lake; but he got no further with it. Nita Prince suddenly interrupted him with a paroxysm of coughing.

"Cough it up, ducky," he said, leaning across and patting her on the shoulders.

Nita Prince did not cough it up, though. The coughing at once turned to a painful choking: the beautiful face was distorted: the eyes desperately stared: Nita's hands clutched and tore at her throat, then jerked feebly in the air before her. They were all staring at her incredulously. Before anyone could move, she had fallen forward across her desk. An ink bottle overturned, rolled slowly off the desk on to the floor, dabbling her bright hair with ink as it went.

CHAPTER III

TRYING to recollect the scene in tranquillity later, Nigel Strangeways found it curiously difficult to piece together. It was as if a bomb had exploded in the middle of the morning, blowing it into grotesque and unrelated fragments. There was the thin, doll-like cry from Alice Lake, "Oh, Jimmy!" There was the Director, staring down at Nita in consternation and muttering over and over again, "Nita, what is it? Nita, what is it?" There was Edgar Billson, taking off his glasses and rubbing them on his sleeve and putting them on again, as though he couldn't believe what he had seen through them. There was Merrion Squires, shivering uncontrollably. There was Harker Fortescue, rigid as a statue in the middle of the room. There was Brian Ingle, the first of them all to move, running across the room, throwing open the window by Nita's desk with a cry of "Give her air!" Then standing protectively over Nita's body as though he could still guard her from what had happened. And there was Charles Kennington, on whose face, before he clapped his hands over it, Nigel had caught an extraordinary expression—a look, he could have sworn, of blind, frantic amazement.

Nigel strode across the room. There were only three things to be done, for the moment. He did them, while the others watched him like sheep. He felt Nita's heart, turned up her eyelids. She was dead. He sniffed at her lips, and her coffee-cup : yes, she had been killed by cyanide ; he laid the bright head gently back on the desk. He dialled Scotland Yard and asked for Superintendent Blount.

"Blount? Thank God you're in. Strangeways here. At the Ministry of Morale. Can you come at once? We've had a death by cyanide poisoning. What's that? . . . Oh, damn your etiquette. Hold on a minute——" Nigel had suddenly thought of a fourth thing to be done. Laying the receiver on the desk, he bent down and sniffed Nita's hands and fingers. "Are you there? It's almost certainly murder. . . . You will? Good. And will you pick up a doctor on the way? It'll be quicker than trying to get one by telephone. Room F 29 of the Ministry. . . . Yes, I'll see to that. 'Bye."

A murmur, absurdly stagey, had arisen when he used the word "Murder", as though they were a crowd of extras in a film registering the appropriate response.

"What the devil do you mean, Nigel?" said Harker Fortescue now in a rasping voice.

And Jimmy Lake, vaguely and sadly, "No, Nigel, you must be wrong."

Brian Ingle, who had been standing away, made a desperate little rush at the body, sobbing as if he was in the last few yards of a close race, and Nigel had to fend him gently off.

"I'm sorry," he said, "but no one must touch her now. And no one must leave the room till the police come." He turned to the Director. "Forgive me taking charge like this, but I've had this sort of thing before. Superintendent Blount is an old friend of mine. Shall we all sit down?"

"What makes you say it's murder?" asked Major Kennington. He seemed a different being: his voice was like a whip; his slight body quivered, and his eyes snapped with intelligence. Nigel caught a glimpse of the man who had captured Otto Stultz.

"Her coffee-cup smells of cyanide. Her fingers don't. If she had taken the poison by putting that trophy of yours straight into her mouth, the coffee-cup wouldn't smell. If she had broken the container into her coffee, her fingers would almost certainly have picked up a smell of the stuff. But there's no smell of cyanide on them. So——" Nigel shrugged.

Major Kennington seemed about to speak, to make some sort of protest. Then he too shrugged his shoulders. Then he did speak.

"Who had Stultz's thing last ? " he snapped, turning upon the group huddled round the Director's desk.

"This is intolerable," said Edgar Billson. "I do not accept Mr. Strangeways' authority."

"You will accept mine, then," said the Director with patient firmness, "and stay in this room. There is no need to answer questions, if you don't wish to, before the police come.'"

Harker Fortescue said, "She might have put the thing in her mouth and taken a gulp of coffee to wash it down, Nigel. And a little of the stuff might have got into the coffee-cup like that."

"It's just a faint possibility," Nigel replied. "That's why I told Blount it was *almost* certainly murder."

"Why are we all talking like this ? " It was Alice Lake's high, tiny voice. "That poor girl was alive just now, and now she's dead."

Jimmy walked over to his wife, an intense, appealing expression on his face, and took her hand.

Presently Charles Kennington said, "Nigel, do me a favour and look in her coffee-cup. See if you can dredge anything up with a spoon. You know what I mean."

Nigel poked about in the cup, which was a quarter full. Then he turned, shaking his head silently at Kennington. The Director, moving restlessly about the room again, hands in pockets, had come near to an open window.

"No ! " said Nigel sharply. "Sorry, Jimmy, but I don't think *any one* had better go near the windows just now."

"Afraid the murderer is going to hurl himself out ? "

sneered Merrion Squires. " Best thing he could do, I should think."

In the shocked silence, Nigel said, " It's not that. It's Stultz's thing." They were getting into the habit of calling it that, not " Charles' thing "—it seemed more tactful. " You see, it's not soluble, and it's not in Nita's cup. So, if somebody did pour the poison into the cup, he's either tucked the container away somewhere in the room or he's still got it on him. And if so, he *might* try to flip it out of a window when no one was looking. We shall all have to be searched, of course."

" This is preposterous," muttered Edgar Billson angrily.

The telephone rang beside Nita's limp, outstretched arm.

" Oh, God, oh, God ! " murmured Jimmy Lake. " This is too much. Nigel, will you—— ? "

Nigel went to the door and spoke to one of the typists in the ante-room. " Please take all the Director's calls out here. There's been an accident in his room. Miss Prince. Now, pull yourself together, Miss Grangely. Take all calls. Say the Director is engaged. Don't let any one into his room. Not even the messengers. When a Superintendent Blount arrives, send him in. *No one* else. Got it ? Oh, yes, and cancel the Director's conference with the Foreign Office people at midday. Ring Mr. Gillespie at the F.O., and say the Director has been compelled to cancel it. Then telephone to my assistant and the Deputy Director's, and Mr. Squires', Mr. Ingle's and Mr. Billson's, and tell them we've been detained. Tell them to carry on."

" Thank you, Nigel," said Jimmy Lake softly.

Harker Fortescue said, " Look here. If that damned stuff ought to have got on to *her* fingers, it ought to have got on to the fingers of whoever——"

" You're right," snapped Charles Kennington. " Nigel, you'd better——"

"I agree," said the Director. "I take it no one objects?"

"If you mean Mr. Strangeways is to go round smelling all our fingers, I must protest. It is a farcical proceeding," said Edgar Billson.

"Not a bit," exclaimed Merrion Squires. "Put us out of our misery. All but one of us, anyway." He held out his hands to Nigel.

The little scene that ensued was bizarre to a degree. The tall, loose-limbed figure of Nigel Strangeways bent over one hand after another, as if at some Court ceremony. Even Edgar Billson gave way, though with a bad grace. Finally Nigel extended his own fingers, first to the Director, then to Charles Kennington.

"Well?" asked Merrion impatiently. "Who is the culprit?"

"Nobody's fingers smell of cyanide," replied Nigel.

There was a general stir of relief.

"May I return to my duties, then?" Billson said.

"Afraid not. For one thing, the stuff is highly volatile——"

"I could have told you that," interrupted Billson.

"——And it's some little time since—oh, well," Nigel sighed, "we must wait and see. And while we're waiting, I suppose we might as well try and find out what happened to Stultz's thing." He said it in a deliberately off-hand way. He wanted to give the impression that he had relaxed. If people were a little off their guard, there might be interesting discrepancies between what they said now and their evidence to the police later when they would be very definitely on guard again—one of them, at least.

"Cook up your stories, boys," said Merrion Squires.

Billson glared at Nigel.

"I cannot concur in this procedure. The matter should be deferred until expert investigation by the police is, h'rrm, set on foot."

"Oh, come, Billson," said the Director, with a return to his normal manner, half-coaxing, half-authoritative. "Don't let's be stuffy. We've got to pass the time somehow."

They were all sitting at one end of the room now, some against the wall, others grouped round the Director's desk. Alice Lake was in the Director's chair, and he himself perched sideways on the desk, holding her hand again. It was as if they wished to huddle together for protection against the dead body of Nita slumped across her table at the other side of the room, one arm outstretched towards them in a stiffening pose of accusation. Between them and her, on the floor, lay the dividing sea of photographs, their groups disordered by the feet that had scuffled over them just now.

"I don't think we need go into *all* this," Alice Lake said. "When Nita came in again with the coffee-tray——"

"Yes, your husband and I went to help her, I remember," said Brian Ingle dully.

Mrs. Lake went on : "Well, *I* had the thing then. You put the tray down on the desk, here "—she laid her fingers on the left-hand edge of the desk—" and I—let me think, what did I do with it ?—yes, I had the thing in my right hand, and I put it down just behind me on the desk : I was standing in front of the desk, at the right-hand corner there. I put it down behind me to take my cup of coffee. Yes, that's right. And then my husband took out Mr. Squires' cover designs and went across the room to prop them up on the bookshelf."

"Did you notice the poison-container there when you took the designs out of your drawer ? " Nigel asked the Director. " It was the top right-hand drawer, wasn't it ? "

"Yes, as a matter of fact I did. It was lying beside my desk calendar."

"You didn't move it or touch it, then ? "

" No."

" Very well," said Nigel. " Now, did you notice the container again after that, Mrs. Lake ? "

" Yes. When Charles pointed to one of the designs and said, ' The murderous type peering out from amidst the bougainvilleas '—I suppose it was an association of ideas—anyway, I glanced round, and the thing was still there, behind me."

" Did any one happen to notice it on the desk after that ? "

A silence.

" Did any one else see it on the desk at any time ? "

" I did," said Brian Ingle. " I mean, I saw Mrs. Lake put it down. That was just after N-Nita told us to come and get our coffee."

" Any one else ? "

Another silence.

" Well, that seems to look after the poison-container. Now, Nita's cup was here "—Nigel indicated the right-hand edge of the desk, near the Director's calendar— " until her telephone rang and she took it over to her own table. From that point she was in full view of every one, and it doesn't seem possible——"

" Don't forget we were all concentrated on the cover designs," said Harker Fortescue.

" That's true. But no one went near *her* desk, except Jimmy——"

Alice Lake cut in quickly, " Well, surely someone would have noticed it if my husband had broken the container into her cup then."

" Exactly," said Nigel. " In fact, she'd have been bound to spot it herself. So we're left with——"

" No," cried Brian Ingle, misunderstanding him. " She didn't ! I—well, I *was* looking at her over there. I'd have seen—besides, she wouldn't have done it ; it wasn't like her——"

His voice broke. Nigel said gently :

" People do kill themselves. People you wouldn't expect to."

" But they don't do it usually in front of a roomful of witnesses," said Charles Kennington. " Nigel, you said the cup was only a quarter full ? "

" Yes. As you see, that's very significant. It means the poison couldn't have been put in till she'd drunk at least half of it—not with a quickly-acting poison like this. And that cuts the murderer's operative period still finer."

Nigel was holding the centre of the floor now, holding them all within the range of his pale blue eyes, which seemed so abstracted but missed so little. He went on :

" Let's get back to the cups. Nita's was on the Director's desk and Jimmy's must have been close beside it. When the telephone rang, Nita said, ' Which is mine ? ' And you, Brian, said, ' This one, isn't it ? ' And Nita said, ' No, that's Mr. Lake's.' "

" You mean, someone picked on the wrong cup to poison ? " asked Merrion Squires, glancing sidelong from Alice Lake to Brian.

" I just want to get the position of the cups clear," replied Nigel. " When did you take up your cup again ? " he asked Jimmy.

" Not till I went over to sit on Nita's table."

" How long between putting it down and taking it up ? "

" Couple of minutes. No, less. About a minute, I should say," the Director replied.

" And we have evidence," mocked Merrion Squires, his long clown's face grinning at them over the back of the chair on which he sat astride, " that, only half an hour prior to the crime, the Director had had a bitter quarrel with M. Squires. Putting two and two together with his well-known genius for mental arithmetic, the astute Strangeways——"

" My dear," broke in Charles Kennington, a jagged edge

on his voice, " my dear, let us under present circumstances try to avoid the more *vulgar* forms of facetiousness."

Nigel observed that Charles' delicate small hands were quivering and white at the knuckles. Nita's death had affected him more deeply than he had cared to betray—that was certain.

Merrion Squires' head had jerked sharply, as though from a physical slap in the face, and he was about to make an angry reply, when the tramp of feet was heard in the corridor.

" That's the police," said Nigel, going to the door.

Presently a doctor was bending over Nita's body, and a uniformed policeman sitting stolidly by her table, while Nigel had a brief talk with Superintendent Blount in the ante-room. A few minutes later he brought Blount and his accompanying Detective-Sergeant into the Director's room and effected introductions. The large room seemed to become even smaller. Jimmy Lake must have felt this too, for he asked if they couldn't clear up the photographs on the floor, which were getting in every one's way.

" Rather leave things as they are, sir, just for a wee while," said Blount in that soothing voice which had given so many criminals so very wrong an idea of him. He broke off, to exchange a few muttered remarks with the doctor, who then took up his bag and departed.

" T'ck, t'ck. Puir young lady." Clucking commiserately, Blount turned to them again, an almost Pickwickian figure with his bald head, glittering spectacles and benevolent smile. " Mr. Strangeways tells me, sir, that none of you objects to being searched."

The Director discreetly glanced round at his colleagues, like a hostess collecting eyes. " Quite right," he said.

" Well, now, that's splendid. Shall we get it over right away? Sergeant Messer here will attend to it, and a female searcher is coming from Scotland Yard for you, madam." He bowed to Mrs. Lake. " Now, let me see,

you're all busy people, I know ; but I'm afraid we must
keep you together in this room till . . . Have you any
screens handy, sir ? "

" Yes, there's a big one in my room ; I'll get it, shall
I ? " said the Deputy Director, beginning to move towards
the door. Superintendent Blount put up a fat hand.

" I won't trouble you, sir," he said. " One of my men
outside will fetch it, if you'll tell me where it is."

" My room's directly opposite this one, across the
ante-room."

Blount went to the door and gave instructions.
Presently the screen was fixed up in a corner of the
Director's room, and the Detective Sergeant started work.
Jimmy Lake, by his own wish, was the first to be searched.
When he came out from behind the screen he was looking
rather white, thought Nigel. Detective-Sergeant Messer
emerged, shook his head almost imperceptibly at Blount.

" You look a bit knocked-up, sir," said Blount,
sympathetically. " A horrible shock for you, I'm sure,
this puir young lady—horrible."

The Director nodded, speechlessly, pulled out a silk
handkerchief and mopped his face. Then he said :

" Well, Superintendent, you'll want to make arrange-
ments for interviewing us, I suppose. Together or
separately ? And I hope you'll let me have this room
back as soon as you can, my dear chap : I've got a lot
of work to do."

Superintendent Blount nodded and clucked. " Most
unfortunate. Most unfortunate. Busy man. Head of
Department. Work of national importance. T'ck, t'ck,
t'ck. Must go over this room *vairy* carefully, though.
Now, sir, what do you suggest ? "

It was finally arranged that Jimmy Lake should carry
on his work from the Deputy Director's room until his
own had been examined, and that Blount should interview
the party one by one, after each had passed the search,

in the room of a member of the staff who was at present away on leave.

At eleven o'clock that night Nigel Strangeways and Blount faced each other over a bottle of whisky. They were in a bed-sitting-room at Nigel's club, where he had lived ever since his wife, Georgia, was killed while driving an ambulance in the blitz of April, 1941.

" No, I really can *not*," Nigel was saying. " These people are my friends, after all ; it's not like those other cases. Besides, in a way I know them *too* well. I've been working with them for five years, damn it, and I can't see them objectively any more."

" Well, your very good health, Strangeways." The Superintendent gazed ruminatively into his glass. " I'm so terribly short-handed, just now, or I wouldn't ask you," he said after a pause.

" And I'm absolutely fagged out. I don't have ideas any more, I only have reflex actions."

" H'm. Shall we play a game of piquet, then ? "

" By all means." Nigel fetched the cards and they cut for elder hand. As Blount dealt, he said :

" Major Kennington ought to be prosecuted for criminal negligence, of course. He'd no business to bring along that poison jigger at all ; and then, to hand it round and let it out of his sight—well, it was a scandalous thing."

" He couldn't have supposed there was a would-be poisoner amongst his old friends and relations, just waiting for the chance to—I'm taking all five," said Nigel, discarding. " Oh, damn and blast this pick-up ! "

" Which suggests that it was he himself who——"

" My dear old Superintendent, you know as well as I do that it doesn't suggest anything of the sort. You're just trying to draw me. All right, I'd rather discuss crime even than play this revolting hand." Nigel flung

his cards on the table and refilled Blount's glass. " Well,
then, where *did* you find it ? "

" We didn't. It wasn't on any of your people. I didn't
expect it to be. But we took that room to pieces this
afternoon—and not a smell of the poison jigger. What
d'you say now ? "

" But it *must* be there."

" Believe you me, Strangeways, it wasn't. We don't
miss things—and it's a bare, bleak sort of room. No, your
man must have flipped it out of the window immediately
after he'd used it. We looked in the street below, of
course, but——"

" He couldn't have done that. The windows were shut
till after the girl died. Then Brian Ingle opened one.
Oh, Lord ! "

" Ah-ha ! " said Blount.

" Nonsense. Brian was devoted to Nita. He'd never
——"

" And that is assuming it was Nita the murderer wanted
to poison. But there were several cups all close together
on the desk."

" Look, Blount, if we're going to discuss this unsavoury
subject, we'd better do it in an orderly way. You tell
me first what you got out of your interviews."

" That's better."

The Superintendent took a gulp of his whisky and
smacked his lips demonstratively. He knew how to handle
Strangeways, he reflected with some complacence.
Drawing a sheaf of papers from his sack-like pocket—
typewritten copies of the interviews with the various
witnesses—and occasionally glancing at one to refresh
his memory, he gave Nigel a résumé of the evidence.
As sifted and docketed in Nigel's mind, it amounted to
this :

First, the poison container. According to Charles
Kennington, Jimmy Lake had suggested he should bring

it along to the Ministry to show his old friends. According to Jimmy Lake, it was Charles' idea to bring it ; but Jimmy agreed that, when he rang up Charles at Claridge's yesterday, he had invited him to come to the Ministry, and that it might possibly have been he who had put into Charles' head the idea of bringing the container then. "When I rang him up," Jimmy's evidence ran, " I congratulated him on capturing Stultz, and in the course of it said something about how I'd like to see the ' This-Way-To-Valhalla '—that's how he described the thing in his letter to me. Then I asked him to come round this morning, and tell us the story, and—yes, I did say, ' Bring all your trophies with you.' " Questioned again, Kennington had stuck to it that his brother-in-law had asked him to produce the container when he came. " Bring your trophy with you," is what he said—what I thought he said, anyway."

Second, the party. Of those present in the Director's room, all but Alice and Edgar Billson had on their own evidence been invited by the Director during the previous day and been told by him that Kennington was going to bring the poison container to show them. It was all over the Division, they said. Billson, however, denied having heard anything about the party until Miss Prince had rung him up, just before eleven o'clock that morning, and asked him to come to the Director's room. Mrs. Lake said that her brother had telephoned to her the previous day, immediately after his arrival in London. No, it hadn't been a shock. A happy surprise, certainly ; but she had never believed Charles was dead. He had told her he probably couldn't come and see her till the next day, as he would have to be closeted with some Brass Hats. Her husband had told her about the party, but not invited her ; she didn't go to his office much, anyway, and she would rather be alone with Charles the first time she met him again. Charles, however, when he turned up at her

home at ten the next morning, insisted on her going along
to the Ministry with him. Neither he nor Jimmy had
mentioned to her that he was bringing the container.
Mrs. Lake's evidence was corroborated by her husband
and her brother.

Third, the coffee-cups. The testimony of the several
witnesses, though it amplified what they had told Nigel
immediately after the event, did not seem to contradict
it at any point. Superintendent Blount had painstakingly
gone into the history of the cups. Miss Finlay had been
immediately behind Miss Prince in the queue at the
trolley, and testified that she had seen her go straight into
the ante-room with the tray. One of the typists in the
ante-room had seen her pass through into the Director's
room. Apart from the obvious improbability of it, there
was eye-witness evidence that Miss Prince could not have
put some private supply of poison into one of the cups on
her way from the trolley. Brian Ingle had been very
insistent, furthermore, that she did not use " Stultz's
thing " to poison her coffee. He had hardly taken his eyes
off her all the time they were in the Director's room : " I
was very fond of her. And she looked so strange—
different, somehow—very excited and beautiful, but
somehow I felt she was terribly unhappy—no, perhaps
not unhappy—uncertain, on the edge of something,
underneath it all."

Fourth, the grouping. Blount had worked on this
point with great tenacity, checking and counter-checking
the movements of each of those present in the Director's
room, from the moment when Nita Prince returned with
the tray, in relation to the coffee-cups of the Director and
Miss Prince. The gist of this was that, unless Mrs. Lake
and her husband and Brian Ingle were all lying, the
poison container could not have been used till after the
tray had been put down on the Director's desk, and Nita
had told them all to come and get their coffee. From that

point there was Alice's evidence that she had placed the container on the desk behind her, and Jimmy's that he had noticed it there when he took the designs out of his drawer. Unless they were both lying, it could not have been used up to that point. If they were lying, Blount's analysis of the grouping showed that every member of the party was at one moment or another near enough the desk to have poisoned Nita's cup, or the Director's, while they were putting up the designs on the bookshelf. But why should Jimmy and Alice have both lied, when the lie would only exculpate the others ? Finally, Alice had repeated her statement that she had seen the container on the desk when her brother made his remark about " the blood-thirsty type peering out from amidst the bougainvilleas." If she was telling the truth, this cleared the Director, who was standing in the middle of the room from that point till Nita's telephone rang, and she carried her cup over to her own table. It also cleared Charles Kennington, who on the evidence of Harker Fortescue had then moved well away to the left of the desk. It did not absolutely clear any one else, for they had all been shifting their positions, close to the desk, to get a good view of the cover-designs, and any one might have poisoned either Jimmy's cup or Nita's, which were standing side by side on the desk. On the other hand, the period between Charles's remark and Nita's telephone ringing was extremely short—less than half a minute, Blount reckoned. But then again, why should Alice Lake lie when the lie only called attention to her own proximity to the two cups and narrowed down the period within which the poison could have been decanted ?

Fifth, the motive. In his first series of interviews, Blount had contented himself with the formal question, did any one know any reason why the dead girl should have been murdered or have killed herself ? The answers had been vague, or entirely negative. Brian Ingle had

E

repeated his statement that she seemed on the edge of something. Merrion Squires said she had been " agitated " that morning and the evening before. The Director, frankly admitting that Nita had been his mistress, said she was very upset when Charles Kennington's letter came, worrying how her ex-fiancé would take it ; she felt they ought to tell Charles the truth, but he had tried to dissuade her from doing this at once—after all, he had said, it was four years since Charles had gone back on active service, and she had not seen him after that, and had had every reason lately to believe he was dead. Charles could not possibly assert any claim over her now, and he might well have lost interest in her, anyway. Major Kennington agreed that he and Nita were " sort of engaged " while he was working at the Ministry, but he said their correspondence had faded out some time before his " death " was announced in the casualty lists, and he had certainly not expected her to " fall into my arms " on his return. Did he know whether her affections had been engaged elsewhere ? " No, not for certain. But I didn't flatter myself a sumptuous girl like Nita would go for long without comforters."

Alice Lake said she had known about Nita and her husband for some time. Jimmy, in fact, had told her. She had accepted it ; as long as it made him happy, she would put up with it.

" So there you are," said Blount," slapping his bald head repeatedly—a sign that he was perplexed. " We have a murder that might just conceivably have been a suicide. We haven't a whiff of motive for either suicide or murder. We have a girl poisoned in full view of eight people, including your own good self. We have a poison container which disappears into thin air—no, we roped off the street underneath that room, and we searched every inch of it for fifty yards, either way, and it wasn't there. It's a wee thing, of course, and might have got stuck to the tyre of a passing car. I've appeals going out on the radio in case any pedestrian picked it up, but I'm not vairy optimistic. And, as if that wasn't enough, we don't even know whether the murderer got the person he wanted to : he could easily have poisoned that puir girl's cup by mistake for Mr. Lake's. And, worst of all, there's the spontaneous nature of the crime."

" Spontaneous ? "

" No one could have known, till the day before, that there was going to be poison available in the Director's room."

" No one but Charles Kennington."

" Granted. And nobody could have relied upon Kennington's letting the poison container out of his own hands. It's almost as though the crime had been unpre-meditated. ' By Jove,' someone says, ' there's that jigger lying on the desk ! Well, since it's going begging, I might as well break it into one of these coffee-cups.' "

" Yes, it does seem a spur-of-the-moment job," agreed Nigel.

" The hell of it is that we should know all about where the poison came from. The usual way we get a poisoner is through his source of supply, as you know—suspect A is recognised by the chemist who sold him the weed-killer. But this crime of yours——" Blount broke off, throwing up his hands disgustedly.

" It is a point in favour of suicide, of course. I mean, a person who is in a state of mind favourable to suicide would be more likely to succumb to the impulse, when she found the means handy. A would-be murderer doesn't wait about, relying on being presented with the means by fortune."

" You'd say that it was suicide, then, or else Major Kennington did it ? " asked Blount with a shrewd look at Nigel through his steel-rimmed spectacles.

Nigel was gazing non-committally at his Bonnard on

the opposite wall. " I'd like to know where and when
Kennington met her yesterday," he said.

The Superintendent positively bounced in his chair.
" What the devil d'you mean ? He said nothing
about——"

" That's just it. Why didn't he ? When he turned up
in the Director's room this morning, he greeted us all very
vivaciously, as long-lost friends. Then Nita said to him,
' You do look different in uniform.' Now, when he was
working at the Ministry, in 1940-41, he always wore
uniform. If Nita hadn't seen him since then—in fact, if
she hadn't seen him very recently, in mufti, why should
she say that ? Kennington tried to cover it up very
quickly. He started babbling away again, said, ' It
seems years since I saw any of you,' and Nita took the cue
and remarked presently that he'd only been wearing one
medal ribbon when last she saw him. I suggest, Blount,
that it would be worth your while to look particularly
close into Nita's movements, and Charles's, yesterday. I
say they met somewhere, and he was in mufti."

" Oh, you ruffian ! " exclaimed Blount, rubbing his
hands in high glee. " Here's the man who doesn't want
to have anything to do with the case ! Routine investigation, mind you, routine investigation. We're looking into
the girl's movements, of course. And her history. We've
been going over her flat this evening. One or two vairy
interesting little finds." He paused suggestively, but
Nigel did not rise to the bait. " And now you've
uncorked yourself, what else have you to tell me ? "

Nigel related the conversation between the Director and
Nita which Merrion Squires had overheard the previous
day, and the quarrel between Harker Fortescue and Edgar
Billson reported to him by Miss Finlay. There were
several little signs and omens filed away in his mind, but
he was not going to lay them before Blount yet.

" Oh, well, now. Miss Prince seems to have been a—

eh—a stormy petrel," said the Superintendent. He mixed himself another glass of whisky, held it up to the light, drank. " Invigorating beverage. Most invigorating. . . . And what did *you* think about her ? " he shot out suddenly.

" I wish you wouldn't use your third-degree tricks on me," protested Nigel. " My nerves won't stand it. I didn't think about my colleagues much. Who does ? What do *you* think about Detective-Sergeant Messer ? "

" A good man. Energetic. Ambitious. A bit of a snob. Clever. But too apt to jump to conclusions—he's young, you see—and when you're young and clever, you get impatient with routine detail ; you see the logical conclusion afar off, so you're apt to jump some of the stages on the way to it."

" He's not thorough, you mean ? "

Blount looked really shocked. " My dear sir, he's a trained man. Our men are always thorough. I said ' impatient ' over detail. He wouldn't live an hour with me if he scamped it."

" Well, let's say he's a human being trained to be a machine, and leave it at that. Now, that's my point. We in the Visual Propaganda Division—we're all human beings, rather clever and unusual ones, for the most part, and we've been trained, or had to train ourselves, in a highly technical, highly mechanical routine. The first principle of our kind of propaganda is the human touch ; but, to keep pace with the demands, we had to mechanise it—to work out a detailed, *in*human sort of routine for delivering the human touch punctually and in large quantities."

" A mass-emotion factory ? " suggested Blount.

" If you like. And the operatives are engaged in producing natural emotions by artificial methods. Bad for them. You can understand the effect this was likely to have on their private lives. It led to a certain unreality, and therefore a certain irresponsibility, in their ordinary human relationships."

" You're thinking of Nita Prince ? "

" No. As a matter of fact, I'm thinking chiefly of the Director." Nigel paused a moment. " Merrion Squires described Nita as a carnivorous orchid. He's too fond of flashy phrases. She's—she was a good deal more complicated than that. But Merrion had the right idea, in one way. I fancy her surface was very deceptive. ' A beautiful blonde '—suppose I say that, what do you think of ?— an easy, decorative, rather nit-witted creature : a pin-up girl with flashing teeth and legs a mile long and a figure that means one thing only : a smooth, golden, varnished, primitive phantasy. Now Nita was all that. On the surface. But something more too. There was something in her eye, and her voice, that said, ' I'm really quite different underneath. Am I fire, or ice ? Wouldn't you like to know ? Come and find out.' "

" And what did you find ? "

" I didn't accept the invitation myself. I don't know who did, apart from Kennington and the Director. Brian Ingle thought her a goddess ; Merrion Squires, a straight bitch. Infinite variety. I dare say they were just painting their phantasies on that smooth, white surface. And suppose—just suppose, Blount—that beneath it she wasn't fire, or ice, but an ordinary woman, vulnerable, foolish and shrewd, a realist about her own feelings, a self-deceiver about others' ; wanting a home and children, maybe—a cosy, humdrum life with hubby coming back from the office at five p.m. and a fortnight at Skegness in the summer. Suppose she hated being a sort of shiny human Odeon, a Palace of Pleasure, a Temple of Mystery——"

" I'm thinking you'd better meet me at her flat to-morrow morning, if Mr. Lake will give you leave off," said Blount.

"Suppose *that* was what she wanted someone to find out," Nigel pursued, "wouldn't you have an interesting motive for——?" He broke off a moment. "That reminds me. A queer little slip of the tongue. Probably means nothing. I told you Charles Kennington used a phrase about one of Squires' designs—'a blood-thirsty type peering out from amidst the bougainvilleas.' A few minutes later, Mrs. Lake repeated the phrase exactly. There was a mild joke—the Deputy Director saying the design was suitable for a volume of Bloomsbury *belles-lettres*. Well, after it happened, I was trying to find out what had become of the poison container. And Mrs. Lake said she had last noticed it on the desk when Charles said, 'The *murderous* type peering out from amidst the bougainvilleas.' One word changed, which she had got right before. It may have been pure accident. On the other hand, that piece of evidence cleared her husband: if the container *was* still on the desk at that point, you'll remember, he could not have poisoned Nita's coffee. But, if she'd seen him do it, or suspected that he might have done it, and wished to shield him, that is just the lie a clever woman would tell. And the slip of the tongue which made her say 'murderous' would reveal what was in her mind."

"E'eh, well. That's too fanciful for me," said Blount, rising to go. "It's terrible late. I must be off. A most interesting chat, Strangeways. I'm obliged to you. And if you should happen to be at 19 Dickens Street at ten o'clock to-morrow . . ." At the door, Blount turned again. "And don't forget, her husband was not the only person in the room cleared by that piece of evidence of Mrs. Lake's."

CHAPTER IV

" So THIS," said Nigel, peering inquisitively about him, " is the love-nest."

It was 10.30 on the following morning. Nigel had gone to the Ministry even earlier than usual and, working rapidly, polished off several jobs outstanding from the previous day. He then went to look for the Director, whom he found in his room talking with the Ministry's Investigations officer, Mr. Adcock—a fat, cheerful, lethargic ex-policeman who, apart from the mysterious outbreak of coat-slashing last winter, had had nothing worse on his hands than the usual lost property and petty pilfering troubles since he was appointed to the Ministry.

" Yes, Nigel ? " Jimmy Lake asked gently. He looked washed out and preoccupied. Nigel told him of Superintendent Blount's request.

" But of course," said Jimmy. " Take the day off. Call it duty-leave. And I'd like to borrow your room and your assistant, if I may : I don't find this room terribly congenial just now."

They had a few more words together. Edgar Billson was creating, the Director said, because he was due to go on leave at the end of the week, and the police had requested that none of those present in Jimmy's room the previous morning should leave London. The work of the Division was going to be seriously hampered by the police investigation, tactful and reasonable though Superintendent Blount seemed to be. And on top of this there was the idiotic little trouble of a missing secret file. However, Jimmy wouldn't bother him with that now :

Mr. Adcock and the Registry would have to thrash it out between them.

Nigel stopped on the way out to tell Miss Finlay that the Director would be using his room.

" You'd better ask now for all his telephone calls to be switched to my extension. Look after him, won't you ? He's just about all in."

Pamela Finlay was relatively subdued this morning. Indeed, the whole floor gave the impression of an uneasy and muted atmosphere, as though someone were gravely ill : voices spoke more quietly, feet trod more discreetly, and the sudden rattle of a typewriter sounded like a quarrel in a sick room.

" Some of the typists are in a flap," said Miss Finlay with a strenuous effort to moderate her usual breezy tones.

" What, afraid they'll be the next to go ? Tell them not to be such asses."

" I will," said Miss Finlay formidably. " It'll be a pleasure. Gossip, gossip, gossip all the time, those girls. Is it true, Strangeways, that you're in with the police ? They're saying——"

" The Superintendent is an old friend of mine. By the way, what's this about a secret file missing. Have you heard anything ? "

" No. Oh, wait a minute. Is that the file the Director was clamouring for yesterday afternoon ? PHQ14/150 ? Haven't they found it yet ? I bet the D.D. is sitting on it."

Nigel remembered vaguely now. Merrion Squires had come in, about five o'clock, asking for some file which the Registry claimed had been charged to the Director, but which he had not received. Nigel had paid no attention to it at the time, beyond asking Miss Finlay to make sure it was not in their room. He remembered her shocked expression, though, when Merrion Squires said, " Secretaries come and secretaries go, but files go on for ever."

" The Irish," he said now, " do not have quite our ideas about the sanctity of human life."

Miss Finlay's eyes widened.

" So it *was* Merrion Squires. Have the police arrested him ? "

" Great Scott, no ! I was thinking about the Irish character, not—you really mustn't jump to conclusions like this, or you'll involve me in an action for slander."

" Sorrow," said Miss Finlay, without any obvious sign of remorse. " Forget it. Not but what I don't think he'd have done it like a shot if—no love lost between him and Miss Prince, you'll have to admit, Strangeways."

" My dear good girl, there's no love lost between myself and Mr. Billson, but we contrive not to murder each other."

Pamela Finlay opened her mouth for one of her usual bellows of laughter, then clapped her hand over it, and looked reproachfully at Nigel, as though he was to blame for the indiscretion. Nigel turned the subject to the day's work and gave Miss Finlay some instructions. Presently he was on a bus, travelling eastward to the Bloomsbury thoroughfare off which lay Dickens Street.

" So this is the love-nest," he said to Superintendent Blount. " Well, what did I tell you ? "

" You'd been here before, maybe ? "

" Never."

" An astute guess of yours, then."

Nita Prince's flat occupied the top floor of 19 Dickens Street. Below it, Nigel had noticed, were on the ground floor a solicitor's office, and on the first and second floors the office of a small publishing firm. There was also a basement, where presumably a caretaker lived, for a dog had barked furiously from below as he climbed the stairs. Very convenient, he had thought, peering at the publisher's discreet brass plate on the first-floor landing :

this chap and the lawyer pack up at five or six in the evening, and after that the whole house is empty : no one to see who visited Nita, unless the caretaker is a busybody. Very convenient for Nita. Very inconvenient for Blount, though, possibly.

The Superintendent had let him in.

" Yes, you can touch anything. My fingerprint chap has been over the rooms," were his first words. " This is the sitting-room. Bedroom and bathroom in there. Kitchen through that door. A homey little place."

Blount had said it. Nothing less like the film producer's idea of a love-nest could be imagined. No seductive divans, no glittering cocktail cabinet, no wardrobe filled with slinky gowns, no signed photographs, no titillating multiplicity of mirrors. No glamour at all. Not even the stale waft of an exotic perfume in the air. If the rooms were stuffy at all, it was only with the stuffiness of an almost aggressive respectability. On the iron, four-poster bed lay a plain white satin night-dress, neatly folded. This note of severity was repeated on the dressing-table, which lacked the usual litter.

" In vials of ivory and coloured glass
 Unstoppered, lurked her strange synthetic perfumes,
 Unguent, powdered, or liquid." . . .

Nigel found himself murmuring, as he eyed the plain wooden-backed hairbrushes, the business-like comb, the simple handkerchief-sachet smelling—of all things—of lavender. Nita's beauty preparations he found tucked away at the back of a drawer. And, at the back of his mind, a new idea of Nita began to form—an idea about her and Jimmy which finally determined him to alter his last night's resolution that he would not become further involved in the case.

He wandered back into the sitting-room, absent-mindedly carrying a threadbare woolly rabbit which he had found on Nita's bedside chair.

" I find all this very pathetic," he said to Blount, who was rummaging in the drawers of a bureau. He put down the rabbit on the mantelpiece, beside a briar pipe which lay there—Jimmy Lake's, no doubt. " It only needs— well I'm blest, and here it is ! " He picked up darning needles and yarn and a man's sock from the seat of a chintz-covered armchair.

" Quite a domesticated sort of lassie, you'd think," said Blount. " But look at this, now."

He held out a sheaf of newspaper cuttings to Nigel. The top one revealed the dead girl wearing a bathing-dress and a photogenic smile, surrounded by a posturing, simpering bevy of nymphs. Underneath ran the caption : " Miss Nita Prince, eighteen-year-old winner of the *Daily Clarion* Seaside Lovelies Competition, with some other competitors." The date of the paper was August, 1936.

" I bet you found these tucked away at the back of a drawer, too," said Nigel.

" As a matter of fact, I did. What's in your mind ? "

" Which drawer ? "

Blount pointed.

" It was the only one locked. You'll see why."

Nigel pulled the drawer right out from the bureau and laid it on the floor. He turned over the contents. Bundles of letters tied up with bright ribbons. A large foolscap envelope, out of which Nigel shook some photographs : these too revealed Nita Prince, but not this time in a bathing-dress. On the back of them was stamped : " Fortescue. Photographic Agency."

" You've noticed this, of course," he asked.

" Yes. She used to model for what they call Art Studies. Mr. Fortescue told me that himself."

" H'm. The body of a well-nourished young woman,"

Nigel murmured. "What squalid phrases the police do use. Anything in the letters ? "

" I'm afraid the puir lassie was rather—e'eh, rather fast-living in her younger days," replied Blount primly.

" No recent letters, you mean ? "

" Well, there are a few notes from Mr. Lake. But nothing from Major Kennington. I doubt that's a little strange, seeing she kept so much. And you'll find a ribbon, same kind as those other ones, in the waste-paper basket." Blount glanced significantly at Nigel. " A ribbon, but no letters to go with it."

" I see your point. But it's rather odd that a person should take away his bundle of letters and leave the ribbon behind, isn't it ? "

" People do silly things. That's how stupid policemen catch up with them."

Nigel began to prowl round the room again. He paused at a Matthew Smith still-life on the wall opposite the fireplace. His eye moved to the chintz covers and the deep maroon curtains, to the E.M.G. gramophone and the albums of records beside it—Beethoven Quartets, Mozart, Sibelius Symphonies, the Enigma Variations. Nita, or Jimmy, had been improving Nita's taste. He moved over to the bookshelf. Yes, relegated to the bottom shelves were the romantic novelettes, the tattered film magazines, the detective novels of Miss Prince's unregenerate days. Above them were ranged more serious reading : copies of the Everyman edition ; a row of the English poets, with Jimmy Lake's favourite Victorians bulking large ; novels by E. M. Forster, D. H. Lawrence, Henry Green.

Nigel picked up a green-covered book lying on the table beside the armchair. " *Poems* by A. H. Clough, sometime Fellow of Oriel College, Oxford." On the flyleaf, " N., with love from J., July 28, 1945." Nigel turned to the pages between which the marker lay. A passage was

marked in pencil—a line at the side of it, and an exclamation mark.

> " Terrible word, obligation! You should not,
> Eustace, you should not.
> No, you should not have used it.. But oh, great
> Heavens, I repel it!
> Oh, I cancel, reject, disavow and repudiate wholly
> Every debt in this kind, disclaim every claim, and
> dishonour,
> Yes, my own heart's own writing, my soul's own
> signature! Ah, no!
> I will be free in this; you shall not, none shall,
> bind me.
> No, my friend, if you wish to be told, it was this
> above all things,
> This that charmed me, ah, yes, even this, that she
> held me to nothing.
> No, I could take as I pleased; come close; fasten
> ties as I fancied;
> Bind and engage myself deep;—and lo, on the
> following morning
> It was all e'en as before, like losings in games
> played for nothing.
> Yes, when I came, with mean fears in my soul, with
> a semi-performance
> At the first step breaking down in its pitiful rôle of
> evasion,
> When to shuffle I came, to compromise, not meet,
> engagements,
> Lo, with her calm eyes there she met me and knew
> nothing of it,—
> Stood, unexpecting, unconscious. *She* spoke not of
> obligations,
> Knew not of debt,—ah, no, I believe you, for
> excellent reasons."

" Listen to this, Blount," said Nigel, and read the passage aloud.

When he had ended, the Superintendent smacked his bald head. " Oh, dear me, dear me. Don't like him. An egotist. A bad case of negativism. Won't take the plunge. Wants to eat his cake and have it. T'ck, t'ck, t'ck."

" He's honest about himself, though."

" Egotists often are. They can afford to be. I mean, they take so much credit for the being honest that it quite obscures for them the unpleasant picture of themselves the honesty has revealed. But this isn't getting us any forrader."

" I'm not so sure. Here's a book Jimmy Lake gave Nita only a few days ago. Either he or she has marked this passage with a query and—hello, what's this ? "

Nigel was holding the book closer to his face. He went over to the window, beckoned to Blount, pointed out to him a faint pencil-mark he had not noticed before in the margin against the last few lines of the poem :

A

" A capital ' A '," said Nigel. " Could stand for Alice. The complacent Alice Lake, who doesn't hold Jimmy to his married obligations. Just read the passage again, Blount, and see how neatly the ' she ' in it fits Mrs. Lake —the unexacting woman who doesn't hold her husband to anything ; who, when he comes in his ' pitiful rôle of evasion ', meets him calmly, takes no notice of his em-barrassment, says nothing of any debt he owes her. Incidentally, the ' he ' is not a bad picture of Jimmy, either. I should imagine he's pretty hard to nail down, you know, in affairs of the heart."

" What you're telling me," said Blount slowly, " is that a man doesn't murder his mistress when he has a complacent wife."

" Exactly. Or suppose this exclamation mark in the margin is ironical, on the other hand. Suppose Alice

Lake is in fact extremely jealous and has been kicking up a fuss, and behaving altogether unlike the woman in the poem. Well, a man may murder a jealous wife because she stands in his way, but——"

"—But he only murders his mistress if she has been carrying on with someone else, or driving him potty with her demands ? "

" And does this pleasant domestic scene look as if Nita was flighty ? No. She'd obviously settled down to be a home from home for Jimmy."

The telephone rang, and Blount went to answer it. After a brief conversation, he put back the receiver. " They've done the autopsy," he said. " The container was not in the body. That seems to dispose of the possibility of suicide. There was just a bare chance she might have swallowed the thing after biting it, though that way it'd have been difficult to account for the traces of poison in her cup.

" Where on earth did the container get to, then ? "

" Well, either Mr. Ingle threw it out of the window, or——"

" Or one of your searchers slipped up."

" I can't think that possible," said Blount, a little stiffly. " I admit that, from my point of view, the personal search was rather a formality. After all, the last thing a murderer would do, after breaking the container into a cup, is to keep it on his person. He only had to drop it anywhere in that big room, and there was plenty of time for him to do it, *after* you'd told them there'd have to be a personal search as well as before. But still, I don't believe my people could have made a mistake."

" It seems to me you're in a proper jam. Means : any one in the room had it. Opportunity : any one in the room had it, unless Mrs. Lake is telling the truth when she says she saw the container on the desk a minute before the girl was killed. So you're left with Motive."

" Quite a classical case of bricks without straw," said Blount dryly. " That's why you've got to come in on it. You're in a far better position than the police to work on the Motive angle."

Nigel, standing by the mantelpiece, gazed at the thread-bare woolly rabbit.

" I'm not sure I won't change my mind," he said at last. " I don't like all this—this pathetic home-making broken up. What about Kennington's movements the day before the crisis ? And Nita's ? " he asked abruptly.

" Kennington is covered from the moment he got back to London till 10.30 that night. He left the War Office at 10.20. A War Office car took him to Claridge's, where he went straight up to his room. All that is checked. He couldn't have met Miss Prince before then. He claims he went to bed. At any rate, the night porters say he didn't go out again. Now for Miss Prince. She left the Ministry at 6.30. Came straight back here. About 6.40 she came in and told Mrs. Humble—that's the caretaker—she'd be having a visitor later and not to bother when the bell rang—she'd open the front door herself. Shortly after eight, Mrs. Humble heard someone let himself in. This, it appears, was Mr. Lake. He volunteered himself that he went to Dickens Street then, intending to spend the night here, but Nita Prince seemed out of sorts and not very welcoming, so he left about nine o'clock, returned to the Ministry, worked late, and slept there. Mrs. Humble assumed *he* must have been the visitor Miss Prince had referred to. So, when the front-door bell rang, a little after eleven o'clock, she came upstairs to answer it. But she heard Miss Prince running downstairs, so she just poked her head round the door between the basement staircase and the hall. She saw Miss Prince open the front door and let a woman in."

" A woman ! " exclaimed Nigel.

" Uh-huh. She couldn't see this woman very clearly—

F

there's only a dimmed electric light in the hall; but she thinks she might be able to recognise her again. Well, Mrs. Humble went to bed. She was awoken by her dog barking; it barks whenever any one goes out or comes in. She heard the front door closing. She looked at her alarum clock. It was ten minutes to one. And the dog only barked four times that night—for Mr. Lake's arrival and departure, and for the second visitor's ditto. So she didn't have any other visitors."

Nigel pondered this for a moment. The second visitor: Nita's girl friends surely would not in the normal way call so late. And why should she so obviously have wished to get rid of Jimmy Lake before this visitor arrived—unless she had something to say to her which she didn't want Jimmy to hear? And, the day after, Nita was murdered. As if in response to Nigel's next thought, Blount remarked:

" Mrs. Humble did say that the visitor—the woman— was small—not so tall as Miss Prince, anyway."

" Have you questioned Alice Lake yet about it ? "

" I'm expecting her here "—Blount looked at his wrist-watch—" in five minutes or so. I rang up her house early this morning, as soon as I'd had my chat with Mrs. Humble."

" She made no objection to coming here ? "

" None at all. Mrs. Humble will bring her up. If she recognises her, she'll nod to me. If she isn't sure, she'll shake her head."

" H'm. Quite a moment. As far as it goes."

Nigel turned back to the bookshelf. No, Nita Prince's education did not seem to have included the novels of Alice Kennington; they were too satirical for her taste, perhaps; too satirical, perhaps, even for Jimmy. If Alice was at all like the novels she wrote under her maiden name, one could understand why Jimmy had taken up with the so very human Nita, the old-fashioned home-girl-at-heart Nita.

" You took all their fingerprints, I suppose ? "

" Yesterday afternoon," replied Blount. " No one objected. Except Billson, who seems to object to everything on principle. But he came round presently. And my fingerprint chap went all over these rooms last night. We'll know the results about midday. Of course," he added grimly, " ladies are apt to wear gloves when they pay social calls."

" No glasses or things lying about ? "

" Mrs. Humble washed everything up yesterday morning. Just Miss Prince's breakfast things, she said. If either of the visitors had a drink, Miss Prince must have washed up the glasses herself. Not much to drink, anyway. A bottle of gin and some lime juice in the kitchen cupboard. That's all."

A few minutes later the bell rang, and footsteps were heard coming up the steep stairs. The sitting-room door opened. Alice Lake stood there, glancing at them a little timidly. Just behind her was a slatternly-looking woman, grinning from ear to ear and nodding her head vigorously at the Superintendent. Blount's face was quite impassive ; but his brow knitted in momentary vexation when Major Kennington stepped into the room after his sister.

" I hope I'm not *de trop*, my dears," he said brightly, " but Alice felt she needed moral support."

" Just so," said Blount. " That's quite all right. I'm sorry to have dragged you along here, Mrs. Lake, but it was simpler. Do sit down, won't you ? "

Nigel was familiar with the spectacle of Superintendent Blount putting a witness at ease. The courtly, considerate manner ; the Pickwickian jollity ; the appearance of slight obtuseness. He had seen clever people fall for it— seen them relax, and a consciousness of intellectual superiority creep into their faces or their words : Ah, yes, not so very formidable after all, I think I can twist *him*

round my fingers all right. And Nigel had seen such
people sadly discomfited. Alice Lake is a clever woman,
he thought, quietly surveying her from the window-seat,
while Blount worked his confidence trick. A clever
actress too—that is, if she *was* in this room two nights
ago—glancing around her with just the right suggestion
of curiosity and faint embarrassment, as if to say, " So
this is where she and Jimmy lived." And an attractive
woman, in her severe, composed sort of way. Nigel eyed
her small, neat profile ; the hair brushed up from the
back in the neo-Edwardian manner ; the delicate features
—long, thin, slightly retroussé nose, ironical mouth,
waxen little ears ; the black coat and skirt and frilled
white silk blouse, small feet and white-gloved hands ; so
crisp and cool compared with most London women after
six years of war.

"—Yes, I'm afraid there's no doubt the puir lassie
was murdered," Blount was saying in his most avuncular
tones. " T'ck, t'ck, a sorry business. Now I'm sure you'll
understand, Mrs. Lake, how much depends on your
evidence."

Alice Lake raised her plucked eyebrows, said nothing.

" That point about the poison container still being on
the desk when you said it was—barely a minute before
Miss Prince took her cup away to her own table. You're
quite sure it was ? "

" Oh, yes. Quite sure."

" No possibility that it could have been used already,
and put back there ? Could you see all of it, or only a bit
of it ? It was lying beside your husband's calendar,
wasn't it ? "

" Yes. I could see it all. Of course, I don't know how
different it'd have looked if it had been used."

" Oh, you'd have noticed the difference all right,"
Charles Kennington put in. " They're fragile, brittle
things. It'd have been broken right across."

" Just so," said Blount. " Your evidence clears your good husband, you realise."

" I'm glad to hear that," Mrs. Lake replied coldly. " And it happens also to be true. I'm not lying to protect any one, I can assure you. I'm not made that way."

" My sister is a madly Victorian girl," said Charles. " She really believes that Truth must always prevail. The blue-stocking type."

" Do be quiet, Charles," said Alice impatiently.

Blount proceeded. " But of course your evidence does not clear *you*. You were within easy reach of the poison container and Miss Prince's cup."

" I realise that too," said Alice. Nigel chalked it up to her—whether a good mark or a bad, he was not sure—that she did not point out how unlikely it would be for a murderer to have volunteered so readily so dangerous a piece of information.

Blount tickled the tip of his nose.

" You would not, in any case, have any strong impulse to protect your husband ? "

" Oh, but I might indeed. I'm extremely fond of Jimmy. Just because I let him live his own life——"

Charles Kennington sighed, rolled up his eyes, lifted his hands theatrically. Alice's policy of *laisser-faire* was clearly a matter of disagreement between them.

"—Yes, Charles, live his own life, it doesn't mean that I am indifferent to him. But there'd have been no point in his poisoning that girl, don't you see ? Therefore, no point in my trying to shield him."

" Quite so," said Blount, with an approving nod. " Now had your husband given any indication to you recently that his affair with Miss Prince was petering out, or that she was—e'eh—not playing straight with him ? Some other man, perhaps ? "

" Oh, indeed no. In fact, a month or two ago, he

sounded me about divorce. In his rather circuitous way."
Alice Lake smiled faintly. " I suppose she'd been nagging
at him a bit. I can quite understand. It couldn't have
been altogether a satisfactory life for her, all this "—her
gloved hand made a slight gesture at the top floor of
No. 19 Dickens Street.

" Well, now, this is most interesting. And what did
you say ? "

" I told Jimmy if he must, he must. I told him I'd
be terribly upset," her high, cool voice continued, " but
he must make up his own mind—I wasn't going to do it
for him. If you want to know, I'd say he dashed straight
along here and told her he couldn't press a divorce on me,
it would break my heart."

Blount blinked a little. " That's exceedingly frank,
Mrs. Lake. And Miss Prince wouldn't accept the situation ? And that's why she wanted to see you, to have a
private talk about it ? "

" A private talk ? "

" Yes, when you came here the other night."

Mrs. Lake's green eyes opened wide. " But—there
must be some mistake. I've never been here in my life
before."

Major Kennington rose from the arm of her chair, on
which he had been sitting, and went to stand with his
back to the fireplace. He glanced from Alice to Blount,
in a quick, amused way, as though they were duelling
over some abstract subject.

" Come now, Mrs. Lake," said Blount. " I have a
witness who saw Miss Prince let you in at the front door
just after eleven o'clock two nights ago."

" But that's nonsense," she replied sharply. " I was
in bed then, in my own house."

" Can you—e'eh, prove that, Mrs. Lake ? "

" I don't expect so. Let me see. Well, my husband
rang me up at 10.30 to say he'd be working late at the

Ministry and sleeping there. But, no, I suppose I can't. I was alone in the house."

" Who is this informant of yours ? " asked her brother in the embarrassed pause.

" Mrs. Humble. The caretaker here."

" Could we not have a word with her ? Identities are sometimes mistaken."

" Surely." Blount rang down to the basement on the speaking-tube. Presently Mrs. Humble arrived, grinning, panting and dishevelled.

" Is this the lady you saw Miss Prince let in two nights ago ? " Blount asked.

" 'Sright. Didn't yer see me nod. That's 'er."

" You're quite sure you couldn't be mistaken ? " Blount asked carefully.

" I 'ope I 'as the use of me eyes still," said Mrs. Humble, bridling. " Same 'eight. Same peekong little fice. A real lady, I says to myself. That's 'er all right, all right, take my ruddy oath."

" Did you notice how she was dressed ? " asked Charles Kennington.

" Black three-quarter length coat, ever so chick. White blouse. White kid gloves."

" What kind of a hat was I wearing ? " asked Alice.

" Get on with you, m'm ! As if you didn't know ! One of them 'alo 'ats, black straw, awiy from the fice."

There seemed no more to be said. Blount told the woman she could go. But, when the door closed behind her, Mrs. Lake quietly remarked :

" I'm afraid it *must* be a case of mistaken identity, Superintendent. You see, I never wear hats. Don't possess one. Any one will tell you."

The Superintendent took it very well. Clucking, beaming, massaging his bald head, he said :

" Well now, t'ck, t'ck, t'ck, that just shows one can't be too careful. Very smart of you, Mrs. Lake, that

question about the hat. Capital. Capital. Puts the lid
on it, as you might say." He chuckled, with the Scots-
man's ripe appreciation of his own witticisms. " It seems
you must have a double, Mrs. Lake."

Nigel spoke up for the first time since the visitors had
arrived.

" Charles," he said. " When we met in Jimmy's room
yesterday morning, Nita said to you, ' You do look
different in uniform.' Implying she'd seen you recently
not in uniform. You said, in your letter to Jimmy, that
you'd been doing one of your female impersonation turns
to catch Stultz. You are the same height as your sister,
and resemble her closely in features. Don't tell me she
has yet another double."

Charles Kennington had buried his face in his hands
during this *démarche*. He now looked up at them all
again, fizzing with laughter.

" Oh, my ! " he giggled. " Oh, what an exposure ! My
' peekong little fice ' ! Too humiliating ! British Major
masquerades as female—I knew it would get me into
trouble with the police one day."

" What is all this about ? Do pull yourself together,
Charles," said his sister sharply.

" *Homo sum*," Charles replied. " Meaning, of course,
' I am the one.' Yes, I will come clean. *Mea maxima
culpa*."

This was his story. Nita had rung him up at lunch-
time the day he arrived in London. She had been very
distressed, and said she must see him alone. He told her
he would have to be at the War Office till late in the
evening. So it was arranged that he should come to her
flat that night, when he had got away from the War
Office.

" But why dress up to do it ? " asked Nigel.

It seemed that Nita had been terrified lest he should
be recognised coming into the house. The caretaker, she

had said, was a fearful busybody : she'd spread it around
that Nita was receiving gentlemen visitors at midnight.

"I told her that was all nonsense. But the poor girl
was in such a taking that—well, it suddenly occurred to
me that I had my female toilette with me, so why not
wear it ? Put her mind at ease. Might even cheer her
up. So I hared back to Claridge's when my conference
was over, and changed and made up and got a taxi to
here."

"And did it ? " asked Nigel.

"Did it what ? "

"Cheer her up ? "

"To be quite frank, no. You see, my little job in
Germany required me to play the woman's part rather
well ; otherwise there'd have been no future in it. So,
when I got into the rig again, I found myself automatically
playing up to it. And this didn't go down madly well
with Nita—I mean, she thought I should become myself
again when she'd got me safely up in her room here, and
I kept lapsing back into Bertha Bodenheim, and in fact
the joke fell rather flat. It's not the sort of joke a womanly
woman would appreciate, anyway."

"What did she want to see you about ? " asked Blount,
rather coldly.

"Oh, but surely you can *imagine*." Charles' high, clear
voice was uncannily like his sister's as he protested.
"Don't you *see* ? We had been engaged. She had taken
up with Jimmy since—*perfectly* right and proper—but she
was terrified that I would assert my claims over her.
She wanted to be the first to tell me what had happened,
not let the truth come *skulking* out when we all met the
next day. And, of course, she wanted to get me on her
side—it's *too* bizarre how naïve women are when——"

"On her side ? Against your sister, you mean ? "
Nigel asked.

"My dear, of *course*. She knew I doted on Alice. She

wanted to be forgiven (*a*) for deserting me, (*b*) for taking away Alice's husband. Oh, yes, we went into the whole thing."

" And did you forgive her ? "

" I think I put her mind at rest, poor sweet," said Charles, with a quick, veiled glance at Nigel. " Not that I *approved* of Alice's life being broken up——"

" It wasn't," Mrs. Lake interrupted.

" Well, you know what I mean. Being broken *into,* dear, if you must be pedantic and proud. But, from what she told me, I gathered that the situation was reasonably in hand, the triangle more or less squared. And she was obviously attracted to Jimmy no end. Quite a changed woman—I was astonished."

" Can you enlarge on that a bit ? "

" So cosy, my dear, so domesticated. *Quite* a different proposition from what she'd been that year I was working at the Ministry. She talked—how shall I say ?—well, like a staid, respectable married woman. Quite *riveting,* the contrast. To tell the honest truth, I found her rather *dull.*"

" Did she talk about divorce at all ? The possibility of Mr. and Mrs. Lake being divorced, I mean ? " asked Blount.

" No."

" There was nothing in her conversation which could help us ?—Think carefully, Major Kennington—nothing to suggest there was some other man, or woman, who might have a motive for making away with her ? "

" No. I must say I find this ' some *other* man or woman ' rather daunting. Meaning my sister and my brother-in-law are the obvious suspects ? "

" No, Major Kennington. As you put it that way. Your sister and *you,*" said Blount in level tones. " You two had more cause for jealousy than any one else, so far as we know yet."

Not a hair of Alice Lake's elegant coiffure appeared to turn at this. She just glanced at her brother, with an ironical twist of her mouth. Charles Kennington studied his finger-nails for a moment ; then he said :

" There are other causes than jealousy, Superintendent, for *crimes passionels*."

" Such as ? "

" Oh, no, you don't ! " replied Charles, with a return to his frivolous manner. " The chief suspect is not going to get himself in deeper by suggesting a few nasty motives for others ! "

Alice was scrutinising him with a puzzled expression. As he said no more, she turned to Blount.

" But surely there's quite a possibility that the wrong cup was poisoned ? I mean, that the poison was intended for my husband ? "

" There is that possibility. Yes."

" Oh, I see," she said, after a pause, making a little face. " And I had an equal motive for killing *him* ? Jealousy again ? The woman scorned ? Charles, you were a silly to put temptation in my way."

" What ? Oh, yes, Stultz's thing. Yes. But how was I to know that publicising it would lead to ?—ah, well, it's a lesson. My poor erring sister, I shall accompany you to the scaffold with spiritual consolation. I shall——"

" I don't think this conversation need be prolonged any further," interrupted Blount, sternly. " You must understand, both of you, that crime is a serious matter. You know my attitude already, Major, towards your bringing that poison container to Mr. Lake's room and then, apparently, forgetting all about it."

" I *know*. It *was* rather *distrait* of me. I couldn't be more sorry. But all those photographs and things took my mind off it. I find photographs so *entrancing*, you see, and——"

" At the same time," continued Blount, " you and your

sister should realise that *everyone* in the room then must be under suspicion. The police are not content with exploring only the obvious motives. I have been frank with you, because you raised the question of ' obvious suspects ' yourself."

" Your sentiments do you credit, Superintendent," remarked the irrepressible Charles. " I feel that, under happier circumstances, you and I could get along whizzingly. Well, my pet lamb, we'd better leave the sleuths to their sleuthubrations."

" We shall, of course, have to check both your statements."

" Statements ? Oh, to make sure it was I and not Alice who came here that night ? Yes, well, Alice's hatlessness should be easily established. And the nightporter at Claridges may remember a seductive female gliding upstairs at about 1.30 a.m.—I had to walk all the way back in my clip-clopping little high-heeled shoes. Or he may not. Wait a minute, though. How silly of me. Did you find a piece of ribbon in the w.p.b ? "

" We did."

" Ah. That saves a lot of trouble. Nita gave me back some old *billets-doux* of mine. They were tied up with the ribbon. Asked me to take them away and destroy them. So I did. So I must have been here."

" Why take away the letters, yet leave the ribbon ? " asked Nigel.

Charles Kennington's features worked themselves into an expression of the most dramatic distaste.

" My *dear* ! How *can* you ask ? Haven't you *seen* the ribbon ? *Magenta!* I could not go about with a piece of *magenta* ribbon—it'd be death to my complexion ! '

" Hum ! " said Blount, when the pair had departed. " Quite a tough nut, that Mrs. Lake. Smooth customers, both of 'em. Very smooth. Hmm."

" I'm inclined to think he was telling the truth."

" Well, he'd better. His story is easily enough disproved, if——"

" I don't mean about coming here. I'm sure he did. I mean when he said that his sister always tells the truth —believes Truth must prevail. I think I must cultivate her society."

" Any other intuitions ? " asked Blount ironically.

" One or two odd little turns of phrase. From Charles."

" Ah, you mean when you asked him did he forgive Nita, and he answered ' I think I put her mind at rest.' "

" That's very perceptive of you, Blount. Yes. It sounds rather sinister now, in cold blood, doesn't it ? But I'm thinking chiefly of—well, first a curious word he used about the poison container ; and second, his extremely uncharacteristic lack of chattiness on one of the subjects that arose."

CHAPTER V

LATE THAT NIGHT, Nigel Strangeways returned to the Ministry. He had spent a fruitless afternoon ; first at Nita Prince's flat, drearily reading through the letters she had kept, which yielded nothing but evidence of her youthful indiscretions ; then, with Blount, trying to extract information from Nita's few women friends. It soon became clear that, after she had taken up with Jimmy Lake, she had forsaken her old haunts and become a home girl. The only woman in whom Nita seemed to have confided recently—Miss Sproule, a Junior Specialist in another Division—said that Nita had been worrying about what would happen to her after the war : the Ministry would close down ; her opportunities for being with Jimmy would be fewer. There was nothing new here. The Director had admitted as much during yesterday's interview with Blount : natural delicacy had no doubt prevented him then from talking about the suggestion of divorce ; but he had said that he and Nita were worried about the future. It must be common enough just now in such liaisons, Nigel reflected—war had prevented people looking far ahead or envisaging the consequences of their private actions : there must be many lovers now wondering if their affairs could last beyond the cessation of hostilities, almost dreading the return of peace. Miss Sproule had told them that Nita seemed determined not to relinquish Jimmy, however. " If he's got to choose between us," Nita had said, " I shall see that it's me he chooses."

Nigel entered the great hall of the Ministry. In deference

to the man at the reception desk who was supposed to scrutinise all passes, he made a perfunctory gesture towards his breast pocket ; but the man was reading a magazine and did not even look up. Nigel marched along the empty, sounding corridor towards the lifts. Presently he was at the top floor. He looked into his own room. No messages for him. He went along to the Deputy Director's room, and found Harker Fortescue, as usual, at work.

" Lay off it," he said. " Come down to the canteen."

The Deputy Director's face looked cadaverous in the light of the green-shaded table-lamp ; hollowed out with exhaustion.

" O.K.," he said. " Ker-rikey, what a day ! Let's see if Jimmy will come too."

The Director, who was back in his own room now, declined. The police investigation had been interfering with his work all day, he said, and the Controller had been nagging at him, and all the efforts of his staff had failed to find the missing secret file, and there was going to be hell to pay for someone ; so they could go and have their midnight feast by themselves.

" He's taking it very hard," said Harker Fortescue as they descended in the lift.

" Well, naturally. After all, Nita——"

" Oh, I don't mean that. Though no doubt he is. But the old boy's been creating all the afternoon about that file."

" I expect it's a way of taking his mind off what happened yesterday."

" Taking all our minds off it. And just as well," said Harker grimly. " I tell you, Nigel, this is a filthy business. After you "—they emerged from the lift and moved towards the basement canteen—" there's going to be an awful lot of muck turned over before the police get at the truth."

" There is indeed."

" Are you working for them ? "

" Well, yes and no. With them, but not necessarily
for them."

" H'm. I suppose you know what you mean by that.
Damned if I do. Anyway, the thing's a nightmare. I
mean, I thought I knew everyone in the Division—*knew*
none of us could do a thing like that. Now it's happened,
one spends half the time telling oneself it couldn't have
happened, pinching oneself, finding one is awake after
all ; and half the time trying to avoid one's colleagues'
eyes. Does a man look any different after he's committed
a murder ? He ought to. But——"

" Don't burble, Hark'ee," Nigel interrupted kindly.
" You're over-strained. What you want is a nice plate of
spam and pickles."

The Deputy Director shuddered strongly, and asked for
his usual glass of milk. They went to a corner table in
the refectory, which was empty now except for a few
teleprinter girls, a handful of messengers yawning over
their dominoes, and a press representative or two awaiting
the next official hand-out. The air-conditioning apparatus
hummed ; the naked electric light glared down on tea-
urns, counter, metal chairs and tables, metallic perms.

" Fancy calling this place a refectory," mused Hark'ee.
" It's more like travelling steerage on a third-class liner
bound for hell."

" You're full of fancies to-night."

" Just whiling away the time, old boy, till you start
on your third degree."

" Oh, I see. Well, you can begin by telling me what
your row with Billson was about."

" Which row was that ? " The Deputy Director's face,
under the glaring lights, looked expressionless, a crude
map drawn on parchment.

" Two Thursdays ago. During the lunch hour. About

Nita Prince. Miss Finlay heard you through the wall."
Nigel stuffed another piece of bread and marge into his
mouth. He repeated the words that his assistant had
heard. " ' Last chance '—what last chance was he giving
you ? And why was he ' in a cleft stick ' ? "

Harker Fortescue's mouth twisted quizzically.

" Your Miss Finlay is a very slap-dash type. Why
don't you train her better ? Always jumping to conclusions and usually the wrong ones."

" In fact you were just having a friendly little romp
with Billson ? "

" I didn't say that. I merely say we were not talking
about Miss Prince."

" But Pamela Finlay heard you——"

" She heard a word which, with her usual inaccuracy,
she interpreted as ' Prince.' The word was prints. I was
telling him off about the dilatoriness of his Unit in
supplying photo-prints for the Production Units."

The Deputy Director was gazing at Nigel, rather in the
expectant manner of one who has told a peculiarly subtle
joke and is waiting to see if the point of it has been taken.
Nigel stared down his nose.

" But, if *you* were telling *him* off, why did he talk
about giving you a last chance ? "

" My dear old boy, you know what Billson is like,
surely ? He's a sea-lawyer. He's a Permanent Civil
Servant. He fights every point, on principle. He refuses
to accept responsibility. When I started ticking him off,
he came back with a long grievance about the Pink
Forms. He said the system was unworkable. He told
me I must reconstruct the procedure—he'd give me this
last chance to do so—or he'd apply for transfer to another
Department. He was quite heated. So was I, I admit.
Billson always did get my goat."

" So you told him he could ' go to the dogs ' for all
you cared ? Strong words, Hark'ee."

The Deputy Director smiled blandly at Nigel.

" I think I really will sack your Miss Finlay. She gets nothing right. What I said was he could go to the *Docks*. The Docks Department of the Ministry of War Transport had a vacancy for a Finance Officer, and that's where he was threatening to transfer. Wish he had. Though God help poor old M.O.W.T., if he did."

" I see. So that explains it." Nigel sighed gently. " How well did you know Nita before the war, when she worked for your agency ? "

" I didn't. She only modelled for us occasionally. I never was one for taking models out to dinner. Though I must say she was a whizzer in those days."

" You realise the police will inquire very closely into everyone's relations with Nita ? And they'll go back some way into the past ? "

" Oh, yes. ' Routine enquiries ' ? I know. Well, my past is a pure white sheet—in that respect. Next ? "

" Why do *you* think someone should want to kill Nita ? "

Harker Fortescue's cold eyes scrutinised Nigel, unwinking. After a long pause, he said :

" Speaking purely in the abstract, there are three possible reasons for killing a beautiful woman." He held up three fingers, and slowly ticked them off. " One, jealousy. Two, satiety. Three, if she's a certain kind of woman, because she's blackmailing you."

" Do you think Nita was that sort of woman ? "

" She was a reformed rake. Reformed, mark you. I take it we're agreed about that ? So not blackmail for money. But there are other things for which a woman may blackmail."

" Go on," said Nigel, his pale blue eyes gazing sleepily at the golden, leaf-metal hair of a teleprinter girl at a distant table, who was chattering away to her companions—no doubt discussing the V.P.D. scandal too.

" Security," said Harker Fortescue. " A reformed rake will go to any lengths to defend her reformation—any lengths of emotional blackmail, I mean. She'll cling to respectability as fiercely as a respectable woman will covet what they call Romance."

" All this, ' purely in the abstract ' ? "

The Deputy Director nodded.

" Well. Very interesting." Nigel sighed again. " And now, while I fetch you another glass of milk, you might be thinking out—purely in the abstract—some slightly less preposterous version of your row with Edgar Billson."

Nigel Strangeways rose and made for the counter, leaving Fortescue goggling at his back. The refectory telephone rang. One of the attendants at the counter answered it.

" Mr. Fortescue ? Mr. Fortescue ? " she called out in a sing-song voice.

The Deputy Director strode towards the telephone. The desultory voices in the canteen, which had been hushed for a little, began again. The next moment, Harker was beckoning to Nigel.

" Jimmy ! Jimmy ! Are you there ? " Nigel heard him say.

" What's up ? "

" He sounded ill. Damn and blast the exchange, we've been cut off ! " Harker jiggled the call lever angrily.

" Never mind about that ! Quick ! Let's get up there ! "

Nigel Strangeways sprinted between the tables, Fortescue at his heels. Faces turned stupidly to follow them, like sheeps' faces when a train is passing. Their hurrying feet echoed through the long basement corridor. Nigel stabbed his finger at the lift button and held it down.

" What did he say ? " he asked, as the light panel flickered—six, five, four——

" He just said, " Hark'ee, is that you ? Come "—and
then his voice faded away. He sounded bloody queer."

The lift door slid open. They tumbled in. Nigel stubbed
the top-floor button. The lift should have gone up, non-
stop ; but at the ground floor it stopped again : the
door slid open, stayed open for the set thirty seconds,
then automatically closed. The same happened at the
first floor. Harker began to curse. But Nigel pushed him
out of the lift, saying, urgently :

" Run down to the Reception Desk ! See that no
one leaves the building. *No one.* I'll ring you down.
Hurry ! "

Nigel stayed in the lift. It had come down to the
basement without stopping. Now it seemed to be going
to stop at every floor. Yes, second floor, stop, pause,
door slides open, pause—curse it, that means someone on
some floor pressed every button on the outside panel,
just before we got into the lift. Someone wants to delay
us. The obvious thing to do is to get out and run up the
stairs. But perhaps someone wants me to do the obvious
thing. Safer not, my boy. Why hasn't this blasted lift
got a non-stop master button ?

At the next stop, Nigel put his head out and looked
upwards. The top floor seemed to be dark. He switched
off the electric light in the lift. He did not want to be a
sitting target, all lit up, when he got there. I'm as bad
as Miss Finlay, he thought ; jumping to conclusions :
childish : probably Jimmy's just got an attack of in-
digestion, or cut his finger, or found the missing file.
Well, here we are, sixth floor, stop, pause, door opens.
. . . He slid quickly through the opening door. Darkness.
Damn the dim-out, the Japs aren't likely to . . . His
fingers fumbling along the wall, found the switches,
pressed them all down. The passage. Quite familiar.
Quite empty. Doors all shut. Walk quietly along it,
then. On my left, Brian's door, Merrion's door, my door ;

on my right, the two doors of the Photographs Library. All in order. Now, the ante-room. Open. On my right, Jimmy's door, shut : a light showing beneath.

Nigel turned the knob and entered. For a moment, his eye naturally going straight to Jimmy's desk, he thought the room unoccupied. But only for a moment. His eye moved to the left. And there, at the table where Nita Prince had died, was Jimmy Lake. What made Nigel catch his breath was that the Director seemed to be engaged in prayer. He was kneeling in front of the table, his head buried between his outstretched arms ; almost as though he were praying to the ghost of Nita who once had sat there, imploring her to return. Then Nigel noticed the thing sticking out of his back. And the situation became normal again, in so far as murder was a normal thing now in this room.

Nigel Strangeways covered the floor in three strides, stood for a moment gazing down at the knife hilt, protruding from Jimmy's back, then took hold of the Director and laid him face downwards on the floor. Kneeling, he slipped his hand inside Jimmy's shirt. The heart was still beating. Nigel took up the telephone receiver, which had been lying off its hook beside Jimmy's outstretched hand. He got through to the Reception Desk and asked for Mr. Fortescue.

"Hark'ee ? Nigel here. Listen. You've got to work quick. Jimmy's been attacked : still breathing : knife —went in a bit too high. Ring up the First Aid Post and tell 'em to send someone up here and to get a doctor, *at once*. Then ring A.R.P. Control, get Lewis to come up here. You're holding everyone at the Reception Desk ? . . . Good, no one's to go out that way, repeat no one, not even the Minister. Get hold of whoever's in charge of the Messengers to-night—he's to rustle out all his men, take 'em out by the side entrance in Manning Street, and post them round the building outside, as many men on

each side as possible, and if they see any one getting out
of a ground-floor window, they're to nab him. That side
door must be locked again, of course. And I want one
man to make sure all the other side doors are locked :
if he finds one open, he must report to me at once. Are
you with me ? Good. Doctor first, remember, and bring
him up yourself the moment he comes."

Nigel rang off, took up the external telephone, and rang
Superintendent Blount's home number. The Superintendent was just going to bed. Nigel told him what had
happened and what steps he had taken. Blount agreed
to come at once, picking up a couple of police on the
way.

Moving back to the door, Nigel turned off the light
switches. The reading-lamp on the Director's desk went
out, as well as the centre light on the ceiling. The room
was pitch dark. He switched on again, went over to the
desk. No signs of disorder, of a struggle. The desk was
tidy—blotter, calendar, pen-tray, ink bottle, one tray of
papers neatly arranged on its broad surface. He tried
the drawers : they were all locked. Straightening up, he
moved away towards Nita's table, peering down at the
carpet. Presently, between her table and the door, he
found a few fresh bloodstains on the carpet ; and looking
closer, his eye almost level with the floor, faint marks
on the carpet as if something had been dragged towards
the door. These he covered with newspaper.

At this moment the nurse from the First Aid Post
arrived. She was a calm, sensible woman, and Nigel at
once took her into his confidence.

" Mr. Lake has been stabbed. You've got a doctor
coming, nurse ? "

" Yes. He'll be here in five minutes."

" Good work. Take a look at him, please. He's alive
still. Can we do anything for him before the doctor
comes ? "

The nurse tried the pulse, nodded to Nigel, and made the unconscious man more comfortable.

"There may be some internal bleeding," she said, "but the knife must have missed the heart. He should pull through all right, if the lung·is not affected. How did——?"

"No questions now. Oh, there you are, Mr. Lewis——"

The door had opened, and the A.R.P. Control Officer came in, a small, alert, red-headed man.

"My goodness, what's this? Mr. Lake, is it?" he asked.

"Mr. Lake has been attacked. His assailant *may* be in the building still. Mr. Fortescue is seeing that all the exits are stopped. Got any fire-watchers on duty to-night?"

"Sorry, Mr. Strangeways. Only three of us. Since the German war ended, we've cut down——"

"Three will do. You know this building like the back of your hand. I want you to start searching it from top to bottom. Start on this floor and work downwards. There'll be some police along presently to help you. Make a list of everyone you find. If any one acts suspiciously, grab him at once. I'll do the apologising afterwards, if necessary. And *make* it a search, like a good chap : anywhere a man, or woman, could hide. Do you know Mr. Ingle, Mr. Squires and Mr. Billson, of this Division, by appearance?"

"Yep."

"And Major Kennington, who used to work in Military Censorship?"

"Yep."

"If you find any of them, bring him straight along here. Never mind about Civil Service etiquette ; I'll cover you. Got all that?"

"Savvy. I'll use this telephone, if I may, and get my chaps up here. Bit of excitement again."

Mr. Lewis and his fire-watchers had just left the room to begin their search when the Deputy Director arrived with the doctor.

" H'm, yes," said the latter, after a brief examination. " Nasty business. He'll do, though, with luck. I'm going to extract this knife first. Nurse, you've got some pads and bandages ready ? Good."

" Use my handkerchief, please. Round the handle," said Nigel quickly.

The doctor gave him a curious glance, then took the handkerchief. He and the nurse knelt down beside the body. Harker Fortescue turned his head away. Presently the doctor gave the knife a strong pull. As he did so, and the nurse applied the pads, Jimmy Lake muttered something.

" What was that ? " asked Nigel sharply.

The doctor said, " I'm not absolutely certain. Sounded like ' Alice. She won't let me go, darling.' Did *you* hear, nurse ? "

" That's what I thought he said, sir."

" Reminds me," Nigel muttered. " Must ring up his wife. Nurse, please tell me anything else he says. It may be vitally important."

Nigel found Jimmy's home number in his address book. Alice Lake answered. She was in bed, but would get out the car and come at once. Oh dear, thought Nigel, I should have done this before. How long since Jimmy telephoned to the refectory ?—ten to fifteen minutes. Taking Harker Fortescue aside, he asked him to ring up Major Kennington, Merrion Squires, Brian Ingle and Edgar Billson at their home numbers. The last three, at any rate, lived too far from the Ministry to have been able to get home yet, supposing——

" He's coming round," said the doctor, who had applied restoratives. " No, stand back please, everyone."

Nigel watched the Director's bloodless face quiver, his

eyes open a little, taking in nothing, close, then open again and survey them in a bewildered way.

"The lights went out," he muttered faintly. "Hello, Nigel old boy."

"Don't talk," said the doctor; and to Nigel, "He mustn't be questioned yet."

"That's all right," said Nigel. "One thing is pretty certain—he never saw his assailant."

"How d'you know that, sir?" the doctor asked, rising from beside his patient and laying a long knife, its handle swathed in Nigel's handkerchief, on the table. Nigel did not answer. He was staring, with consternation in his eyes, at the knife: he drew the handkerchief away from it: yes, it was one of the knives, pointed, thin-bladed, eighteen inches long, used in the Art Work studio to slice drawing-paper—as effective a substitute for the stiletto as a modern assassin could hope to find.

"And now, sir," the doctor was presently saying to Harker Fortescue, "if you've finished with that telephone, I must ring up for an ambulance. Hospital for this gentleman."

"No," said Jimmy, who had been lying with eyes closed. "No. Not hospital. Take me home. Send for Alice."

"But my dear sir——"

"She's on her way, Jimmy," interrupted Nigel. He took the doctor aside, spoke a few words to him urgently.

"No, I cannot take the responsibility. He must have trained attention."

Nigel shrugged his shoulders. Jimmy spoke again, his voice startling Nigel, so much had it resumed its normal, rather tired, infinitely patient, inexorably firm intonations.

"I am *not* going to hospital. So let's have no more of that. Alice, my wife, trained as a nurse. She's perfectly competent. I'm sorry, doctor, but——"

The latter gave him a searching look, then turned away to telephone for the ambulance.

" Well, Hark'ee ? " asked Nigel.

" They are all at home, except Merrion."

" Did they answer—in person, I mean ? "

" Brian and Charles Kennington did. Billson's wife answered for him, said he'd been in all the evening."

Nigel's brow knitted. He began whistling a dreary little tune between his teeth. Firm steps were heard in the passage : Superintendent Blount, two uniformed constables and a plain-clothes man behind him.

" T'ck, t'ck, t'ck," he clucked briskly. " How's he doing, doctor ? "

" He'll be all right, provided that——"

Jimmy, thinly but firmly, interrupted. " Superintendent. Tell this excellent doctor, please, that I am *not* going to hospital."

" Well. Dear me, now," Blount patted his bald head. " An impasse, eh ? An impasse ? "

" Shall we wait till Mrs. Lake arrives, before deciding ? " put in Nigel. He took Blount aside and spoke to him. In a minute, the two uniformed policemen had gone off to assist in the search of the building, while Harker Fortescue was deputed to return to the Reception Desk and ring back if the net of Messengers round the Ministry caught anything : he would also find out from the official at the desk whether he had noticed any other member of the Visual Propaganda Division entering the Ministry earlier that night.

" And now, doctor," said Blount, " I must ask your patient one question."

Brushing aside the doctor's remonstrances, he knelt down beside Jimmy.

" Just this one question, Mr. Lake. Did you see the person who attacked you ? "

" No. The lights went out, I tell you."

" Have you any notion who it might be ? "

The Director's head shook wearily, then rolled to one side.

" He's fainted," exclaimed the doctor angrily. " I must insist that no more——"

" That's all I wish to ask," Blount said : then, turning to Nigel, " You were right. But I don't just see how——"

" I'll explain later. Hallo, what's this ? "

The red-headed Mr. Lewis had come in, bristling with excitement. He held up a long white overall-coat, which Nigel recognised at once as the type of garment worn by the people in the Art Work Unit. Mr. Lewis tossed it over to him, bundled up.

" Found it in the Gent's, fifth floor, stuffed down one of the lavatory bowls. Thought you might be interested. Take a dekko at the right-hand sleeve, Mr. Strangeways."

Nigel shook out the dripping coat. On the cuff a red stain was visible. The stain, when Blount tried it, was still damp : the rest of the cuff, which could not have been immersed, was dry. Blount turned to the inside of the coat collar, put his finger on the label there, pursed his mouth. Over Blount's shoulder, Nigel read on the label, indelibly marked, *M. Squires*.

Blount gave instructions that the search should be continued, with Merrion Squires as its main objective. Five minutes later Mrs. Lake arrived. Jimmy Lake, who was conscious again, gave her a strangely appealing look as she entered—a look, thought Nigel, such as a small boy might give to his mother when he had injured himself in some parentally-forbidden exploit ; a mixture of pathos and bravado and uncertainty. Alice Lake took it all pretty coolly : no flutter, no flood of tears or questions. Her husband once again insisted that he should be taken home and not to hospital.

" Very well, Jimmy," she said in her high, detached

little voice. " If you really want to. And the doctor agrees."

The doctor, now he had met Mrs. Lake, was rather more amenable. After a few words with her, he consented, on condition that he should send a trained nurse in the morning to assist her. The ambulance having just arrived, Jimmy was put on a stretcher and brought away, Mrs. Lake and the doctor following.

Blount and Nigel were alone in the room, the plain-clothes man having been sent off to Merrion Squires' lodging to keep an eye on it supposing he had escaped from the building.

Nigel now gave Blount a fuller account of the evening's work, as far as the known facts went. When he had finished, Blount asked him how he had known that the Director never saw his attacker.

" First, because of the lift buttons. Second, because Jimmy was not dead."

" Now go easy with me. It's well after midnight, and it's getting terrible cold in here, and my brain won't function at its best."

" Well then. The fact that the lift buttons were all pressed *after* the lift had got to the basement suggests that the criminal wished to delay us in order to make his own escape."

" Yes, I *can* grasp that," said Blount dryly.

" He would not try to delay us unless he knew we were on our way. After all, he'd not have dared to attack Jimmy at all if he didn't think this floor was unoccupied, as it usually is at that time of night. Now, how could he know someone was going to come up from the base-ment just then, unless he had heard Jimmy make his telephone call to the basement refectory ? "

" So far, so good."

" Right. We have the criminal *after* he has stabbed Jimmy, hearing Jimmy telephone. The criminal couldn't have been in this room still, or he'd have prevented Jimmy telephoning. But, when he heard him using the telephone, and knew he hadn't succeeded in killing him, why didn't he go back and finish the job properly? The only possible reason is that he was afraid of being recognised. He knew we'd be on our way up. He couldn't be certain that, if he attacked Jimmy a second time, Jimmy might not survive for the minute it would take us to get up here, and give us his name. Besides, of course, he'd left his knife in the body. But, if Jimmy *had* seen and recognised him when he first stabbed him, then it was absolutely imperative that—at whatever risk—he should return here and finish him off before we arrived. But he didn't return and finish him off. Therefore Jimmy had *not* recognised him."

" Q.E.D. Yes, that's—e'eh—vairy ingenious. How do you reconstruct things, then ? "

" The criminal opens this door, puts his hand through, switches off the lights, all in a twinkling. One of those switches, by the way, controls Jimmy's desk light. The room is pitch-dark. I tried it. Jimmy—you remember him saying just now ' the light went out '—Jimmy would naturally make for the switches, assuming it was a boyish joke by Hark'ee or someone. The criminal has slipped into the room. He gets behind Jimmy, feels for him, strikes. Then he goes out. There are blood-spots on the carpet there, within a few feet of the door. That's where Jimmy went down. There are also marks of dragging. Under the newspapers there. Jimmy was not quite out. Dragged himself to the switches, turned them on, dragged himself to the nearest telephone, on Nita's table. I suggest that the criminal saw the light under the door, or heard Jimmy moving. Too late to do anything about it, without being recognised. He tears down the passage, slams down the lift buttons, turns out the passage lights—if he hadn't done so on his way in, runs down one flight of stairs,

hides his coat in the Gent's, and then——" Nigel snapped
his fingers.

" And then, presumably, runs down the remaining
flights and tries to get out of the building."

" He'd not have time to get past the Reception Desk
before Hark'ee was there."

" Plenty of windows on the ground floor.   Your
Messengers don't move very fast, I've noticed.   No, I
don't fancy we'll find your Mr. Squires here to-night."

" My Mr. Squires ?   No.   I fancy you won't."

Something in Nigel's tone made Blount glance at him
keenly.

" I noticed you kept talking about ' the criminal.'
Very correct.   I doubt it's not like you to be so correct."

" Well, I ask you——"

" Och, I know what you're going to say," chuckled
Blount.   " A man doesn't attempt a murder with a knife
that can easily be traced to him : and, if he does, he
will not leave it in the body for us to find.   Nor does he
wear a white coat with his name clearly marked on it,
to attempt a murder in a dark room where it's the one
kind of garment that might make him visible.   Nor does
he stuff the coat down a lavatory one floor below, carefully arranging that the cuff with his victim's blood on it
shall remain above the water.   It's all vairy deplorable,
oh my, oh my, it is !   But then, where is your Mr.
Squires ?   Why isn't he at home in his pure white bed ? "

" Blount," pronounced Nigel, " there are times when I
come near to misjudging you."

" I'm not so gullible as I look," Blount conceded.   " At
least, I hope not.   Well, we shall know before long—
Simpson is going to ring me from Squires' lodgings when
he gets there.   And in the meantime, I'll take a look
round this room."

Curled up in the arm-chair Blount vacated, his eyes
half closed, Nigel watched the Superintendent at work,

moving solidly, purposefully, from one part of the room to another, shifting the newspapers to peer at the carpet, measuring, making marks with white chalk, taking notes, standing back as if to see the puzzle in perspective, muttering and clucking to himself the while. After a quarter of an hour of this, the very room began to look browbeaten, exhausted and guilty.

" You ought to go on the films, Blount."

" Uh-huh ? "

" And everyone in the country be compelled to attend the picture. Prophylactic measures. An awful lot of people would be inoculated against crime for ever if they could see one police investigation—the real thing—from beginning to end."

" Crime Doesn't Pay series, eh ? "

" No. They're too dramatic, too box-office. It's the slow, tireless, meticulous, cumulative, boring side of an investigation ; the spectacle of a stout, fatherly-looking gentleman in a bowler hat leaving not a single pebble on a whole beach unturned ; that's what would unnerve any misguided person who was contemplating a felony."

" The professional criminal hasn't that much imagination. He's a stupid fellow, on the whole—a one-track mind."

" But we're not dealing with professionals now. You'll never hear the last of it from Establishments Division if you cut a piece out of that carpet. Has it occurred to you, Blount, that the method of this attack on Jimmy, compared with the last——"

The telephone rang. Blount took up the receiver.

" Yes, Blount here . . . He's not at his house ? Went out at 10.25 ? . . . Very well, Simpson, wait there till you hear from me."

He turned to Nigel.

" What do we make of this ? "

" Search me. Brrh, it *is* cold in this arm-chair—it

must be the dawn wind. One might be sitting on a
mountain ledge awaiting the rescuers. *Oh, my God!* "

Blount positively started. Nigel was on his feet and
had whipped round to face the window behind the arm-
chair. Silently he moved towards it, opened a crack in
the curtain and peered through.

" Blount, this window is unlatched. That's where the
draught was coming from."

" Well, shut it then," said Blount irritably.

" No. I fancy perhaps there *is* someone sitting on a
mountain ledge to-night."

Nigel drew the curtain right back, opened the window
wide, put out his head and called into the darkness.

" Merrion! Merrion, you idiot! Hadn't you better
come in ? "

" Is he there ? Can you see him ? "

" No. But he used to sit on the ledge, outside his
room, when the flying bombs were coming. Blount, go
and pull back the curtains and turn on the lights in
all the rooms on this side, will you ? If he's out there,
I'll go after him."

" No, that's my job, Strangeways."

" Please. I know him. He may take some handling."

" Very well. Watch yourself, though."

Nigel was already clambering out of the window. The
ledge was at least two feet broad, but the well of darkness
beyond made it seem more like two inches. Just as his
eyes were growing used to the darkness, and he could see
the traffic lights at the corner far below to his left, the
light from Harker Fortescue's room sprang out, carving
a little bay in the night, making the darkness around it
blacker still. Then, the light from his own room, Merrion's,
Brian Ingle's. The ledge, flood-lit now, seemed deserted.
Already one or two angry cries were coming up from the
street below : people had been conditioned for so long to
the black-out that although it was no longer necessary,

they still made their automatic protests. Nigel found himself filled with a quite insensate rage against these busybodies in the street. "Bloody fools," he muttered, and then, keyed up by his rage, began to walk smartly forward along the ledge.

If Merrion was there at all, he must be at the corner of the building, where the ledge stopped. The lights, streaming out from the rooms in between, cut him off from view as effectually as would total darkness. Nigel walked through the successive bays of light, hoping that Merrion —if he was there—had not gone mad ; hoping he was not there ; yet hoping in a way that he was there, so that his own conjecture might be proved right.

A gust of wind tousled the tree-tops in the park opposite, and seemed to bounce off the canyon wall of the Ministry, twitching maliciously at Nigel. He was passing Brian Ingle's window. There was the end of the ledge, no figure crouching on it, nothing beyond but a dark drop.

And then Nigel saw, with an odd mixture of fear, relief and irritation, the knuckles white on the coping. He went deliberately to the edge, knelt down and looked over.

He was looking into the upturned face of Merrion Squires, more clown-like than ever, dead pale as if it had been coated all over with liquid white. He was hanging by his hands over an abyss. Far below, the traffic lights flicked from green to red.

"So you *are* here," said Nigel inadequately.

"Don't try and touch me, or I'll let go."

Nigel's accumulated irritability burst inside him.

"All right, let go, then. Dash your god-damned brains out—it doesn't matter to me," he said furiously.

He could not, if he had pondered conversational gambits for an hour, have hit on a more successful one. The wild look went out of Merrion's frantic, upturned eyes. A sort of resentment took its place.

H

" That's a nice way to talk to an old friend," he gasped.

" If you don't pull yourself up soon," Nigel remarked coldly, " you'll not be able to."

" Well, who cares ? You don't."

" Jimmy has been stabbed, and——"

" Yes, I know that. With my knife. So I'd better take the high jump now, hadn't I ? "

" You'd better come up and tell me what you know about it."

The eyes rolled in the chalky, clown's face ; they were beginning to look mad again. " I don't know anything. I——"

" This is the most ridiculous conversation I've ever had. I'm getting cold and I want to go to bed. Jimmy is not dead ; he won't die. *You* will, if you try and stay there much longer. It'll take you about fifteen seconds, after you've let go, to hit the street. You'll be conscious all the time, and it will seem much, much longer than fifteen seconds. And when you do hit the street, you will not necessarily be killed outright. People have fallen greater heights, and survived for some days afterwards, in extreme agony. Why go through all that when neither I nor the police are at all convinced that it was you who attacked Jimmy ? "

Merrion Squires, beads of sweat on his face, peered up at Nigel. At last he said :

" D'you swear that, now ? "

" Yes."

" All right. Help me up."

Nigel lay down full length on the ledge and took hold of Merrion's wrists. Merrion's feet began to scrabble on the smooth wall. His breath came in sobs : " I can't ! I've got no strength left ! I——"

" Pull, damn you ! Don't be such a snivelling baby ! "

The insult seemed to brace Merrion. He swore back at Nigel furiously, made a new effort, and scrambled out of the abyss of darkness on to the lighted ledge. There he collapsed for a few seconds, sobbing again.

" Are you ready now ? " asked Nigel briskly. " We'll have to crawl back to Jimmy's window ; the rest are locked inside——"

Merrion Squires interrupted him strangely.

" Nigel, you asked me a question just now."

" Well, *are* you ready ? There's no hurry. Take your time——"

" Not that. You asked, ' Why go through all that ? ' " His body shuddered convulsively. " I'll tell you. Because I don't know. I don't know whether I stabbed Jimmy or not."

CHAPTER VI

" I KNOW it must look bad, after that shindy I had with the Director over my lay-outs for the Pacific job," said Merrion Squires.

" You don't inevitably attempt to kill the boss just because he ticks you off."

Merrion gave Nigel one of his glancing looks, half-challenging, half-defensive.

" Ah, but think of the Irish temperament, my boy. Vindictive. Never forgets an injury."

" Well, if you've got a confession to make, you'd better keep it for the Superintendent. He'll be here any moment."

Nigel Strangeways rose from the breakfast table and began prowling round Merrion's room. It was 8.45 on the morning after the attack on Jimmy Lake. When they had got him off the ledge, Merrion had been in no shape for questioning. With Blount's consent, Nigel had accompanied him back to his lodgings in a police car and stayed the night. The plain-clothes man, whom the Superintendent had insisted on keeping at his post there, had just been relieved by another as they began breakfast. The search of the Ministry building had disclosed nothing more than an unlatched window on the ground floor—which might mean something or might not. No doubt the police were working on it now.

" I must say, it's very odd to think of you as a detective," Merrion Squires was saying. " I'm not sure I don't prefer your normal rôle—the stern but just Jehovah of the Editorial Unit. Don't you find it embarrassing having to snoop around your old colleagues ? "

" I prefer it myself. On the other hand, I do quite enjoy snooping. Born inquisitive, I suppose. I collect human frailties like Hark'ee collects. . . . Now *this* is very nice, a quite enchanting piece of work."

Nigel held up a pencil drawing of Merrion's, with an air of delighted discovery which effectually concealed the fact that he had already found it earlier this morning, while Merrion was asleep, and Nigel poking about in the magpie litter of his sitting-room.

" Did Mrs. Lake sit for this ? " he asked.

" Is this the sort of ' human frailty ' you collect ? " replied Merrion, a sharp edge on his voice.

" Why be so evasive about it ? Nothing morally culpable about drawing a head-and-shoulders sketch of a pretty woman, is there ? "

After a pause, Merrion said, rather sulkily :

" Yes, she did sit for it. I can't draw from memory."

" You know her well ? "

" I *have* made a pass or two at her, if that's what you mean."

" I didn't mean it at all. However, as you approach it from that angle——"

" What other angle would you prefer to approach a pretty woman from ? "

"—With what results ? "

Merrion Squires' evasive glance flickered from Nigel to the portrait he held. He seemed to be making up his mind whether he should take offence or not. Then he gave an exasperated kind of grin.

" Nothing very striking. I did not ' make ' her, as you'd put it. A few kisses. She's a very deep, cold little pond, that one."

" A case of deep meeting deep, that must have been. Is she still in love with Jimmy, would you say ? "

" I doubt if she could love any one distractedly, except herself." Merrion was talking seriously now. " No, Jimmy was the peaked and pining lover of the two."

" Yes, poor Nita seems to have——"

" Poor Nita, nothing ! It's Alice his emotional capital has always been sunk in, my boy ; don't you get that wrong."

" He took a queer way of showing it, then," said Nigel, genuinely surprised.

" Ah, don't be so naïve ! Nita was a substitute for him—a substitute for the womanly affection and admiration, all the cosiness he couldn't get at home. Clever of her to see that's what he wanted. But of course he didn't *really* want it—not in the depths of him. And he was beginning to realise this."

" He did, and he didn't, want it ? "

" Yes, my innocent friend. Jimmy's not capable of sustaining a deep, whole-hearted emotional relationship. He's the type that, in the last resort, hates being fully involved. I know. I'm that sort myself. Now, Alice never made such demands on him ; she gave him room to breathe. That's why I say his emotional capital is sunk in her. He took up with Nita because there's always a hell of a dualism in his sort of nature. Part of it wants to lose itself utterly in someone else—wants to defy the other half, which is all for keeping its own integrity and remaining irresponsible. Jimmy's setting up with Nita was the first part of him, making a dash for full emotional responsibility. But the other half would always have been stronger and hauled it back. In fact, it's a wonder Nita lasted so long—great tribute to the girl, when you come to think of it."

" Did Nita convey all this to you ? " asked Nigel, after a meditative pause.

" Oh glory, no ! I was on far from intimate terms with the deceased, I'm glad to say."

" ' Glad ? ' You've always been very hard on her, haven't you ? "

" I see Jimmy's fate, and I says to myself, ' There, but for the grace of God, goes M. Squires.' "

" Well, how do you know all this ? Pure reason ? "

" Oh, no," said Merrion. " Alice told me. Gave me the clue, anyway." His voice became a startling mimicry of Mrs. Lake's high, cool tones : " ' I know he'll regret it. He doesn't like exacting women. He'll find her absolute hell before long, Merrion.' "

The thought shot across Nigel's mind that, if Merrion and Mrs. Lake were in a conspiracy together, this could be a very subtle manœuvre by Merrion to direct suspicion away from them—if they had been in a conspiracy against Nita, that is to say. On the other hand, if Jimmy Lake had been the intended recipient of the poison, why should Merrion admit even a mild degree of intimacy with her ? And the fact that a murderous attempt should have been made on Jimmy, so soon after the poisoning, suggested that he had been the real target for the poison too.

Nigel had no time to follow up this thought, for Superintendent Blount was announced. Blount was very business-like and impersonal this morning. He administered the official warning to Merrion Squires, then asked him to give his account of the previous evening. With a wry glance at the sergeant, who was all set to take down his evidence, Squires began.

His story was that, after lunch on the previous day, he had found on his desk a note from Nigel, asking him to come back to the Ministry at eleven in the evening, as he had some important matters to discuss, and to wait in his room till Nigel turned up. He did so. He must have arrived only a few minutes after Nigel and the Deputy Director went down to the canteen. No, he had not seen any other member of the Division when he came in. About ten or fifteen minutes later—Merrion could not be

at all sure—he had heard feet running past his door
towards the staircase, and a moment afterwards he could
see through the transom over the door that the passage
lights had gone out. He left his room to investigate, and
was attracted by a queer sound from the Director's room.
He went in and found Jimmy Lake very much as Nigel
had found him, kneeling before Nita's desk, his body
sprawled over it. Protruding from Jimmy's back was the
hilt of a knife which Merrion recognised as his own, or one
of the same pattern. He assumed Jimmy to be dead. But
he was approaching the body to make sure, when he heard
the whine of the lift ascending, heard the lift door opening
and feet coming down the passage. He was trapped in the
room, with a body which had apparently been stabbed by
his own knife. There was nothing for it but to scramble
out of the window, push the window to from outside, and
hide on the ledge, awaiting events.

" I lost my head, of course," he concluded. " If I'd had
any sense, I'd have pulled out the knife and taken it
with me."

" It's extremely lucky for you that you didn't," said
Nigel—a remark which earned him a nasty look from
Blount.

" I take it you wrote no such note to Mr. Squires ? "
the Superintendent asked Nigel, who shook his head.
" What did you do with the note ? "

" Scrumpled it up and put it in my pocket. Here it is,"
said Merrion Squires.

" Ah. Typed. I see it's got your initials, Mr. Strangeways."

" That's easy," said Nigel, looking at the typewritten
sheet over Blount's shoulder. " We all initial everything
in the Civil Service—including the Attendance Book.
Nothing simpler than to forge someone's initials when
you're seeing them every day on odd bits of paper."

Blount took Merrion Squires over his story again,

asking a number of innocent-seeming questions, which would have been dynamite if the story had been fabricated. But he could not shake Squires at all. In spite of that sliding eye, which often prepossessed one to doubt Merrion's veracity, he did seem to be telling the truth now.

" Was it generally known in the Division that Mr. Lake would be working late last night ? "

" I couldn't say. I didn't know myself. He often did, of course," replied Squires.

" And the Deputy Director ? You see what I'm trying to get at, Mr. Squires ? If your statement is correct, or, for that matter, if it is not, I have to ask myself how the criminal could rely on finding Mr. Lake in his room, yet be sure there'd be no one else about the place."

" There I can't help you. Not being the criminal, as it so happens," replied Merrion Squires.

" Hark'ee—the D.D.—is very regular in his habits. He always goes down to the canteen about eleven o'clock when he's working late," put in Nigel. " And presumably the criminal had made sure, somehow or other, that Jimmy would be on the spot. Made an appointment with him, perhaps."

" If *that* is so, we shall know soon enough who it was. I'm going to see Mr. Lake this afternoon. The doctor says he is fit to be interviewed." Blount held Squires with a steely look.

" No, you won't bounce me *that* way," said Merrion, flushing. " If I stabbed Jimmy, it was quite unpremeditated, I assure you. Nothing was further from my mind when I came to the Ministry last night." He held up a hand to check the question Blount was about to ask. " And, if I may make my modest contribution to human knowledge, the obvious thing for X to have done was to wait in the Photographs Library—its door is directly opposite the Director's ante-room—wait there in the dark, with the door slightly open, till he'd seen Hark'ee depart for his nightly orgy in the canteen, and then slide into Jimmy's room."

" Just so, Mr. Squires. Did you miss your white coat when you went into your own room last night ? "

" No. Didn't notice it was gone. I was feeling rather dreamy."

" So dreamy that you aren't sure whether you attacked Mr. Lake or not ? " Blount put all his weight and impetus behind the question, like a Rugby forward charging into a loose scrum.

Merrion Squires was silent. His eye roved uneasily over the magpie litter of his room, the books higgledy-piggledy in their shelves, the guitar leaning in a corner, the pencil and wash studies pinned to the walls, the floor scattered with magazines and shoes and artists' materials, as though seeking from them advice or support.

" Come now, Mr. Squires," said Blount peremptorily. " You told Mr. Strangeways last night—this morning, I should say—that you didn't know whether you'd stabbed Mr. Lake or not. You have just now repeated something in the same sense. Surely it must be clear to you that——"

" All right, all right. Don't nag. Yes, I suppose you'd better know the worst. Are you acquainted with the word ' schizophrenia ', by any chance, Superintendent ? "

" We hear it quite often in the Courts," replied Blount icily. " From the lips of Counsel for the Defence."

" You remember the coat-slitting epidemic in the Ministry last winter, Nigel ? "

" Yes."

" Well, you see in me Jack-the-Coat-Ripper."

The epidemic had caused a brief sensation in the Ministry. Several of the women in Visual Propaganda Division, to which the outbreak was confined, had found their coats hanging in their rooms slit from collar to hem. This wanton, malicious damage was naturally even more unpopular at a time when coupons were so short, and an

ugly spirit of suspicion had spread, trembling on the edge
of panic and very nearly pushed over it by Miss Finlay's
tactless remark that "One of these fine days someone
will be inside a coat when it's slashed." The outbreak
ended as suddenly and mysteriously as it had begun, Miss
Prince's coat being the last to suffer. No clue to the
perpetrator was found. There had been a strange epilogue
a fortnight later, though, each of the three victims finding
on her desk an envelope containing money and coupons
enough to purchase a new coat.

Merrion Squires, looking sick with self-disgust, his
hands trembling on the back of the chair he was sitting in
his usual equestrian pose, now revealed that he had been
the cause of it all. He had had no idea that he was the
culprit, he said, until a member of the staff had caught
him at work, the knife in his hand.

"It was as if I'd been sleep-walking, and someone had
woken me up. I mean, I had no idea what I was doing
in the room, with a knife. The last I remembered was
sitting at my own desk working on some rough lay-outs.
But *there* was the knife, and *there* was the coat, all muti-
lated. It was a pretty nasty awakening, I can tell you."

Merrion went on to say that he supposed the flying
bomb, which had blown him off the ledge, must have
created something equivalent to a geological fault in his
unconscious. However, the counter-shock of being discovered in the act seemed to have re-established equilibrium. Or so he had hoped, since there were no further
cases of coat-slitting—until last night brought the whole
nightmare down on him again.

"You can imagine what I felt like. In the same room.
Staring at the same knife. But this time there *was* a
person inside the coat. And I'd felt sleepy while I was
sitting in my own room, waiting for Nigel to turn up. Oh,
God, I don't know yet! Did Mr. Hyde take control
again?"

Merrion Squires buried his head in his hands. The Superintendent asked, in a kinder voice than he had used so far, " And who was it that discovered you that time ? Miss Prince, I take it ? "

" Oh, no. It was Billson."

Blount and Nigel exchanged questioning glances.

" Billson ? But I'd have thought he was the type who'd have reported it at once," said Blount.

" So did I. But our Edgar turned out to be quite an opportunist. Or quite human, if you like to put it that way."

According to Merrion, Billson had promised him that the matter should go no further if he made restitution. He offered to make up the required number of coupons, as Merrion had not nearly enough. Billson was even so kind as to propose, if Merrion gave him the money in £1 notes, to put it with the coupons into three envelopes and place them on the desks of the three victims himself, so that there should be no doubt that the full price of a new coat was in fact given to each.

" Good Lord ! " exclaimed Nigel. " This is a new light on Billson."

" Yes, indeed. I found it most illuminating. But I must say, for a Finance Officer, his Simple Division of Money was a bit faulty."

" Oh ? "

" He asked me for £200. Each of the girls found £25 in her envelope. Actually, £25 was adequate for buying a new coat. But £125 seemed to me rather heavy as an agent's fee."

" But that was pure blackmail ! " Blount exploded.

" You bet your life it was. But what could I do ? Even if I'd been willing for the coat-slitting story to come out, I couldn't have brought blackmail home to Billson. It was a remarkably cunning arrangement on his part. In fact —I suppose I'm very ingenuous in some ways—but, when he asked for the £200, I genuinely believed he was going to divide the whole sum between the three girls—you know, give them more than double the value of their coats as a sort of sweetener."

" But—but Mr. Billson is a Permanent Civil Servant," said Blount.

" And therefore incorruptible ? I know. I can't expect you to believe my story. And I've no way of proving it."

" Has he attempted to get money from you since ? "

" As a matter of fact, he has. Last week. He didn't get it, though. You see, it suddenly occurred to me that, although I couldn't prove blackmail against him, it was equally impossible for *him* to prove that it was I who had slashed the coats. It would be his word against mine, in either case."

" May we go back to the coat-slitting a moment ? " asked Nigel. " Have you any idea why you slit those particular coats and not any other ones ? "

Merrion Squires' hands began to shake again, his eyes to slip and slide restlessly over his room.

" They were all three rather pretty girls, you remember," he said at last, forcing the words out painfully. " And—oh, to hell with it ! Let's put it that, not long before, I'd had a row with Nita : she rejected my advances, as they say. And the others . . ." He shrugged his shoulders significantly. " But you see "—the words came tumbling out now—" you see why I was in such a stew last night ? A couple of days ago, as you know, Nigel, *I had a row with Jimmy. . . .*"

Ten minutes later, Nigel and Blount were speeding in a police car towards Pinner, where Edgar Billson's home was. An idea had been forming in Nigel's mind, during the interview with Squires, and he wished to test it.

" What did you think of all that ? " he asked.

" Well, now. Very specious. May be true. We can't prove it, of course. Billson wouldn't be likely to confess." Blount's eyes glittered behind the steel-rimmed glasses. " But supposing it isn't true. Suppose it was not Billson but Nita Prince who caught him in the act of slashing her coat. Suppose it was she who had him in her power—perhaps blackmailing him. Now *there's* a possible motive for the murder of Miss Prince. And it might be that Squires found afterwards she had betrayed his secret to the Director. So Mr. Lake has to go, too. If that were the truth of it, the whole of Squires' story would be a very ingenious plan to draw us away from the danger area—from his hidden motive for poisoning the girl."

" That's sound enough, up to a point. And I must admit, before you came along, he'd been saying things which could be interpreted as an attempt to throw suspicion for Nita's death on someone else." Nigel gave Blount a resumé of the conversation. " But," he went on, " if Merrion is the criminal, why, why, why should he confess to having had a row with Nita before the last coat-slashing incident ? The rest of his confession tended to isolate the attack on Jimmy—whether Merrion actually did it or not. But, as soon as he volunteered of his own free will that a row with Nita—her rejecting his advances —might have been his unconscious motive for slashing her coat—why, he walks straight into what you call the danger area ; he links up the attack on Jimmy with the murder of Nita."

" I doubt he's a bit daft, your Mr. Squires. I don't like his eyes. Slippery."

" Well, there's this to be said for him : poisoners usually stick to the same weapon."

" But this case is different. There was but the one poison container. Supplied free and gratis by that nincompoop, Kennington. It just so happened to be handy. Like Squires' knife happened to be handy last night. And you could say Squires was well advised just now to feed us with schizophrenia. And you could argue that, having been a genuine victim of it when he slashed the coats, he would use that method on Mr. Lake with the assurance that his defence was already established supposing he was caught."

"Why didn't he use the same method on Nita, then? By the way, talking of poison containers," whispered Nigel, "I see you've got a new sergeant."

Blount looked his grimmest.

"Yes. Sergeant Messer is going back into uniform. I will not stand for carelessness."

"He didn't search 'em properly?"

"He omitted to examine carefully some of the possible places of concealment—bodily concealment," replied Blount primly.

"But, damn it, we were all in the room. No one undressed. How could any one have concealed the thing that way?"

"So Messer reasoned. But it wasn't his job to reason. Anyway, you don't have to undress in order to put a thing in your mouth."

"No one would be crazy enough to put the poison container in his mouth, surely? Why, there might well have been some drops of poison left in it. And anyway, the fumes——"

"That is all quite true. Nevertheless, Messer fell down on his job."

"What about your woman searcher?"

"She was thorough."

"H'm. Well, I still *cannot* understand why the criminal should have bothered to remove the container, however he did it, at such a risk of discovery, when he need only have dropped it on the floor, or——"

"Maybe he was afraid it'd take fingerprints."

"A tiny thing like that?"

" The identity of a criminal has been reconstructed from a mere fragment of a fingerprint before now, thanks to photo-micrography. Not that our suspects are likely to know this—they're amateurs, after all."

" All except one, Blount," said Nigel slowly. " I should think there's nothing Charles Kennington doesn't know about—well, concealment. And subterfuge. And throwing dust in eyes. He did catch Stultz, after all."

" There's no use beating our heads against that wall just now. When we get to Billson's house, I propose——"

The Superintendent outlined his plan. . . .

Mrs. Billson was dusting the front parlour when the bell rang. Drawing aside the muslin curtain, she peered out sidelong. A fat gentleman in a bowler hat and a blue suit ; a tall gentleman, hatless, with tow-coloured hair. Couldn't be commercials—they didn't go about in pairs. She hastily slipped off her flowered apron, bundled it behind the sofa, patted her greying frizzy hair, and went to the door. Might as well face it. If it wasn't now, it'd be later. Did you have to feed duns, bailiffs, whatever they were called, when they encamped in your house, she wondered distractedly.

" Good-morning, gentlemen. If you've come about that account at Shoolbridge's, I can assure you Mr. Billson will be sending a cheque very shortly."

" Madam, I think there must be some mistake. I am a police officer, and I would like a word with you. May we come in ? " Blount held out his official card.

Mrs. Billson hardly looked at it. Oh, dear, she thought, now I've given it away, and Edgar will be furious. Why did I blurt it out ?

" Of course. Please step inside. Pardon the untidiness. One can't get a maid nowadays for love or money," she said in accents so refined that Nigel's teeth were positively set on edge.

" Now, madam, it is rather a grave matter—no, I will

stand, thank you—but I hope you may be able to clear
it up satisfactorily."

"I can assure you, I——"

Blount held up a hand which, to the flustered woman,
seemed as large as doom.

"If you will allow me. Last night we arrested a pick-
pocket. He was found to be in possession, amongst other
things, of a wallet we believe may belong to your husband.
The man admitted having just stolen it——"

"Oh dear, Edgar didn't say anything about——"

"Now, it has been brought to my attention that, later
last night, an Officer of the Ministry of Morale rang up
this house, and was told by you that your husband had
been at home all the evening. You will appreciate,
madam, that this puts the police in an awkward position.
We should wish to restore Mr. Billson's wallet. On the
other hand, how could it have been stolen from him,
some distance from here, if he was at home all the time?"

"Oh, I can explain that. Edgar—Mr. Billson, that is—
doesn't care for the Ministry gentlemen to know that he
goes to the Sta——"

"Has an occasional flutter at the dogs, eh?" Blount
beamed upon her like an appeased shark. "Quite under-
standable. One has to be careful in the Civil Service,
naturally. So he asked you to say he was in all the
evening, if any one rang up. Had he in fact returned
home when Mr. Fortescue telephoned?"

"No. He got back about half an hour later. He had
stopped at a friend's house on the way."

"Quite, quite. I'm glad we've cleared that up. Can't
afford to lose wallets these days, eh? What stadium was
he at, by the way?"

"Harringay, he said he was going to."

"Hope he made a haul."

"Well, I couldn't say, I'm sure. I was in bed when he
got back. We—hem—have separate rooms. And this

morning he overslept, and had to dash off to work without
hardly touching his breakfast, so I scarcely had a word
with him."

" I only hope, for your sake, we're right about Billson,"
said Nigel, as the police car tore back towards Central
London. " Or else he'll raise an almighty stink about that
interview with his wife."

" Let him try. Did you notice, Strangeways, his wife
took us for duns at first ? It all fits in."

" Yes. And it does seem to strengthen Merrion's story.
If Billson had been playing the dogs and getting into debt,
that would account for his taking the £125 off Merrion
instead of reporting him to the authorities. No doubt he
got the extra coupons off some shady Black Market friend.
Well, it quite revives my spirits to know that the correct
Billson has been leading a double life."

Blount looked worried. " But it doesn't account for
his attempting to murder Mr. Lake."

" You think it was he ? "

" I've an open mind. We want more facts yet. But I'll
grant you this : if Mr. Squires was telling the truth, the
man most likely to have made the attack on Mr. Lake is
the man who knew that Squires was behind the coat-
slashing, and who therefore would use Squires' coat and
knife in an attempt to frame him. But why should
Billson try to kill Mr. Lake ? Suppose Lake *had* found
out about his debts and his dog-racing—you don't kill a
man for that, not even in the Civil Service. After all, it
wouldn't prevent Billson's creditors coming down on
him."

" Blount, I have an idea. It's been taking shape for
some time. Listen."

As Nigel unfolded his theory, the Superintendent's face
began to light up as briskly as a technicolour dawn. At
one point he even went so far as to remove his bowler

hat in order to slap his bald head—a sign of excitement now, not of perplexity.

"Ah, well now, well now! That's vairy interesting, vairy suggestive. Let's hope Mr. Lake is in a fit state to corroborate. Now, supposing he does . . ."

They began to lay their plans. Here, Nigel's inside knowledge of Ministry procedure proved useful. It was agreed that there should be no questioning about the events of last night, beyond a formal routine inquiry by Blount into the movements of each of the suspects, ostensibly to confirm the alibis which Fortescue's telephone calls had given them. The problem of lulling Billson's suspicions was a difficult one. It was decided that Blount should take the offensive about his last night's alibi, for Billson's wife would almost certainly telephone to him about the police visit. Billson would then, presumably, fall back upon his second line of defence—that he had been at the Stadium. This alibi Blount would, subject to the usual checking, be apparently prepared to accept. If Billson had any lingering doubts, they should be dispelled by what would happen later in the afternoon.

On their arrival at the Ministry, Nigel went straight to the Deputy Director's room. He noticed a policeman sitting stolidly upright outside the Director's door, an object of some giggling and eyelash-fluttering on the part of the typists in the ante-room. Nigel asked Fortescue if he would send his secretary away for five or ten minutes: he had some private words for him. When this was done, Nigel lay back in the armchair, and began:

"Hark'ee, we want some co-operation from you. You must call an Emergency Progress Meeting for this afternoon. No trouble about that, with Jimmy hors-de-combat —re-assignment of work, and so forth."

"To say nothing of the Head of the Editorial Section waltzing around with policemen when he should be——"

"Keeping his fingers on the strings, to prevent bottlenecks. I know. In the course of this meeting, you must say two things. First, that an arrest for the attempted murder of the Director may take place any moment; and you've been assured by the Superintendent that, as soon as it does, the police will all be removed from the building and we can get on with our war effort unimpeded."

" Is this true ? "

" In a way. The second thing is, you must give out that, first thing to-morrow, there's going to be a check of the Q photograph files."

Harker Fortescue's cold and fishy eye lit up with something near to animation. He stroked the side of his chin. He opened a drawer, took out a packet of cigarettes, flipped one across to Nigel, and lit his own. Or rather tried to light it ; but his lighter seemed recalcitrant, and in the end Nigel had to supply a match.

" What's the idea of that ? " he asked at last. " One of your subtle manœuvres ? "

" Yes and no. A check of the Q files certainly must take place as soon as possible."

" But, damn it, man, not now. The Division is understaffed as it is ; and if you're dragging off one of us this evening for Jimmy's——"

" You've only got to *announce* the check. At present. It may be that M.I.5 will *do* it for you."

The Deputy Director eyed Nigel thoughtfully.

" Oh, it's like that, is it ? Well, I wish them luck. You know that PHQ Secret File Jimmy has been fussed about ? It's still missing. And it contains the complete list—the *only* complete list—of the Q.W. tray of canned photographs. They can't very well check them without it."

" Yes, I know that. You must say that the file has been found."

Seeing Hark'ee still looked rather unco-operative, Nigel added

" We're seeing Jimmy this afternoon, early. If necessary I shall ask him for a chit requesting you to check the Q files to-morrow morning."

" My dear Nigel, there's no need to jump me like this. Of course I'll announce it. I'd be glad to have a note from Jimmy about it, though. I take it he's on the road to recovery, then ? "

" Yes."

Jimmy Lake was lying in bed, his shoulder heavily bandaged, his face still as pale as the bandages, but evidently in full possession of his senses, when Blount and Nigel turned up at his house. The nurse said they might have fifteen minutes' conversation with him, and left the room with a brisk glance at her wrist-watch. Alice Lake was sitting at the bedside. Blount first asked the Director to tell him what had happened the previous night. Jimmy said he had not made an appointment with any one to see him then. When the door had opened, he had not looked up instantly (this, Nigel could well imagine : when Jimmy was deep in a piece of work, you could often come into the room, sit down and light a cigarette before he looked up to see who it was). The next instant, said Jimmy, the lights had gone out. He sat still for a few moments, supposing it to be Hark'ee back from the canteen. He said something like, " Turn 'em on again, you silly ass." Nothing happened. So he got up and moved over to the switches. Yes, he had thought there was someone in the room, but still assumed it to be Hark'ee. When he was near the door, he felt a hand fall on his shoulder from behind. Then the blow came, pitching him forward on to the floor. He was dimly aware of someone gliding out of the room, shutting the door behind him. He did not call out, for fear his assailant might return, but dragged himself to the door, turned on the lights, and

then managed to get Hark'ee on the telephone before
he passed out.

All this seemed to fit in with Nigel's reconstruction of
the scene. But Blount's further questions proved that
Jimmy could give no clue at all to the identity of his
assailant ; and there was the awkward though not
unexpected fact that he had made no appointment to see
any one that night. How could the attacker have relied
on his being there ? This was easily answered. Both
Brian Ingle and Edgar Billson had rung him up in the
afternoon, asking to see him about certain jobs of theirs
he had on his desk for approval. He had told them both
that he hadn't dealt with them yet, but hoped to get
them done that night, and have them ready in the
morning.

Nigel studied the Director's face while he gave this
evidence. Jimmy Lake looked innocent, defenceless,
irresponsible, as people do lying in bed. The square,
handsome head ; the voice weak, but collected ; the
familiar mannerism of running his tongue round against
the inside of his lips before he spoke, as though it were
an aid to deliberation : all this was unchanged. Yet
Nigel seemed to perceive an unwonted air of anxiety
behind it. Jimmy Lake, he obscurely felt, was straining
to catch some implication from the Superintendent's
questions at the same time as he answered them at their
face value. From time to time Jimmy's eyes turned to
his wife ; and then a different sort of anxiety seemed to
come into them. It was as though he were in a dream,
trying to grope his way to her, but unable to reach her,
thought Nigel. Alice Lake, for her part, was cool and
quiet as ever. Her husband's condition, so frail and
appealing, did not modify her air of detachment. She sat
at his bedside more like a nurse than a wife. When his
right hand went out to her affectionately, Nigel almost
expected her to take his pulse.

Blount was now asking about the missing Secret file. Nigel had already explained to the Superintendent the general procedure of the PHQ files. Throughout the war, photographs from every theatre of operations, at home and abroad, poured into the Ministry. Every photograph was submitted to the appropriate censor—Naval, Military or Air ; if necessary, to all three. All photographs passed by the censors were filed and indexed under subject headings in the Photographs Library, whence they could be issued to the Press or drawn upon for the Ministry's own productions. Any photograph stopped by the censors was put away with its negative, in a special department of the Library.' These stopped, or " canned " photographs were the subject of the PHQ files. Each file contained a list of canned pictures numbered, indexed and keyed to the number of the trays in Q Department, where negatives and specimen prints were put away, together with a brief note on their subject, date of receipt, date of censorship, etc., and any internal correspondence about them. Such photographs had usually been censored on security grounds : it might be that a picture gave away information about the position of an unexploded bomb in London, or of bomb damage, or the number of a ship or the shoulder-flash of a Division, or some secret apparatus such as radar.

It sometimes happened that these canned photographs were more dramatic, or of better quality, than the sets on any given subject released for general publicity purposes. And it could also happen that the original reason for their being stopped was no longer valid. So it was the custom of Nigel's editorial unit, when collecting photographic material for a new production, to examine the Q files for any relevant pictures ; and if an exceptionally good photograph was found there, he would re-submit it to censorship. A year ago, browsing through the Q files, he had made a note of a most sensational

picture, Q 5339, taken in the Pacific theatre. When he
had recently got to work on his new production in the
Pacific series, he had remembered this photograph and
put through an order for six rough prints, in the hope that
the censors might now be prevailed upon to release it.
This was the picture which had caused his row with
Billson on the morning of Nita Prince's death.

Now Nigel was painfully aware that, if the Secret file
relevant to any group of canned photographs were
missing, it would be extremely difficult, if not quite
impossible, to check the originals. Each group of prints,
it is true, was numbered in serial order. But, very
occasionally, a print proved to be too dangerously
revealing to be kept even in the locked files of Q Department, and the censor requested that it should be destroyed,
together with its negative. In the absence, then, of the
relevant Q file, it would be very difficult to prove that a
given photograph had not been thus destroyed ; and,
but for Nigel's having taken a note of Q 5339, there would
have been nothing to indicate that this photograph and
negative were in existence a year ago, and therefore had
not been destroyed by official request.

Nigel, it now transpired, was not the only person who
had worried about this. On the day of Nita Prince's
death, file PHQ14/150 had been sent up to the Director
from the Registry, but had never reached him. He had
sent for it, he said, that morning, wishing to discuss with
Merrion Squires some changes in the lay-out for the
Pacific job and hoping that the list of canned photographs
in the file might give them some ideas for new material.
The Ministry's Investigations Officer had traced the file
as far as the In-tray in the Director's ante-room. A
Messenger had placed it there—he remembered it because
of the red Secret tab on the envelope—just before eleven
o'clock, when the senior officers of the Division were
assembling in Jimmy's room to greet Charles Kennington.

From that point, it had been seen no more. It was unlikely that it could have been abstracted after the party had assembled, for a typist was in the ante-room all the morning from then on, and she protested stoutly that she would have noticed any one tampering with the In-tray. But there had been a period of five minutes, just after eleven o'clock, when she had left the ante-room.

Jimmy Lake had been too preoccupied the rest of that day to draw conclusions. The following day, however, he remembered how Charles Kennington had asked Nita to invite Edgar Billson to the party. This had been just after eleven o'clock, when the rest of them were already met in Jimmy's room. Theoretically, it would have been possible for Billson to take the file from the In-tray then and conceal it in his room, without being seen, before coming to the party. At Jimmy's suggestion, the Investigations Officer had been making tactful inquiries round the Division, with a view to testing this theory, during yesterday—the very day when the Director was attacked. Jimmy remembered, as did Nigel, how, less than an hour before Nita's death, Jimmy had asked her to ring Mr. Billson and tell him that he must supply within twenty-four hours the Q.W. prints requested by the Editorial Unit, over which he had been so queerly obstructive. Did all this link up, the Director wondered. Had Billson somehow lost the negatives in question? Or had they been damaged? How else could one account for his recalcitrance over providing prints from them, or his making away with the PHQ file—supposing it was he who had done so?

Jimmy now agreed that all the Q files must certainly be examined the following morning, and scribbled a note to the Deputy Director, instructing him to put this in hand, signing it with his initials.

"And now, Mr. Lake," said Blount, "that nurse of yours will be turning us out any moment. But I must ask you one more question. You spoke of these photographs as having been lost perhaps, or damaged. Did no other possibility enter your head ? "

Jimmy frowned. An expression of anguish came over his face.

" I cannot believe that any member of my Division would——"

" It is vairy painful for you, sir. Don't think I don't appreciate that. But those photographs, or their negatives, might have been of the utmost value to an enemy power. And—e'eh—let us suppose that the poison Miss Prince took was intended for you, as the knife certainly was— you see what a motive we have now for the criminal ?— a man will go to great lengths to protect himself from a charge of high treason, Mr. Lake."

CHAPTER VII

FROM: MR. BILLSON
TO: DEPUTY DIRECTOR

THE PROGRESS MEETING was in full blast. Sitting at his desk, the Deputy Director ran his finger down to the next item on the Production Schedule.

"This job seems to be very sticky," he said. "Went to the Studio on the 20th of last month, and we still haven't got an approved lay-out. It's a scandal. Merrion?"

"The Director didn't like two of my double spreads," said Merrion Squires, sitting astride his chair and contemplating Hark'ee ruminatively over the back of it. "So he bunged the job back to me, and I've been trying to find some new pictures."

"It's absolutely scandalous. Here's a job in a standard format—no technical difficulties about it. The Admiralty are clamouring for it. And you talk to me about new pictures. What about the captions?"

"Oh, they're d-done," stammered Brian Ingle eagerly. "And Nigel has p-passed them. All except for those two openings, I mean."

"Finance?"

"That's cleared," said Mr. Oddie, the officer who was responsible for printing costs.

"Well, there seems to be only one bottleneck. In the Art Work Unit. Let me see, delivery is scheduled for the 31st of August. And it's now—my word, we'll have to get cracking! The Controller gave Priority A. for this job, and it's got to be delivered on schedule. That's basic. Nigel, you're supposed to push the work through every stage quickly," he rapped out at the apparently unconscious figure in the deep leather arm-chair, Miss Finlay busily taking notes by its side.

"We've been held up by Photographs Library. I ordered some new pictures for Merrion over a week ago. One of them, from the Q files, hasn't turned up yet. Billson's girls have lost it, I suspect."

"I take exception to that remark," said Mr. Billson frigidly, his pasty face set in an expression not unfamiliar to his colleagues. "I queried with Mr. Strangeways the necessity of supplying *six* prints of the photograph in question. It is a matter of principle. Mr. Strangeways does not seem to grasp, even after five years' experience of Civil Service procedure, the necessity for economy. I am responsible to the Treasury for——"

"Yes, we know all that," interrupted Harker Fortescue. "I also know this is a rush job and the Budget won't unbalance itself if a few extra prints of one photograph are made. What did you want them for, Nigel?"

"Submission simultaneously to the three Service censors."

"Very well. Let him have them double-quick, Billson."

"Mayor cuts red tape," murmured Merrion Squires, very audibly.

Edgar Billson gave the Deputy Director a queer look. "Are those definitely your instructions? Six prints of Q 5339?" There was some undertone in his voice which Nigel could not interpret.

"Yes," snapped Hark'ee. "And while we're on the subject of the Q files, they are to be checked to-morrow morning, Billson."

"Oh, no, I'm afraid that's out of the question. Several of my staff are away on leave, and I can't waste my time just now with routine checks." Billson's white face looked as obstinate as a mass of dough that refuses to rise.

"Can't help that," said Hark'ee. "I've a note from the Director giving firm instructions. Like to see it?"

He passed the piece of paper to Edgar Billson, who took off his glasses and wiped them before reading it.

"I cannot accept this," he said at last. "I must come back at the Director with a firm request for postponement on the score of—h'rrm—lack of staffing facilities."

"Oh, God, now we're off!" came another stage whisper from Merrion.

"I'm sorry. It's got to be done," said the Deputy Director coldly. "So there's an end of it. The missing PHQ file has been recovered, by the way. And it's not a routine check, Billson. I understand that a representative of M.I.5 may be present."

Nigel opened his eyes wide. He had not intended Hark'ee to come out with this extra piece of bait: but, seeing the consternation on Billson's face, he was quite glad of it. A little hum of surprise and interest had started in the room, soon silenced by Hark'ee saying:

"Well, that's the lot, as far as the Production Schedule goes. We'll turn now to the Commissions Pending sheet. Where's my sheet, chump?" he called to his secretary at the far table. While she was taking it out from a folder, Hark'ee went on:

"Commissions Pending. Yes. I'm afraid, in the Director's absence—you'll be glad to hear he's out of danger, but he'll not be back for a week or so—some work will have to be redistributed. And there's another thing. The police inform me that they will be making an arrest any moment now for the attempted murder of Jimmy. Let us hope," said Hark'ee bleakly, "it isn't one of our number. If it is, we shall be still more short-handed. On the other hand, the Superintendent promises to withdraw his men from the building as soon as this arrest has been made: so at least those of us who *are* left will be able to get on with our work in peace."

There was a shocked silence in the room. At last, Brian Ingle said:

" Does that mean that—that, well, N-Nita's death will be cleared up at the same time ? Was it the same p-person who did it, I mean ? "

" Couldn't say. I'm not that far in the confidence of the police. Now, item 368 on the sheet," Hark'ee announced, in the manner of a parson giving out the number of a hymn.

" ' Lead us, Heavenly Father, lead us,' " murmured Merrion Squires.

The meeting got down to the discussion of work commissioned by other Departments but not yet at the stage of production. They were engaged on it ten minutes later, when Superintendent Blount came in, a uniformed sergeant behind him. He advanced formidably to Hark'ee's desk, bent over, murmured a few words in his ear. Hark'ee was seen to nod. Blount turned to the rest of them.

" I must ask you to come with me, Mr. Squires," he said.

Watching Edgar Billson covertly, Nigel saw his body relax and beads of sweat starting from his forehead. No one spoke. They might have been the guests at the feast when Perseus flashed the Gorgon's head at them. Merrion Squires cast one look of infinite reproach upon Nigel; then, without a word, strode to the door, Blount at one elbow, the sergeant at the other.

The Deputy Director raised his eyebrows interrogatively at Nigel.

" Yes," Nigel said, " I'm afraid so."

" I think, ladies and gentlemen, we'll end this meeting," said Hark'ee.

As he went out, Nigel looked round. The Deputy Director's head was buried in his hands. . . .

Five hours later, at ten o'clock that night, Blount and Nigel were sitting in the latter's room at the Ministry. They were sitting in the dark and speaking in whispers. Blount had removed the disguise he had used to enter the building again undetected by any eyes that might be on the look-out for him. The door was slightly ajar, so that they could hear any footsteps that might pass along the passage to the Photographs Library on the other side.

The telephone rang. Blount took up the receiver, listened a moment, said " O.K."

" That's my man," he said to Nigel. " Billson has left his house in a car."

" Let's hope he's not off to Dublin or somewhere."

" Don't you worry. I've got a mobile patrol out there. They'll be following him now. If he bolts, we've got him. If he comes back here, we'll get him. He's in a cleft stick."

" So Hark'ee told him not long ago. Funny how one always takes things metaphorically nowadays. When Miss Finlay overheard Hark'ee telling him he could go to the dogs for all Hark'ee cared, I never thought of the literal meaning. Hark'ee must have known about Billson's passion for gambling."

" Aye, that's how it started, no doubt. Billson got badly into debt, and one of his race-track friends was a bad lot—in touch with enemy agents, and Billson began selling them prints of those secret photographs of yours. I suspect that he must have accidentally destroyed the negative of the one you've been fussing about, while making a print from it : others, too, maybe : he'd never be fool enough to let the Germans have the negatives, when he might be called on to produce them here any time. Well, we'll get it out of him all right."

" If he hasn't taken fright."

" Not he. Our little act this afternoon was bound to put him off his guard."

" And what about our visit to his home this morning ? "

" Oh, I talked to him about that earlier to-day. As I expected, he told the same story as his wife. Said he'd been at the Stadium last night, and didn't want it to get round the Ministry. Gave me the names of one or two witnesses. No doubt he did go there earlier in the evening, and slipped out. I pretended to swallow it. Said I'd have to check up on his story, of course. Apologised for the tale I spun his wife about the wallet—aye, the fellow had the audacity to tell me he'd a good mind to have an official inquiry launched into my methods. He's got some nerve, under that pasty face of his."

" Well, I wonder what he's going to do with his nerve to-night. *If* he comes."

" He's going to try and rig those Q files so that M.I.5 don't find anything wrong with 'em."

The telephone rang again. It was the mobile patrol following Billson, to say that he had stopped at the house of one Solly Hawks : Solly, Blount explained to Nigel, was an unamiable character, well known to the police, who had been boss of a racecourse gang, served a sentence for gravely injuring a bookie, and was now believed to be mixed up with Black Market activities.

" What exceedingly low friends our Edgar has got," said Nigel. Then presently, " You know, Blount, there's one thing that's been puzzling me. That Secret file. Secret files are always circulated under cover : in an envelope, that is, with a red tab on them. How on earth could Billson know that the envelope in Jimmy's In-tray contained the file he wanted to get rid of ? "

" Yes, I thought of that, when I was having a chat this afternoon with your Investigations Officer. In fact, he told me that no one else had called for the file that day, which is a bit awkward."

" It is indeed," said Nigel. " The only way Billson could have known the file was on its way to the Director, was if he had rung up the Registry to ask for it himself."

" Oh, well, it'll all come out in the wash, no doubt," said Blount.

They continued a desultory, whispered conversation in the dark. Nigel felt his nerves strung tighter. Any moment now. Would their trap be sprung, though ? If Billson did enter it, he wouldn't escape as he had escaped the previous night, anyway : the exits from the Ministry were well covered, this time—Blount had seen to that.

Suddenly, without warning, like the blink of an eye, the passage lights went out. Someone had come up the stairs, in uncanny silence. Blount was at the barely-open door. Nigel could just hear the faintest pad of footsteps outside. They passed the door. And then the first unexpected thing of that very surprising night happened. A door further down the passage opened, and they heard the intruder moving about, not in the Photographs Library, but in the Deputy Director's room. There followed a sound like that of a drawer being opened.

" Did you see who ? " whispered Nigel in Blount's ear. " No."

A minute later, they heard the footsteps moving back through the ante-room, into the passage again ; the sound of a key turning, another door opening. Yes, he had gone into the Photographs Library now, by the door opposite the ante-room. Acting on their preconceived plan, Blount and Nigel stole out. There was a second door to the Photographs Library, at the other end of the passage : Blount had a key to it, and had taken the precaution of oiling the lock earlier that night. Nigel crept towards the door by which the intruder had entered the Library and put his ear to it. He heard, as he had expected, an inner door closing. The intruder had entered the Library annexe where the Q photographs were stored. Nigel moved back along the passage very slowly, step by step ; felt for Blount ; gripped his elbow. Very.

K

very slowly, Blount inserted his key in the door, turned it, and silently, inch by inch, pushed the door open.

They were in their stockinged feet. They crept into the Photographs Library, feeling their way along the nearest filing cabinet in the pitch darkness. These steel cabinets, their sliding trays each containing sets of photographs in foolscap envelopes, were arranged transversally across the long room, with aisles between them. Peering round the end of their cabinet, Blount and Nigel were looking down the central aisle, the door of the Q annexe directly opposite them, at the far end. They could see a sliver of light now underneath this door.

They paused there. And then the second unexpected thing happened: which was, that nothing happened at all. The partition wall between the annexe and the Library proper was so thin that any movement in the annexe could not fail to have been heard by them. Yet the anticipated sounds, of metal drawers sliding open, of feet shuffling around the annexe, simply did not occur. The intruder appeared to be sitting in there, doing nothing at all; or maybe he was reading an improving book, or going into a trance, thought Nigel irritably.

Blount touched his arm. They began to creep towards the annexe, one on each side of the aisle, feeling their way cautiously across the gaps between the ends of the ranks of steel cabinets, in case any stools had been left lying about in their way. After what seemed to Nigel a large segment of eternity, they had got half-way down the long room. It was like some game of musical chairs in slow motion: at any moment the annexe door might open, a torch flash into the Library; and they must be hidden behind one of the ranks of filing cabinets if that happened.

But still nothing happened. The person in the annexe might have been dead, for all the sounds of activity that could be heard. The pair began to creep forward again, only to dodge back behind the cabinets the next moment, for the whine of the lift came to them through the silent building, and then the noise of the lift doors opening, and then footsteps advancing firmly up the passage at a normal gait—the new-comer must have switched the passage lights on—and entering the ante-room ; and a door was banged shut, either Jimmy's door or Hark'ee's.

It was extremely disconcerting—this altogether un-furtive new arrival. It seemed to make nonsense, to make farcical melodrama of their present proceedings, thought Nigel. But now, as if those inappropriate foot-steps had lifted a spell, the light in the annexe went out, the annexe door opened and feet whispered through the darkness, moving towards the Library door, which was very quietly opened. Nigel cursed the steel cabinet, which cut off his view ; for, in the light from the passage, he could otherwise have seen who it was. After about thirty seconds, the Library door as gently closed again, then the annexe door, and beneath it the sliver of light reappeared. Billson, Nigel assumed, must have crept out for a moment to assure himself who it was that had just entered the Director's ante-room. Cautious bloke, Billson. No, he wasn't being so cautious now. At last, from the annexe, the long-expected sound was heard of metal trays sliding open, and, with it, a noise half-way between a rustle and a crackle. Negatives, said Nigel to himself, advancing more rapidly now, under cover of that noise, towards the annexe door, keeping pace with Blount on the other side of the aisle.

They had reached the last of the rows of cabinets between them and the annexe, and Blount was about to cross the intervening space, when a new noise came to them—a sort of plop and hiss, startling and somehow venomous—and the light beneath the annexe door sud-denly intensified so that it resembled a rod of white-hot steel. The next instant there came a violent whishing

and crackling, and at the same moment the annexe door
flew open and a figure appeared there, outlined against
an inferno.

" Edgar Billson ! I——"
Blount dodged back behind a steel cabinet just in time.
The figure, now at the Library door, had whipped out a
revolver and fired. The bullet, with the sound of a steel
wire breaking under high tension, twanged diagonally
across the room and slammed into a cabinet behind
Nigel. The Library door banged shut.

" Get this fire out ! I'll follow him," shouted Blount,
darting to the door, turning on the switches, then disap-
pearing into the passage. Nigel could hear the blasts of
his police whistle, and footsteps pounding down the
emergency staircase to his right, where so often the staff
had hurried downstairs on the approach of a flying bomb.

He raced for the Deputy Director's room, cannoned
into Harker Fortescue in the doorway.

" What the devil ? Who's been shooting ? "
" Fire in the annexe, Hark'ee ! Get those fire buckets
at the end of the passage ! Got to telephone ! With you
in a minute ! "

Nigel plunged for Harker's telephone...
" A.R.P. Control ! Jump to it ! . . . Lewis ? Strangeways here. Fire on the sixth floor. Bad one. Send some
Messengers up to help with the buckets—there's only
two of us. Send for the fire brigade. And get that mobile
pump out into the back courtyard—play the hose up—
you'll see the blaze all right, don't worry. O.K ! Get
cracking then ! "

He ran back into the Photographs Library. Harker
Fortescue was in the act of hurling a bucket of water into
the heart of the flames : as he did so, the magnesium-
white centre seemed to burst open and send feelers out
in every direction.

" My God ! " exclaimed Hark'ee, reeling back from the

doorway, "that's an incendiary in there, I'll swear. Water's no good. Get the sand buckets."

They raced to the end of the passage and fetched them. But the heat from the blazing piles of negatives prevented them from emptying the sand over the fire's centre, and the flames were now dribbling out everywhere, leaping on to furniture and black-out curtains, fanned by the draught between door and open window.

"It's no good," panted Nigel, drawing Hark'ee back. "Lewis is sending up some chaps to help with the buckets. Stay here and direct 'em, will you? Stop it spreading into the Library, if you can. That's the best we can do, till the Fire Brigade comes."

Nigel knew he could safely leave it to Hark'ee, who had been a part-time A.R.P. instructor during the early blitzes. He tore down the passage, reached the lift just as Lewis' reinforcements were coming out of it at a sedate jog-trot—the fastest gait at which he had ever seen a Ministry Messenger proceed, and took the lift down to the ground floor.

In the lobby by the Reception Desk, a small mob of Ministry staff was collecting, talking excitedly, and getting in the way of the fire-pump team Lewis had gathered, who were trying to ram their way out into the back courtyard where the mobile pump was housed. A policeman recognised Nigel and forced his way to him through the crowd, shouting "Stand aside, please! Stand aside! Break it up!"

"Have you seen the Superintendent?"

"No, sir. Heard his whistle, though. All our men are on the alert. We've got the exits covered, and the patrol car is shining its headlights along the front of the building."

"Good-oh. Don't let any one out."

Nigel leapt on to the Reception Desk, bawling for silence.

" Any ex-fire-watchers here ? Ministry ones ? "

Six or seven men stepped forward.

" Follow me."

Nigel led them swiftly downstairs to the basement
floor, along the catacomb-like passages, till they reached
the foot of the emergency staircase. They were now at
the back of the building.

" Two of you stop here. Nab any one who tries to go
up or come down. If it's Mr. Billson—know him ? Right
—watch out. He's armed. Come along, the rest ! "

Blount's whistle was blowing again. Nigel ran towards
the sound. He found Blount, panting, dishevelled, but
intact, at the entrance of the basement sleeping quarters,
fifty yards away.

" I've got him cornered in here. He ran this way.
We'll beat him out now."

These sleeping quarters, where many of the Ministry
staff had slept during the blitzes, were a series of rooms,
divided up by blast-baffle walls so that they formed a
kind of underground maze. The walls were still lined
with two-tier wooden bunks, and a few of these were still
occupied by old habitués who had not grasped that the
German War was over—or else their own houses were in
ruins and they had nowhere else to sleep. Here and there
a face looked out from under the blankets, muttering
bilious curses against the disturbers of the night's rest,
as Nigel's party, reinforced now by a couple of policemen
who had come in response to Blount's whistle, proceeded
methodically to comb the labyrinth, two men having
been left at the entrance to stop Billson's retreat if he
tried to double back.

It was easy to see how Blount could have lost his man
here. The blast-walls made these underground rooms
as intricate as the wards of a key. One man could dodge
another here till Kingdom Come. But he couldn't dodge
a whole search-party, sweeping cautiously yet inexorably

forward, examining every bunk, scrutinising each occupant to make sure that their quarry was not foxing under the blankets, switching on the lights in each successive compartment so that in the glare of the unshaded bulbs the whitewashed walls more than ever resembled the walls of some labyrinthine catacomb.

It was only a matter of time now. And a question whether, coming round one of the blast-walls, you might not be picked off by a bullet. Billson's revolver presumably had at least five left, thought Nigel queasily. But the party reached the last compartment, after Blount had peered very cautiously indeed round the end of the blast-wall. And the compartment was empty.

" Damn it, it's impossible. He must be here. This is a dead end."

" No, sir," said one of the fire-watchers. " Emergency exit in the wall. Behind that bunk."

Blount plunged for it. The bunk was dragged aside, revealing a metal plate, rather like an oven door, in the whitewashed wall. Blount depressed its handle, pulled, then pushed : the door swung outwards into darkness.

" What's outside ? "

" Back courtyard," replied the fire-watcher.

Blount struggled through the hole in the wall. Nigel came behind him, and in a moment was gazing at a remarkable scene. In the centre of the courtyard stood the Ministry's mobile fire-pump. Lewis, at the branch, was directing a jet of water at a sixth-floor window : it was as though the flames were trying to climb out of the window, and the steely arm of water to push them back. At the same time a clanging could be heard from the street at the far end of the courtyard ; and a policeman unlocked the gate in the ten-foot-high iron railing which separated the courtyard from the street. The gate swung open to admit the approaching fire engines. And, as it did so, Nigel realised that this was what Billson must have been banking on if he had come out through the emergency exit. The air was full of shouting and clanging, the drumming of the mobile pump's engine, the hissing of the hose. The eyes of Lewis's men and of the approaching firemen were fixed on the blaze overhead. Then, in the sudden glare of the fire-engine's headlights as it turned in from the street, Nigel saw a figure slinking along by the railings towards the open gate. Blount saw it in the same instant, yelled, and ran towards the gate to shut it. But it was nearly a hundred yards away, and Billson was only twenty yards from it, and Blount had not yet, in all this clamour, attracted the attention of the policeman at the gate.

Nigel snatched the branch of the hose from Lewis, leant all his weight on it as the pressure of the water tried to buck him off the hose, and swung the jet down and round in a streaming arc. Billson was now ten yards from the open gate, silhouetted against the fire-engine's headlights. The jet seemed to feel for him, to waver, then to leap at him. Billson was dashed against the railings by the jet's pressure, and pinned there, spread-eagled and impaled on a quivering spear of water.

Ten minutes later they were sitting in a Conference room on the ground floor of the Ministry. Edgar Billson's pallid face emerged from a chrysalis of blankets : the fight had been knocked out of him by the hosing which had saturated his clothes : his eyes, watery enough at normal times, seemed to be swimming now with exhaustion and self-pity. Nigel had asked Blount that the Deputy Director should be present at the questioning of Billson, ostensibly on the grounds that a senior Ministry official should hold a watching brief in the matter of the Q photograph files.

Blount had charged his prisoner with arson, and given him the official caution. Edgar Billson—the old Billson

so familiar as a champion obstructionist, an arguer of
every toss, a professional splitter of the hairs of procedure
—was hardly recognisable in this shivering creature
before them. He did not even claim his right to legal
advice. He was evidently determined to make a full
confession. And he announced this determination with a
vicious look at Harker Fortescue which confirmed the
theory that had taken shape in Nigel's mind.

Rather more than a year ago, said Billson, he had
sustained a series of gambling losses and fallen heavily
into debt. Not long afterwards he had been approached
by a certain person, with the suggestion that he should
" lend " this person from time to time the negatives of
any particularly interesting photographs in the Q files.
Small sums were to be paid in cash, for the loan of each
negative, and the negatives to be returned on the following
day.

" The name and address of this person ? " asked Blount.

" I shall come to that later," replied Billson in a voice
which almost seemed to gloat. At first, he continued, he
had not suspected anything wrong, for the negatives
requested had been of the type censored on policy grounds,
not on security.

" You mean, an official photographer snapped some
Allied Leader with his pants down ? That sort of thing ? "
asked Nigel.

" Precisely. But after a bit this person to whom I have
alluded came back with a request for another class of
photograph. Photographs showing detail of secret
apparatus—radar devices on aircraft, for example. I protested vigorously. I pointed out that, if such photographs
got into the hands of enemy agents, they might reveal
vital information. You will appreciate, gentlemen, when
I tell you who this person was, why it had not yet dawned
upon me that he was an enemy agent himself."

" Oh, do let's stop all this circumlocution," said Nigel

impatiently. "It's quite obvious that the 'certain person' is our esteemed Deputy Director."

The Sergeant taking down Billson's evidence snapped the point of his pencil and swore under his breath. Blount bounced in his chair, as if a small charge had exploded beneath it. Billson showed his teeth in a rat-like grimace and nodded. Harker Fortescue, his face still grimy from the fire-fighting, gazed coldly at Billson, saying :

"Don't be a prize ass. Look here, Superintendent, I'd better explain——"

"We'll come to you later," said Blount grimly . "And I must warn you now that anything you say may be taken down and used in evidence. Now, Billson, will you be prepared to swear on oath that Harker Fortescue was the person to whom you supplied negatives of the Q photographs ? "

"Yes. With pleasure."

"Never mind about the pleasure. Get on with your story."

When Fortescue had asked for a second selection of security-censored negatives, Billson continued, he began to entertain the gravest suspicions of him. But he himself was now in the toils. Having already supplied one set, he had laid himself open to the charge of complicity in a very serious offence. Besides, he was still badly in debt, and his creditors were putting on pressure—and, in short, he succumbed to the temptation. Imagine his consternation when Fortescue told him, the next day, that four of these negatives had been ruined : a V.2 had fallen in the vicinity of Fortescue's house, and the concussion had spilt a bottle of acid over them in his dark room. Fortescue, he asserted, had made no further requests for negatives thereafter : Billson imagined he had been frightened off. Transactions between them had then ceased and no mention of the secret photographs was made.

"Until you started trying to blackmail me about them," interrupted the Deputy Director.

"I object to that term," said Billson.

"Now, at last, we know what you and he were quarrelling about in his room, at lunch-time, three weeks ago," said Nigel.

"My financial position had become—h'rrm—somewhat embarrassing again. I decided to ask the Deputy Director for a loan."

"'Ask for a loan' is good," drawled Fortescue. "You threatened me with exposure, and I pointed out that if I went to the Tower, you'd certainly go with me. You were in a cleft stick, my poor Billson, and you knew it. Even if it hadn't got as far as a trial for high treason— and it wouldn't have—your conduct would certainly have had you shot out of the Civil Service. I was *not* a Permanent Civil Servant, so why should I worry?"

"You——!" Billson came out with a string of abuse more fitted to the race track than the Conference room. "You dragged me into this! Why didn't you take the negatives yourself? It'd have been simple enough. You have a key to the Q annexe."

Nigel leant forward eagerly. Much depended upon the answer to this hysterical question.

"There are a number of possible reasons," Harker Fortescue drawled, his fishy eyes dispassionately fixed upon Billson. "Perhaps I was afraid you might catch me borrowing the negatives. Perhaps I wished to test the integrity of one of my subordinate officers. Perhaps I was just pulling your leg."

Billson swore at him again, foully. Blount, who had astutely decided to let the pair rip, now interposed.

"This is all vairy instructive. But I think you had better get on with your evidence, Billson. When did you first plan to get rid of Mr. Lake? Was Fortescue your accomplice in that, too?"

From the back of the building they could hear the occasional shout of a fireman, and the rattle of the appliances. The fire had been under control when they entered the Conference room, and it should not be long now before it was extinguished.

The crisis had come, said Billson, when Strangeways put in an order for several prints, amongst which was a Secret photograph whose negative was one of the four destroyed in Fortescue's dark room. Billson had stalled as long as he could. But, when the Director sent a peremptory order that the prints in question must be supplied within twenty-four hours, he was in a most dangerous predicament. He could probably explain away the disappearance of one negative—it might have been mislaid or lost. But the search for it would inevitably reveal that three others were missing. M.I.5 would certainly be brought in, and Billson admitted he was in a panic lest the investigation should then disclose the treasonable purposes to which these negatives had been put.

His first thought had been to destroy the PHQ file without which a check of these particular photographs would be at least seriously hampered. But he found that this file had already disappeared.

" What's that ? " exclaimed Blount. " You did *not* take the file yourself ? "

Billson strenuously denied it, and Blount failed to shake him on this point. Nigel felt sure Billson must be telling the truth : having confessed so much, it was inconceivable he could be lying about the file. And it was *after* the murder of Nita Prince that the Director's hue and cry about the missing file had started. Nigel had not time to pursue this thought further, for Billson was now accusing Fortescue of having made away with the file.

" Of course he must have. He stood to lose as much as I did, if the whole business came out."

On the afternoon of Miss Prince's death, Billson continued, he began to fear that the Director was hot on the track of the missing negatives. Jimmy Lake was kicking up a great fuss about the file, throughout the Division ; and that he should do so only a few hours after his secretary had been murdered, at a time when so terrible an event might have been expected to drive everything else out of his mind, seemed to argue that his gravest suspicions had been aroused in the matter of the Q photographs. But the Director, as far as Billson knew, was the only person in the Division who could have any inkling of the real truth. His confidential secretary was dead : the Deputy Director—the only man whom he would consult at this stage—was not likely to give anything away. If the Director were silenced, investigation into the Q prints would go no further : would go no further, at any rate, provided that his death could be thrown upon someone else.

Billson accordingly laid his plans to implicate Merrion Squires. His discovery of Squires some time back, in the act of slashing Miss Prince's coat, put the idea into his head. He typed the note to Merrion, signing it with Nigel's initials, to ensure that he should be on the Ministry premises that night ; took Merrion's knife and white coat : the Director had already told him he was going to work late, and it was generally known in the Division that, when the Deputy Director worked late, he took a break in the canteen about eleven o'clock. Billson said he had first intended to wear the coat when attacking the Director. But then he feared that, even in the pitch-dark room, it might show up. So he left it outside the door. When he realised that the knife had not done the job instantly, having heard Jimmy Lake stir and seen a strip of light appear beneath the door, he did not dare enter again. Listening at the door, he heard Jimmy telephone. He then picked up the coat, raced for the lift,

pressed all the buttons to delay those who were coming
up, ran downstairs into the lavatory a floor below, made
a cut in his leg and let some blood fall on to the sleeve of
the coat, which he then hid where he hoped it would
soon be found. He knew that his own blood was of the
same group as the Director's, both having volunteered
for the Ministry's blood-transfusion scheme. He had
finally walked down to the ground floor, entered one of
the rooms on the front of the building, and jumped into
the street through a window. As he walked away, he
had seen the Messengers pouring out to form a cordon :
it had been a narrow escape for him.

During this stage of Billson's confession, there were
points where Blount had to press him pretty hard. But
on the whole it flowed freely. And Nigel imagined this
was so because, Jimmy Lake now being out of danger,
Billson had no murder charge to fear, while in the matter
of the photographs he had aimed to turn King's Evidence,
and thus receive a more lenient sentence. Presumably
he had a fair chance of this, for without his evidence a
treason charge against Fortescue could not possibly stand.
But, if Billson confessed to the attack on Jimmy simply
because it had been unsuccessful, he must logically be
innocent of the murder of Miss Prince, if the poison she
drank had been intended for Jimmy. The last thing
Billson would do, had it been he who poisoned the coffee,
would be to confess so readily to a second attack on the
Director.

Blount was now taking Billson through the events of
to-day. The Director's instructions that the Q files were
to be checked did not come as a surprise to him. It was
inevitable, since Jimmy was still alive. But the pretended
arrest of Merrion Squires for the attack on Jimmy, and
the withdrawal of the police from the building, had per-
suaded him that he was under no immediate suspicion in
the matter of the Q photographs. Moreover, the Deputy

Director had said that the PHQ file had been found again, and a check of the photographs would be easy. He decided that the Q files must be destroyed—he did not think he could rig them to stand investigation by M.I.5. An accidental fire ? The idea of fire put a whole scheme into his head. He knew that Harker Fortescue had a practice incendiary bomb in his cupboard—a souvenir of his A.R.P. instruction days. He was burning to get his own back on Fortescue ; determined that, if he himself had to be ruined, he would drag Fortescue down with him.

He called at the house of Solly Hawks, to arrange that an alibi should be set up for the night's work, and to borrow a revolver in case Fortescue should try to interfere. He had previously made sure that Fortescue would be sleeping, as in fact he usually did, at the Ministry. He had gone into Fortescue's room, taken the incendiary bomb, and also taken a small fountain-pen-size torch from one of Fortescue's desk drawers, intending to drop it in the Photographs Library as a faked clue against the Director. Then he had gone into the annexe and waited. This accounted for the period of inactivity which had surprised Nigel. It was essential to Billson's plan that the fire should not break out before Fortescue arrived in his room ; otherwise he might have an alibi for it. Billson had waited till he heard footsteps in the passage, crept into the ante-room to make sure Fortescue was in position, then returned and set off the bomb in a heap of the Q negatives. At one stroke he hoped thus to destroy the evidence of the treason against himself, and to throw the guilt of the arson on the Deputy Director. If an investigation into the Q photographs could get anywhere, with the evidence destroyed, it would only be Fortescue's word against his own. And it would be Fortescue who had incriminated himself by setting fire to the negatives, while Billson would have an alibi for the night supplied by some accommodating friend of Solly Hawks.

" I was only obeying his instructions, after all," Billson concluded. " He had told me to get rid of the evidence."

" What the devil is he talking about now ? This gets crazier and crazier," said Fortescue calmly.

" You know well enough," replied Billson, glowering at him. " During the Progress Meeting, just after you'd announced there was to be an examination of the Q files, you turned to Commissions Pending. You repeated the phrase and then said the police would be withdrawn from the building this afternoon. And you added that those of us who were left could get on with our work in peace. I suppose you'll deny this was your subtle way of conveying to me that I could set to work at once on destroying the Q file evidence."

" I certainly do deny it. Never heard such nonsense in all my life."

" Nevertheless," said Blount, " it seems to me you have a good deal of explaining to do. You are at liberty, of course, to refuse to answer questions before obtaining legal advice."

The Deputy Director looked steadily at Blount, at Nigel, at the venomous face of Edgar Billson, in turn. When he spoke, it was in the trenchant, almost autocratic manner with which he was wont to address his subordinates on the more official occasions.

" It would be perfectly open to me to deny the whole thing. It is Billson's word against mine ; and one is not likely to give much credit to the word of a self-confessed murderer—or would-be murderer. Apart from this, there is not a shred of evidence against me. Nor would you ever find it. You and M.I.5 could work yourselves black in the face trying to discover any contacts of mine with the enemy, any evidence that I passed on secret infor- mation to them. You'd never find it. Because I didn' t

However, I do not propose to deny the whole of Billson's statement. What I would like to know "—Hark'ee's eye twinkled for a moment—" is how Strangeways picked on me as the sinister Mr. X whom Billson kept hinting at."

Leaning back in his chair, Nigel appeared to be studying a chart on the opposite wall, which illustrated the public response to the Eat More Potatoes campaign. His eye still fastened upon it, he said.

" It's probably as true as any other generalisation that every collector is a potential criminal. No doubt a great number of them are actual criminals. I wouldn't know. Blount, you'd better ask the Deputy Director to say a few words about his collection of filthy pictures."

If a Superintendent of the C.I.D. could ever be said to gibber, Blount gibbered now. Hark'ee stroked his bald head, grimy from fire-fighting still : his thin mouth twitched.

" Strangeways is an extremely useful member of my staff," he said : " it is fortunate that he has such a good memory. This isn't the first time I have profited by it." He then proceeded to relate his version of Billson's story.

After explaining to the Superintendent the nature of his collection of " feelthy peectures "—that gallery of the Great in unguarded moments and ill-considered postures, which he had described to Nigel one night in the canteen —he went on to tell how it had occurred to him to adorn this gallery with selections from the policy-censored Q photographs. He had been far too busy himself to examine them for suitable material ; so he had thought, why not put Billson on to it ? At the outset, it was a pure fantasy thought. But the idea of the correct and rigid Billson searching his files for photographs of the Great in, so to speak, undress—this idea so tickled Hark'ee that he did approach Billson, " just to see what he'd say, really." To his surprise, Billson consented, demanding to be paid a certain sum for each print ; he, Billson, would make

L

the prints himself, as he did not care to let the negatives
out of his possession. Harker had not told Billson why
he wanted the photographs. After a bit of haggling the
bargain was sealed.

Hark'ee, thinking it over, found his suspicions aroused
by Billson's ready consent, no less than by his demand
for money. He made a few tactful enquiries, and learnt
that Billson, was an habitué of the race tracks. Now,
strictly speaking, what his officers did in their spare time
was no business of the Deputy Director's, provided there
was nothing illegal about it. But it occurred to him that
an officer of, the Ministry, whose conduct suggested that
he might be in debt, and who was responsible for the safe-
keeping of secret photographs, might conceivably be a
source of disquietude. So he decided to test Billson's
integrity by asking him to supply a set of security-
censored photographs, showing certain secret apparatus.
Billson had at first refused, with a great show of righteous
indignation. But presently he gave way, stipulating that
he would not make the prints himself but only " lend "
Hark'ee the negatives, and that a high price must be
paid for the loan.

At this point, said Hark'ee, he had suddenly realised
that Billson had suspected *him* of being an enemy agent
from the start of the transactions. He now agreed to
Billson's terms. Two sets of negatives were "loaned" to
him. When some of the second set were accidentally
destroyed, he perceived that things had gone too far.
What had begun as a joke, and continued as a test of
Billson's integrity, might now, if the facts came out, put
Hark'ee himself in an awkward position. " The mists of
collector's mania cleared away for a moment, and I saw
how very odd the whole thing would look to an outside
observer," was how he put it to Blount.

He had at once called off the transactions. He had not
paid, and had no intention of paying, the high sums

demanded by Billson for the two last sets of negatives. And it was this refusal that was the subject of the quarrel between them, overheard by Miss Finlay. On the other hand, knowing that his own share in the transactions would be difficult and embarrassing to explain, and feeling that—unreliable though they had proved Billson to be—it would be " a bit low " to expose Billson now on this account, he had not passed on the facts to the Director.

" Ah," Blount interrupted. " That's a crucial point. You divulged the facts to no one else."

" No one. I told Billson—that was the day after Miss Finlay overheard our little dispute—told him the truth, why I'd asked him for the pictures, and made it clear to him that he'd have to watch his step in future. And the silly ass didn't believe a word of it——"

" Bluff ! Who'd believe a cock-and-bull story like that ? " exclaimed Billson viciously.

" You see ? He still doesn't believe it. He's got it into his thick head that I'm a male Mata Hari, and nothing'll ever get it out now."

" You have no means of proving your story, I take it ? " asked Blount.

" None at all. Except that I can show you the prints in my private collection. But no doubt you'll tell me this might only be my shop window, and I'd been passing other copies under the counter to our late-lamented enemy."

The Superintendent faced him formidably.

" You are not well advised to treat the matter lightly, Mr. Fortescue. You may be telling us the truth. You may not. You can be sure that if there have been any contacts between yourself and enemy agents, it will be brought to light now. There will be a most stringent investigation into your movements throughout the war, and before it. But, if you are proved innocent in this respect, you must still realise that your actions have been indirectly responsible for an attempted murder, for the destruction by fire of Crown property—and, it may be, for the death of Miss Prince."

" I didn't do it ! " shouted Billson suddenly. " Not that ! I'd nothing to do with that ! I swear it ! "

Harker Fortescue coldly waited for the outburst to end. Then he said, " I cannot accept responsibility for anything this little rat did after I'd told him the facts, explained why I originally asked him for the photographs. I'm terribly sorry that such things should have happened. But I'm not wasting any sympathy on Billson. A man who could try and frame Merrion Squires, as he's confessed to doing—well, he can take what's coming to him. It makes me sick just to think of it. As for myself—do *you* believe me, Nigel ? "

" *I* think it's all in character. Yes," replied Nigel noncommittally. " On the other hand, Hark'ee, you'd better realise now how other people will see it. They may argue that your collection of ' feelthy peectures ' has from the start been a cover for traitorous activities. It *would* be a good cover, you know. And they will ask themselves what you were doing before the war, when you travelled all over Europe, *including Germany*, to add to your collection. And they may doubt, not knowing your peculiar sense of humour, whether such a hobby could really be enough to explain so much expense of time and money. No, Hark'ee, I'm afraid M.I.5 will put a very large question mark to your story."

CHAPTER VIII

(1) MR. STRANGEWAYS : TO SEE
(2) MR. INGLE : TO DISCUSS

SO, TO ALL intents and purposes, we are back where we started, thought Nigel.

It was the afternoon following the arrest and confession of Edgar Billson : a Saturday afternoon. Most of the Ministry staff had left the building by one o'clock, to make the best they could of the short war-time week-end. Just as Nigel was himself about to leave, Brian Ingle had come into his room and, after some blushing and stammering, asked if Nigel could do him a favour. Brian, it turned out, wanted a keepsake of Nita Prince's—a book he had once given her. He had been fond of her ; and he possessed nothing by which he could remember her. It seemed a pleasant, if old-fashioned, act of piety. Nigel had accordingly rung up Blount, and asked if there was any objection to his meeting Brian in Nita's flat that afternoon, and letting him have the book. Blount told him it would be in order. He added that the police inquiries at Nita's bank had disclosed only a small balance of £350 odd, that she had as far as they could discover died intestate, and that her next of kin was a married sister living in New Zealand. So money was clearly not a possible motive for her murder.

Nigel had made an appointment for Brian Ingle to meet him at the flat at 3 p.m. He himself, after picking up some sandwiches at a pub nearby, had gone straight to Dickens Street, where the slatternly caretaker let him in. She thought he was a C.I.D. man, having seen him

last with Blount, and he had some difficulty in staving
off her ghoulish enquiries about " Who'd done in that
poor girl ? " Alone at last, in the rooms from which
Nita's presence, like a ghost at the old trysting-place,
seemed reluctant to vanish, Nigel ate his sandwiches and
fell into uneasy speculation.

To all intents and purposes we're back where we
started. On the face of it, of course, Billson might now
seem the likeliest person to have poisoned the coffee-cup.
But there's so much to be said against it. First, the
evidence all seems to show that Jimmy did not start to
get worked up about the PHQ file till after the poisoning.
Surely Billson wouldn't have poisoned Nita's cup, believ-
ing it to be Jimmy's, unless he felt *certain* that Jimmy
was hot on his track. Now the first sign that Jimmy was
getting warm was his sending for the file. But Billson
didn't know that the file was missing, hadn't attempted
to obtain it for his own purposes, and therefore couldn't
have suspected that Jimmy was hot on the track, and
therefore couldn't have planned to poison him, *till after
the poisoning took place*. That isn't perfectly logical, my
boy. I know it isn't. Let's take the hypothesis, then,
that Billson *did* get in an unwarranted panic, *before* the
poisoning, lest Jimmy had discovered his secret, and
therefore planned to kill him. You see, my good chap,
the whole conception at once collapses on the word
" planned." Billson was not invited to the party in
Jimmy's room. He'd never have been there at all if
Charles Kennington had not, only a minute before coffee-
time, taken it into his head to invite him. Nor, until a
few minutes before the crime took place, had Billson so
much as set eyes on the instrument with which it was
committed. How could he *plan* a murder with a poison-
container he had never seen ? And, if the murder of
Jimmy was intended, surely Billson wouldn't be such a
fool as to get the cups mixed up ? All right, my boy, I

grant you all that. But suppose Billson wanted to, knew he *had* to get rid of Jimmy double quick : suppose he then found himself in a room with his victim and a poison container. Might he not have acted impromptu ? That is possible. Yes. But it's not in character. Look at Billson's subsequent crimes. The second attack on Jimmy, the burning of the Q files in the annexe, and the calculated attempts to throw the guilt for them on Merrion and on Harker, the alibis prepared for himself— everything cold, cautious, cut and dried, and the very opposite of the poisoning. Besides, what did he do with the poison container after he'd used it ?

Well, then, given 'that the poison was intended for Jimmy, who else had a motive ? Hark'ee. But only if (*a*) he is in fact a traitor and was lying last night, which I don't believe, and (*b*) if he knew that Jimmy had suspicions about the secret files. But when I rang up Jimmy this morning, he was absolutely definite that he'd suspected nothing fishy about the Q photographs till the PHQ file disappeared. He'd sent for it, on the morning of Nita's death, simply to glance over the list of canned photographs which might be available for the Pacific job, if the censorship stop could be lifted. He had not imagined for a moment that there was anything more in Billson's recalcitrance over the Q print I'd ordered than his usual official stickiness ; not until the disappearance of the file began to put ideas into his head. He had not discussed his suspicions with the Deputy Director even then. And if, by some extraordinary feat of clairvoyance, Hark'ee was enabled to see into the future state of Jimmy's mind, and therefore attempted to poison him in order to forestall the suspicions which Jimmy did not yet entertain, what did Hark'ee do with the poison container after he had used it ?

Merrion Squires, then ? His only possible motive for wishing to get rid of Jimmy is that he's deeper involved with Jimmy's wife than he admitted. Blount will ferret that out, if there's anything in it. But it doesn't make sense, in any case : for Alice Lake was free to get a divorce from her husband—he had even sounded her about it. And the same holds good for Mrs. Lake herself having attempted to poison him, in order to be free to marry Merrion.

Charles Kennington ? A quixotic gesture ? Murdering Jimmy because he had been unfaithful to Charles' sister ? Absurd. Because he had stolen Charles' fiancée ? Not quite so absurd, but absurd enough.

Brian Ingle ? Because he loved Nita : and, with Jimmy out of the way, she might have come to him. No. It's too thin altogether.

The other hypothesis, then—that there was no accident with the cups, and Nita Prince was the intended victim.

Edgar Billson. No apparent motive. Harker Fortescue, ditto : Blount had failed to find any association between Hark'ee and Nita, except that she worked for Hark'ee's agency some time before the war.

Merrion Squires ? He didn't like Nita. She had rejected his advances, he told us. But Merrion makes a pass at almost anything in skirts—it's automatic with him. And if everyone who pushed him off was to get murdered, London would be littered with dead females. No real link between him and Nita has been discovered. Count him out, for the present.

Brian Ingle ? In love with Nita. A forlorn hope for him. A good-hearted little chap. Inconceivable, after knowing Nita for several years, and therefore presumably knowing about her affair with Jimmy, he should suddenly up and poison *her*.

Charles Kennington ? On the face of it, he's the best bet. We've only his word for it, that he was prepared to hand over his fiancée to Jimmy without a murmur. He provided the poison. His Secret Service training and experience make him the most likely person to have been able to get rid of the poison-container afterwards. What did that silly old Messenger say, the morning before ?—" Millions of young men, trained to kill. Proper artful, too." It was artful enough certainly. At least it could have been : a carefully staged murder, rigged up to look like an impromptu one. Kennington has the dramatic instinct well developed, that's obvious enough. If only these walls would tell what he really said to Nita that night. She confessed to him about her relationship with Jimmy—that's why she asked him to come along. Did he just give it his blessing, as he told us ? Or did he cut up rough ? Or did he pretend to accept it quite calmly, and go away with murder in his heart ? Nita was still in a state the next morning—the crumpled handkerchief, the distrait air. But there's one gigantic obstacle to all this. Charles Kennington is not, by any sign or symptom, the jealous type. Just look at him. Think about him for a moment. Can you imagine him as an Othello ?

And the same applies to his sister. They are both highly civilised creatures. Why should Alice Lake, after accepting her husband's mistress for years, turn round and kill her ? If she was a neurotic or a wildly passionate woman, if she was madly in love with Jimmy still—well then, something might have happened just before Nita's death to explode her accumulated resentment. But surely she isn't ? Think of her, sitting equably at Jimmy's bed-side, holding his hand as if she were a nurse feeling his pulse. I ask you ! Nevertheless, I must get to know her better before I can be sure. And Charles.

Jimmy Lake himself ? His only possible motive, since his wife knew about his relations with Nita and was apparently complacent, is that he wanted to free himself from Nita but could not do so in any other way. Don't underestimate that motive, my boy. Under certain conditions, it could be immensely strong. What con-

ditions ? First, that Nita should be an insinuating, cling-
ing, tenacious character : well, we have fair evidence
that she was. Second, that Jimmy was tired of her : no
proof at all ; one or two very shadowy suggestions,
which might be interpreted quite differently. Third, that
there was no other way of releasing himself from her
grip : on the face of it, preposterous ; why shouldn't he
just walk out ? Pay her off ? Psychologically, though,
not so preposterous ; a weak character, a morally unrobust
character might be incapable of freeing himself except by
such violent means. But is Jimmy a weak character ?
What is Jimmy really like ? The fact is, you don't know.
Find out, then. And find out, incidentally, if he's the
sort of man who, having poisoned his girl, would publicly
slap her on the back and tell her to cough it up, ducky.
It seems impossibly macabre, utterly incredible, that any
one—and besides, *how did he get rid of the poison container ?*

   To that insoluble question, again and again, the problem
reduced itself ? And it applied equally to all the suspects
except Brian Ingle. Brian *could* have thrown it out into
the street when he opened the window. It could then
have been carried away on someone's boot-sole or the
tyre of a car. But Brian was the one person who seemed
to have no adequate motive for murdering either Nita or
Jimmy. Charles Kennington's experience put him next
on the list in this respect. But how could even the
capturer of Stultz convey a broken container out of that
room ? Blount had dealt very severely with Sergeant
Messer. But in fact, Nigel now knew, the Sergeant had
been at fault only in one point of his search. He had
examined the suspects' clothes most thoroughly, after
they had stripped behind the screen ; then searched the
possible hiding-places on their bodies, although none of
them had had an opportunity to secrete the thing in that
way. The only point where he could possibly have slipped
up was in his examination of their mouths. He had

glanced into their mouths, but not run his finger round their teeth. The poison container might, theoretically, have been concealed from him in a gap between the back teeth—in the very place where, as Charles Kennington had told them earlier that morning, the Nazis kept these containers lodged if danger seemed imminent.

But there were two crushing objections to this possibility. First, who but a lunatic would have tried to hide the container thus, knowing there was going to be a rigorous search by the police, and when he only had to drop it anywhere in the room, after wiping it with his handkerchief in his pocket, for his association with it to be entirely sponged out ? And secondly, supposing some-one *had* been lunatic enough to hide the thing in his mouth, he would inevitably have betrayed himself : for the container must have been broken to decant the poison into Nita's cup, and there were bound to be traces enough of the poison left in the container to cause at least a severe fit of choking, from the fumes, when it was put in the mouth. It was the certainty of this, in fact, which had led the too-intelligent Sergeant Messer to his slight carelessness over the examination of the suspects' mouths.

Nigel, now lighting another cigarette, set himself to grapple once again with this problem. It faced him as two blindingly enigmatic questions. *How* was the container hidden from the police and conveyed out of the room ? Why was it *necessary* to the murderer to convey it out of the room ? The first of these questions he had run his head against, hard and often, and it yielded nothing. Maybe if he could find the right answer—no, if he could get as far as imagining a *possible* answer—to the second question, it would throw some light on the first.

Well, then, why does any murderer remove the weapon from the scene of the crime ? Because it might be identified, and incriminate him. But in this case we had all seen the weapon : it was positively on display a few minutes before the murder. Therefore it was unnecessary for the murderer to remove it. But the murderer *did* remove it. It's a vicious circle, absolutely unbroken, no way to break out of it. . . . Oh, my sainted ancestors down to the seventy-seventh generation ! I've got it ! I see how to break out of the circle !

Nigel floundered up from the arm-chair and began pacing the room excitedly, his mind full of the image which an idle phrase had presented to him. A clear, visual image : absurdly simple, yet revolutionising his whole conception of the case. What it implied was perfectly logical—the only logical answer to his second question ; and with mounting excitement he realised it also gave a rational answer to the first. What it did not give, he soon ruefully admitted, was any definite clue to the identity of the murderer. Still, that could wait. He took up the telephone and got through to Superintendent Blount at New Scotland Yard.

" Blount ? Strangeways here. A most extraordinary idea has come into my head . . . Yes, about the poisoning of Nita Prince. I think I know why and how the murderer spirited that poison container away . . . No, I don't know who it is yet. . . . No, blast you, I haven't got any evidence for it yet—I did it by an exercise of pure reason. . . . Don't be offensive, Blount old boy. Getting the evidence is the job of the plodding policeman, meaning you. May I suggest this for a start—find out which of the suspects had access to poison. . . . Yes, I know they all did, I'm not a half-wit ; I mean access to some *other* supply of cyanide . . . What ? . . . Yes, on the whole no harm at all in letting them know that you're looking for it. It'll shake X to the wick, whoever he is, and he may do something silly. . . . No, not just a bluff ; it *is* essential to find out if any of them had another supply. The point is this——" but Nigel had not time to start unfolding his theory, for the doorbell rang, and Brian Ingle was shown in, and Nigel had to ring off.

Brian sat down gingerly in the arm-chair Nigel had vacated. His eyes flickered about the room, screwed up as if the light, or what he saw, hurt them.

" You've not been here before ? " asked Nigel at a venture.

" Oh, no. No. I couldn't, could I ? Feeling as I did for Nita, I mean."

After a pause, Nigel said, " I wish you'd talk to me about her."

" Yes, I've been meaning to. But you were busy. And—I s-say, Nigel, have the police—I mean, do they suspect any one particularly yet ? Was it Billson ? I see Merrion's back at work this morning, so it can't be him."

" Funny. You're almost the first person to ask me about that. The self-control of our colleagues is remarkable."

" It's n-not self-control," burst out the little man. " It's sheer callousness ! What do they care ? One more death. We've had so much death these last years, our reaction to it is atrophied. We're not interested."

" Including Jimmy ? "

Brian Ingle went into one of his trance-like silences. Nigel knew well enough not to break it, or try to hurry him. It was like watching a mouse bring forth a mountain.

" I don't know," said Brian at last. " He used to love her, of course. But—I wish I knew."

" ' But,' " prompted Nigel.

After another protracted silence, Brian came out with, " She was very unhappy, latterly."

" Did she confide in you much about it ? "

Brian Ingle's eyes roved round the room, more boldly now. " He was good to her. Yes, I must admit that." Long pause. " You know, Nigel, I simply couldn't bear

to talk to that Superintendent much. Oh, he's a very
decent fellow, I'm sure. But it all seemed so irrelevant.
She was dead. What did it matter who killed her ? And
—well :

> " ' The sweeping up the heart
> And putting love away
> We shall not want to use again
> Until eternity.'

I had an awful lot of sweeping up to do. And all this
police investigation—questions, questions, questions—it
was like being interrupted by lawyers and telephone calls
and letters of condolence when one "—his voice choked
a little—" when one is trying to tidy up."

"Yes, I know. But there's this to be said : perhaps the
happiest part of her life was over, anyway."

"*I* could have made her happy," replied Brian, with
affecting simplicity. "You see," he smiled crookedly,
"I could take any amount of domesticity."

"And Jimmy couldn't ? "

Brian Ingle fell into his fit of abstraction again. When
he spoke, it seemed, as so often it did with him, at a
tangent to the subject.

"She used to come and see me sometimes, in my
rooms—I always refused to come here—about the only
thing I ever did refuse her. She knew she could rely on
me to listen, to console her. About her life with Jimmy."

"That was rather cruel of her, wasn't it ? "

"Oh, yes, I suppose so. One is cruel when one's in
love. To everyone else, I mean, if one's as much in love
as Nita was with Jimmy. The single-minded person is
bound to ride roughshod over everyone's feelings. And
I tell you, it'd have killed her if Jimmy had left her."

"She'd had lovers enough before him," said Nigel with
a deliberate roughness. Brian Ingle did not wince.

"That's why," he said, following some enigmatic thought of his own. " You see, they all left her, sooner or later. None of them offered to marry her."

" Why ? "

" Because she was too beautiful. Her beauty misled them, Nigel. They thought they'd got the perfect—well, the perfect courtesan. And presently they found out it was a sort of trap : you walked into the Temple of Aphrodite Pandemos, and you found yourself in a snug domestic interior with knitting lying about and the Hoover humming away. Like this." He gestured round the room with his hand.

" It seems to have suited Jimmy all right, though."

" Nita thought so too, at first. For quite a time. So did he, I expect. He and his wife are sophisticated people. They're what's called ' modern ' : easy come, easy go. Nita was something quite different. Her passion for domesticity—well, it'd be a sort of new, delightful game for him, at first. And then he'd begin to realise that for her it wasn't a game, it was in dead earnest——"

" And no chance of ' easy go ' ? "

" Well, can you blame her ? I know it's easy to talk about a woman getting her claws into a man, suffocating him—oh dear, that word ' suffocate,' how it does bring back all the novels by lady novelists of a certain type I used to review. But people who talk like that never put the other side of the case to themselves—the woman's side. It was just because Nita *had* led a rackety life, just because all those men wanted her as a mistress, not as a wife, that she grew to put so high a value on security. Every woman wants security, of course : it's biological. But Nita was dotty about it. I used to laugh at her. Gently, of course. She'd no sense of humour, though, poor darling. Why should she anyway, on that subject ? Oh, yes, she looked so poised and invulnerable and successful, didn't she ? And beneath it there was panic and chaos. She'd no more belief in herself : thought there must be something terribly wrong with her, because no one would marry her and give her security."

" But Jimmy did ? Give her security, I mean ? "

" He gave her all the accessories of it, yes," replied Brian with another long look round the room. " And therefore the sense of it, for a while—you know how women have to deceive themselves into taking the shadow for the reality, when the reality isn't there—making emotional bricks without straw. And because he'd given her so strongly the *sense* of security——" Brian broke off suddenly.

"——her disillusionment when she discovered he'd only been playing at home-making was all the more painful ? " suggested Nigel.

Brian Ingle appeared to contemplate this from every angle, like a housewife turning over a prospective purchase on a stall, before he answered.

" I wonder is that quite right. I wonder. I'd say there *was* a time when Jimmy only played at home-making. But then a point was reached when his home-making with Nita became so real that it started to challenge his real home, with his wife, if you see what I mean. A con-flict was set up within him. And a very painful one it'd be. He'd know then that he must choose between the two—the equilibrium couldn't be preserved any longer. From that point he was a divided mind—and Nita began to be unhappy."

Nigel found all this of absorbing interest. Brian's comments were so much more solid than, for instance, Merrion Squires' dashing but superficial strictures on the two persons in question.

" So you think Jimmy was trying to break free ? "

" Unconsciously, yes. Mind you, Nita must have had a great physical hold over him, too. I'd say he was a morally weak man : infirm of purpose : the Micawber streak too—waiting for something to turn up which would cut the knot he hadn't the resolution to cut himself."

" In this case, the end of the war ? "

" No doubt. It would force him to act one way or the other. I dare say he didn't know which knot it would cut for him, either."

" The Nita knot or the Alice knot ? "

" Exactly."

" And Nita was aware of this conflict in his mind ? "

" She knew he was on edge. And she tried her best to pull him over the edge on to her side."

" Hence the request for a divorce ? "

" That. And other things. She was fighting for her life, poor girl, after all."

" Other things ? "

" I don't know—I've never experienced—but I can imagine how a woman might create a blazing inferno for a man she was determined to keep, every word fanning a flame, every look and gesture and silence a reproach or an appeal, every trick in the bag used. I bet she had plenty, too."

" But, if she was in effect making things so hot for him, why shouldn't he just walk out ? "

" Oh, my dear Nigel, life isn't as simple as that. She was in his blood. He loved her. Oh, yes, he really loved her. He wouldn't get rid of her just by walking out—he was far too intelligent a man to suppose that."

" He wouldn't be rid of her, of his problem, his conflict, till she was dead ? " asked Nigel purposefully.

Brian Ingle shrank back in the chair, holding up his hands as if to ward off the question.

" No," he exclaimed. " No, no ! Please. This is dreadful. It sounds as if I'd been meaning to accuse him of—— Honestly, I didn't."

" But the thought has occurred to you, perhaps ? "

M

The longest of all Brian's silences ensued. He might have been in an epileptic trance, dumb and insentient. At last he spoke, almost to himself :

" Nita *was* frightened."

Another pause.

" Frightened ? Recently ? "

" The morning she died—was murdered."

" How was that ? " asked Nigel, gently, delicately, as if humouring a child.

" I didn't tell the Superintendent," said Brian slowly. " When he interviewed me, I wasn't in the mood, I didn't care two pins *who* had killed her, it didn't seem to matter. That was wrong of me, no doubt. Anyway, the morning she died, she came into my room at the Ministry, early. I could see she was very upset—almost incoherent, trying to tell me something. ' Oh, Brian, what am I to do ? What am I to do ? ' She kept saying. Wildly. You know, when that sort of woman gets in a panic, she's like an animal. It's terrifying. The mental anguish communicates itself to her body : you see her body, her face—it's like an animal in a trap—you see it actually struggling, jerking, twitching one moment, and the next absolutely inert, frozen, in a sort of coma, like the animal shamming dead."

Brian Ingle broke off abruptly, silenced by the pain of the recollection.

" What did she say ? " asked Nigel.

" I've been trying to remember. It's awfully difficult. You see, she really was—well, like a person in delirium. Her words hardly made sense. She kept repeating, ' It's my last chance. He said it was my last chance.' ' Last chance to do what ? ' I asked. ' To give him up.' ' Give Jimmy up, you mean ? ' She nodded. ' But I won't,' she said : ' I won't, I won't, I won't.' And then she burst into a terrible fit of sobbing. I tried to soothe her. She did quieten down a bit. And I asked her—I don't know why—*when* he'd said this. 'Last night. He came to my flat. Brian, I'm so frightened, I don't know what to do.' I couldn't talk to her any more, because Jimmy came in—I suppose he'd heard her voice from outside—and he said he wanted her straight away to type some letters for him.''

"Do you remember anything else she said? Anything. Doesn't matter how wild it was."

"No. . . . Wait a minute . . . Yes, there was one very curious thing she said—really delirious it seemed. She muttered, 'It startled me so when I saw him. I knew he'd be like that. But it was horrible, Brian. You wouldn't understand, though.' And then, after a bit, she went on, 'I wish I could trust him. There's no one I can trust now.' So of course I said she could always trust me and tried to comfort her. And of course she said, 'I know, Brian: but you're different.' Oh, yes, I was always different. Just the faithful little dog to take out for a walk when there was no one else——''

Brian broke off, clearly ashamed of this little touch of bitterness.

"And this 'he' she kept talking about. The 'he' who was giving her a last chance, whom she wished she could trust. Whom do you suppose she meant?"

"Well, that's obvious, surely." Brian's eyes opened wide in astonishment. "Who would she be talking about but Jimmy?"

"But why should Jimmy 'startle' her so when she saw him?"

"Well, I dunno. I suppose she wasn't expecting him, or something. Who else would come to her flat at night —who else, I mean, with that power to upset her?"

"Who indeed?" replied Nigel, gazing down at his feet and the mellow Persian rug on which they rested. The 'he' whom poor, frantic Nita had spoken of—it *could* be Jimmy, it *need* not be Jimmy; she might, for

that matter, have been talking about two separate he's.
It all depended.

But further questioning extracted no more meat from
this egg. Brian Ingle was beginning to look about him,
in an absent, impatient way.

" You'd like to take your book now ? "

Jumping up from his chair, Brian went over to the
book-shelves and ran his eye along them.

" Ah, here it is." He gazed for a moment at the inscription on the fly-leaf, then put the book in his pocket.

" Hallo," he said, " I didn't know any one read Clough
nowadays." He took up the poems of Clough, still lying
on the table beside Nigel's chair, and opened it at the
marker. " Well now, that's an interesting passage," he
said presently. " He'd have made a good novelist,
wouldn't he ? ' Like losings in games played for nothing.'
Funny we should have been using that word just now."

" What word ? "

" ' Games.' The idea, anyway. ' Playing at home-
making.' "

" Oh, yes. Yes, to be sure."

" I say, Nigel, you'd think Clough had known Jimmy
personally, wouldn't you ? Extraordinary. A life-size,
life-like portrait of him, this is. Or of Nita's idea of him,
anyway."

" But it must have been another likeness in the passage
that caught her attention. How does it go ? ' Lo, with
her calm eyes there she met me and knew nothing of it
—Stood unexpecting, unconscious. *She* spoke not of
obligations.' That's Alice Lake, I take it."

" Mmm. Yes. I suppose it is. But what makes you
think that was the bit Nita was interested in ? "

" Look at the margin. She wrote a capital A there.
A for Alice."

" Sounds like a bomber. Yes, so she did. It's so faint,
I didn't notice it at first. No, she didn't, though. This

isn't her writing. She always made a sort of printed A.
This is an A with a squiggle. Look."

Nigel jumped up and almost snatched the book from
him.

" Yes, by Jove, you're quite right. Can't think how I
missed it. I've seen her initial A often enough. She used
her full name, Anita, when she signed minutes, didn't
she? Well, I must say that's very odd. And the only
other person who'd have been likely to mark the book is
Jimmy himself."

" And his capital A is quite different from this one."

" Yes. Oh, well, it probably doesn't mean anything at
all. I must be getting along now. Nothing else you'd
like to take away ? "

Brian Ingle said no. His eyes lingered sadly over the
room for a minute. Then he turned away and left. As
soon as the door closed behind him, Nigel went back to
the bookcase and began looking through the fly-leaves of
the books. At last he found what he wanted—a book
with an inscription to Jimmy from Nita. He brought it
to the window and compared it closely with the letter in
the margin of the Clough.

It had suddenly occurred to him that, if you took a
capital 𝐽 and added to it ⅗ , you would produce an 𝓐
precisely the same as appeared in the margin. Provided
it was the right kind of J. And now, on the fly-leaf of
the book he had found, was " Jimmy, with all my love,
Nita." And the J of Jimmy seemed identical in shape
with the left-hand J stroke of the letter 𝓐 in the margin.
The natural deduction was that Nita had originally
written a J there, because the passage had reminded her
of Jimmy, and it was presumably she who had pencilled
the question-mark beside it, too. Then someone had
come along and turned the J into an 𝓐. Who ? And
why ? Nigel could not, as yet, be sure. And anyhow, it
might well just be an idle, meaningless bit of doodling.

But possibly the scientific boys at New Scotland Yard would be able to detect whether the 𝒜 was in fact a composite letter, made by two different hands. It would help to be quite sure of that. Nigel left the flat, carrying the two books under his arm, and walked in the direction of New Scotland Yard.

A few hours later, as he was dining at the Club, a servant called him out to the telephone. It was Blount at the other end.

" That book you left for me. Our people tell me they think the 𝒜 is composite. The J part is slightly less indented than the rest, anyway. And there's a slight thickening on the down-stroke of it, which you'd expect from the normal way of writing a J—starting at the top, I mean, and ending with the curl. To write a capital 𝒜 of that kind, you'd normally start at the curl and go upwards, and then do the right-hand side of the letter with a down-stroke, and——"

" All right. I'm ahead of you. What about the second source of poison ? Have you had time to get on to that ? "

" Yes. At least four of the suspects had access to some form of cyanide."

" Gor lumme ! Now I've done it ! That's too much, Blount."

" Billson used it for photographic purposes. Mr. Lake and Mr. Fortescue possess, or rather say they once possessed, capsules of the poison. Mrs. Lake had access to Mr. Lake's capsule. Billson had signed for his supply in the ordinary way : we're checking the amount he received from the chemist with the amount he has left. Mr. Lake and Mr. Fortescue say they got theirs privately in the autumn of 1940, when the invasion scare was on : they both believed they were on the Nazi Black List, so they wished to be prepared."

" But they say they haven't got their capsules now ? "

" Mr. Fortescue claims that on V.E. Day, he—e'eh,

pulled the plug on his : had a solemn little ceremony all
by himself. Mr. Lake—I went to see him—had his capsule
carefully locked away :   at least he thought he had ;
but when I opened the drawer with the key he gave me,
it wasn't there.   Mrs. Lake protested that she knew
nothing about the existence of this capsule, and couldn't
account for its disappearance. So there you are. And
now you'd better tell me what's on your mind."

" Just a minute. All of them volunteered this information quite freely ? "

" Yes. Ye-es. Mrs. Lake was a bit rattled, I doubt :
she was with her husband when I asked him. But there
was no attempt at prevarication or concealment."

" Did Lake and Fortescue know about each other's
acquisition of cyanide capsules ? "

" Yes."

" Has Fortescue no other source ?   Doesn't he use
potassium cyanide, too, for photographic purposes ? "

" He says no. We shall check this, of course."

" You realise, Blount, that his admission about the
capsule is a point in his favour as far as the Q Photographs are concerned ? He would hardly need to furnish
himself with poison if he was an agent of the Nazis."

" Not to take in the event of the Germans occupying
Great Britain, I agree. But he'd need it if the British
counter-espionage caught up with him."

" In that case, why should he destroy the capsule on
V.E. Day ? He might well have still needed it."

" We've only his word that he destroyed it."

" Certainly. But it'd be to his interest to produce it
now, if he still had it. However, my only point at the
moment is that Hark'ee's possession and alleged destruction of the capsule works in his favour over the Q photographs but against him over Nita Prince's death."

The telephone yammered a bit.

" But, my dear sir, are you suggesting that Major

Kennington's poison container was *not* the means of her death? This is absolutely——"

" Oh, talking of Kennington, surely he had some quick means of suicide, for his espionage work in Germany ? "

" Yes," said Blount gloomily. " You could float a duck on the amount of cyanide that's pouring in just now. He volunteers that he did possess a capsule, but says he handed it in at his Headquarters when he left Germany. I'm checking this, of course. The War Office have sent out a signal for me."

" I take it that these three capsules—Lake's, Fortescue's and Kennington's—would all be of the soluble type ? "

" That is so."

" And what about Squires and Ingle ? Didn't they have a few pints of poison salted away somewhere ? "

" According to their own statements, none," replied Blount with gravity.

" Too bad. No doubt you'll be circularising the chemists. Don't leave any one out. Well, Blount, I wish you'd do something for me."

" What's this, now ? " asked Blount suspiciously.

" Try and find some more poison."

The telephone yammered in a quite demented way, and Nigel held the receiver away from his ear for a few moments. When Blount had unburdened his bosom, Nigel said :

" I think it would be a good plan to get a search warrant and start searching our suspects' belongings for a poison container—a poison container so like the one Kennington took off Stultz as to be indistinguishable from it."

There was an awful silence on the line. Nigel could almost feel Blount struggling to master his emotions. At last, in a sternly-controlled voice, the Superintendent asked :

" Where do you suggest I should begin this—this wild-goose search ? "

" Oh, begin with the Lakes. Or Charles Kennington."

" You know Kennington has moved into the Lakes' house ? "

" He has, has he ? Well, well, well. I'll invite him here to lunch to-morrow, so you can have a free hand."

" And now—e'eh—in this little formality of a search warrant, perhaps you'd be kind enough to tell me on what grounds I should apply for it," said Blount with heavy sarcasm.

" My dinner's getting cold. Never mind. It's like this, Blount——"

And Nigel explained to the Superintendent the idea which had come to him that afternoon in Nita Prince's flat—the answer to the question why it had been necessary for the murderer to spirit " Stultz's thing " out of the Director's room after the murder, and how he had been able to do it.

When Nigel had finished, Blount agreed to ask for a search warrant.

CHAPTER IX

REFERENCE : MRS. LAKE

ELEVEN O'CLOCK the next morning, Sunday, found Nigel
Strangeways on his way in a bus to the Lakes' house at
Regent's Park. He had already, the previous night, secured
Major Kennington for lunch. But, before he talked to
him, there were certain things which he wished to ask
Jimmy and Alice Lake. And certain things which,
though he could not ask them, he hoped to discover.
Nigel believed that he now knew the identity, the motive
and the method of Nita Prince's murderer. But he had
no proof, nor did he see how proof could be obtained,
unless the murderer was flustered into some ill-judged
action. Blount's inquiries about a second source of
poison might do this ; or again, it might not : it depended,
really, upon the murderer's nerve—would this person,
who so far had remained so cleverly quiescent, who had
made so little attempt to cover up, or to trail red herrings,
and therefore had avoided the most flagrant kind of self-
betrayal, would this person be goaded into action by
Blount's last inquiry, which must convey the hint that
the police now had come perilously near to discovering
the murder method ?

Jolting up empty Baker Street on the top of his bus,
Nigel was thinking desperately hard. From now on,
every word of his must be directed to one end, to prising
the murderer, like an otter from his holt, out of the
security of silence, inaction, acquiescence, out into the
open. He knew that he was dealing with a mind of great
intelligence and subtlety. Indeed, it was one of the
difficulties which had faced the police all through their
investigation—that, as far as the death of Nita Prince

went, there had been a general lying low, a relative
absence of the gossip, the exhibitionism, the hysteria, the
bogus confessions, the charges and counter-charges, on
which they would normally rely for information. And
this was because the suspects were all, with the possible
exception of Edgar Billson, persons of high intelligence :
moreover, they had been working together for some years
now in a small, successful group, whose *esprit de corps*,
though they would not all admit it, had affected each of
them as individuals, creating a certain resistance to any
influence from outside which tended to criticise or
threaten the group as a whole.

How far was it true to say that the Director himself
had been responsible for this *esprit de corps* ? Without
question, his was the creative mind of the Division. His
flair for the kind of visual propaganda with which they
were concerned was extraordinary : he had created, one
might almost say, a new mode of propaganda, and the
productions of the Division were all stamped with his
personality. His charm and tact, besides, had proved
indispensable, not only in keeping the wheels of the
organisation well oiled, in smoothing over the differences
which sometimes arose between the temperamental
members of his staff, but in " selling " his own conception
of propaganda to other Government Departments. It
was not difficult to understand his success, before the
war, as chairman of the National Committee for Public
Relations in Industry—that cumbrously-named body
which had been set up in the middle thirties to boost
British products abroad. But, in so far as *esprit de corps*
meant fighting spirit, Nigel inclined to think that the
Division owed it more to Harker Fortescue than to
Jimmy Lake. It was Hark'ee's driving power which had
got them through the blitzes and the long hours of work,
Hark'ee's painstaking examination of every detail of
every job which had kept them all up to the mark,

Hark'ee's firmness and pugnacity that had fought Jimmy's creative ideas through the resistance so often in the earlier days manifested by Government Departments, each of which possessed its own Public Relations Staff suspicious or jealous of the growing prestige of the Ministry of Morale.

Such were Nigel's thoughts as, alighting from the bus, he walked through the July sunshine round the curve of the noble crescent at the far end of which stood the Lakes' house. The stucco was discoloured and peeling, the magnificent row of houses was gapped in two places where bombs had fallen; but its grandeur had not departed from the place.

Nigel rang the bell of Number 35. Alice Lake herself answered it. She did not look particularly surprised at his visit, though she could not have been expecting it.

" Oh, hallo," she said in her cool way. " Do you want to see Jimmy ? He's up. He got up yesterday, though I don't suppose it's very good for him, so soon after——" Her voice trailed away, as though she had already lost interest in the subject.

" I really want to see you both."

" Oh. I was writing. It's a damned nuisance, my daily woman not coming on Sundays. I like to write every morning, you see, when I'm at work on a book. Otherwise I lose touch with my characters. Is it important ? "

" Well, yes. It is rather. Though I wouldn't like to say it was more important than one of your novels."

" I hope you don't use ' important ' in the reviewers' sense. I should hate to think I was an ' important novelist.' It opens up such dreary vistas of social realism, and starkness, and well-meant tedium." She opened the door of Jimmy's study. " Here's Mr. Strangeways. He wants to talk to us," she announced.

Jimmy rose from his chair. His left arm was in a sling.

Without seeming to make any effort, he created a warmth
of welcome, of solicitude almost, for Nigel, very much in
contrast with his wife's off-hand manner. He had that
magical touch which comes from inherited good breeding
and acquired success : there was something hypnotic in
it—soothing and stimulating at once.

"This is a nuisance about Hark'ee," he said. "The
Superintendent was telling me. Of course it's idiotic to
suppose the old boy was trafficking with the enemy : but
one can understand they're not very keen for him to stay
in his job while he's still under the faintest suspicion.
What can we do about it ? The Minister is rather fussed
too."

"I don't really know. I'd be in favour of hushing it up
and keeping Hark'ee on. After all, it's not for much
longer. And no doubt he'd be under surveillance of some
kind."

"Ye-es. The fact is I can't do without him. The
Division can't. Things are disorganised enough as it is,
and the doctor won't let me go back for a week at least.
I feel pretty well all right again, but I suppose being
stabbed does take it out of one more than one supposes."

Nigel got the impression that Jimmy was angling for a
little wifely comfort and solicitude here. If so, he did
not get it. Alice Lake, sitting at the opposite side of the
fireplace, hands folded in her lap, hardly seemed to be
attending at all. Her eyes were abstracted, inwardly
brooding perhaps upon the characters she had left
upstairs in her writing-room. There was an aimless
moment of silence, which Nigel broke by saying flatly :

"It's rather a nuisance about that cyanide capsule of
yours, too."

"Oh, my pill ? Yes." The Director laughed gently.
"Though I must say I can't think what the police are
driving at. Do they believe the—the poisoning was not
done with that thing Charles brought along ? I can't

make sense of it. Or is it just what they call routine investigation ? "

" Blunt has some theory he's very keen on. Did you have just the one capsule—in the house, I mean ? "

Nigel's question produced a queer change of atmosphere. There seemed something apologetic in Jimmy's affirmative reply. Alice sat quite still, her delicate small head turned away from them.

" But, my dear girl "—Jimmy was now addressing her directly, a faint note of exasperation in his voice—" *you* weren't on the Nazi Black List. Alice feels bad because I hadn't provided a pill for her as well," he explained to Nigel.

" I don't think Mr. Strangeways can be interested in these domestic shortages," said Alice in a voice like a tinkle of ice.

She has wit, but no sense of humour, reflected Nigel : a genuine satirist.

" You didn't know of the existence of this capsule ? " he asked her.

" Not till yesterday afternoon."

" Did any one know about it ? "

" Hark'ee did. I mean, we arranged our suicide pact together," replied Jimmy, smiling gently. " I don't see how any one else could have known. I kept the thing in a locked drawer in my dressing-room. In a little pill-box with ' Poison ' written on it. Just in case any one should——"

" And the key of the drawer ? "

" Oh, that's on my ring. And my key-ring stays in my pocket. Except at night, when I put it on my dressing-table."

" When did you last look in that drawer—look in the pillbox, I mean, to make sure the capsule was there ? "

" Ages ago. About a year ago, I should think it was."

" Did Hark'ee tell you he'd destroyed his one ? "

" No—yes, of course he did. On V.E. Day."

The Director shook with one of his silent laughs, remembering no doubt Harker Fortescue's ceremony of disposal.

" I'm sorry to be asking all these tiresome questions over again. No doubt the Superintendent asked them all yesterday. But would you mind telling me, Mrs. Lake, when your brother came to fetch you along to the Ministry, the morning Miss Prince was murdered, did he stay long ? I mean, was he here for long before you set off ? "

" What you really mean," said Alice Lake, with her cold clear eyes fastened directly upon him, " is, did he go up alone to my husband's dressing-room, I suppose ? "

" Well, did he ? "

" No. He was only here for five or ten minutes, and he was with me all the time, and then we left."

" Did he say anything to you about Miss Prince that morning ? Anything about having visited her the night before ? Or their engagement being broken off ? "

" I don't know that I care for these questions very much," said Mrs. Lake.

" You certainly don't have to answer them. I've no official standing in the case. I realise they're rather impertinent. But I do want to find out who killed that girl."

" Oh ? Why ? " Alice Lake shot it at him flatly, her delicate features quite impassive. The question might have been one of pure intellectual curiosity, for all the emotion she showed.

" My dear girl," Jimmy put in, " don't be so Bloomsbury."

His wife entirely ignored this, continuing to gaze full in Nigel's eyes as if waiting for a rational answer to her question, but with small expectation of there being one.

" Because," replied Nigel, " if Blount's theory is

correct, a person I like and respect is guilty of a peculiarly atrocious murder. I should prefer that Blount was not correct."

For once, Alice Lake seemed a little disconcerted.

" Aren't all murders ' peculiarly atrocious ' ? " she said hurriedly. " No, I suppose not. What they call the crime of passion—I dare say there may be excuses for that. Poor girl, she must have been very trying, by all accounts."

" All whose accounts ? "

" Oh, Charles'. And Jimmy's."

The Director, who had been stirring uneasily in his chair, said :

" Alice, if you persevere with these disinterested reflections on the case, you'll find yourself accusing *me* of a *crime passionel.*"

" Well, Jimmy, I should be almost relieved to know you had it in you. Surprised, anyway. You've taken the poor girl's death so calmly."

" Why, damn it, do you expect me to be in a permanent state of hysterics ? That's the last thing *you* would like."

" No, but——" She bit her lip. " Mr. Strangeways must find this all very embarrassing and interesting. Of course I know you didn't do it, Jimmy "—her husband's face lit up, rather pathetically, but the light went out the next moment as she continued—" because I saw that poison-container thing on your table, and you couldn't have used it after that because Miss Prince had taken her cup away before you came back to the table."

" It might have been nice," murmured Jimmy, " if you could have brought yourself to believe in my innocence without having to have it proved to you by the police."

Nigel was conscious, more acutely than ever, of an invisible gulf yawning between the pair—a gulf across which the husband made gestures of conciliation, tenderness, appeal, only to find the figure on the other side either disregarding or coldly analysing them. Nigel at this moment felt genuinely sorry for Jimmy Lake. He said :

" I'm afraid it isn't so simple as that, Mrs. Lake. If Blount's theory is correct, Nita Prince was not poisoned by means of that container of your brother's at all. So everyone is under suspicion again."

" Oh, lord," said Jimmy, in some consternation, " I *thought* all that stuff about the poison pill wasn't just routine inquiry. But why ? It's mad. Why should any one bring his own poison along when there was poison there, on tap, so to speak ? "

" I can't imagine," said Nigel, who was inwardly reflecting how fluently—in his own case, at any rate—one lie led to another. " But Blount is a remarkably intelligent and pertinacious sort of chap, and if he——"

" I think," said Alice Lake, whose hands were now folded deeper and tighter in her lap, " I think if you don't mind, Jimmy, I'd better have a little talk with Mr. Strangeways in private. Would you come up to my room ? " she asked, rising briskly from her chair.

Turning back at the doorway, Nigel caught a curious expression on the Director's face. Anger, was it ? Or disappointment ? Or fear ? Or a kind of brooding disillusionment ? A bit of them all, may be.

" I'm afraid it's at the top of the house," said Alice Lake, as she started up the stairs.

" What a lovely house it is. Difficult to warm in winter though, I should think."

" Oh, we have quite a good boiler for the central heating."

" But no fuel or boilerman nowadays, I suppose ? "

" Jimmy stokes it up in the evening. When we have it on, I mean. We ration ourselves to three hot baths a week. It's a nuisance not having a geyser."

N

After climbing several flights of stairs, the rooms on the third and fourth floors being all shut up, Mrs. Lake told him, for the duration of the war, they reached her eyrie, a work-room composed of two or three servants' bedrooms knocked into one. Here, from the top of the house, there was a magnificent view over Regent's Park. This view seemed the only concession made to the æsthetic sense, for the room itself was bare, almost anti-septic in the impression it made upon the visitor. A large kitchen table, littered with notes and sheets of foolscap paper, to which Alice Lake's eye at once automatically turned: an electric fire: a battered basket chair and a few hard ones: a few built-in book-shelves: the walls were cream-washed, and not one picture hung upon them.

"It certainly *is* a work-room," said Nigel.

"You find it rather forbidding? That's the idea. It keeps people—my husband's friends—out. I need a barbed-wire fence on the landing, really. You've no idea how, if you're a writer—a woman writer specially—people assume your time is all at their disposal. One has to fight tooth and nail for it. I don't mean you, of course. Do sit down. There are cigarettes on the mantelpiece."

Alice Lake sat on the hard chair by the kitchen table. Her eye roved once again to the papers on it; then she firmly pushed them away, like a temptation.

"Tell me, Mr. Strangeways, do you—is it my husband the police suspect?"

"I don't know who their chief suspect is at the moment. Honestly."

Alice clasped her hands in her lap, and turned to him full-face.

"You were asking about my brother just now. I didn't like to talk about him in front of Jimmy. That morning he came to fetch me—he did say something about Nita Prince."

" What did he say ? "

" Well, there wasn't much time to talk : he was only here ten minutes : and then in the taxi to the Ministry. But he did ask me if I intended to press for a divorce. I didn't, of course, as you know."

" He'd been discussing the situation with Nita ? "

" Yes, the night before. He told you so."

" I mean, he told you *then* that he'd discussed it with her the previous night ? "

" Oh, I see. Yes, he did say he'd seen her since returning to England, though he didn't tell me the circumstances."

" Circumstances ? "

" That dressing-up nonsense."

" Did you get the impression that Nita had tried to enlist him as an intermediary over the divorce ? "

Alice Lake seemed to consider this, as an abstract proposition, or a possible situation, it might be, in one of her own novels.

" No. Not exactly," she replied after a pause. " I thought he was sounding me about it for—well, for his own interest."

" He was still interested in Nita himself, in fact ? "

" You could interpret it that way, I suppose. Yes, of course he was. But I'm sure he had no idea of holding her to her engagement."

" If Jimmy had left her, gone back to you, would Charles have married her, do you think ? "

" Oh, that's pure speculation," she said, reprovingly almost, in her high, light voice. " It's difficult to think of him as the marrying type—difficult for me, I mean. But I'm probably too close to him to see him clearly."

Nigel came back to the point from another angle.

" Charles would actually do all he could to preserve *your* marriage ? "

" If he thought it worth preserving—yes, I suppose he would."

" Did *he* tell you, that morning, that the night before he'd given *Nita* a last chance to give Jimmy up ? Or suggest that he *had*? "

A look of fear and *perplexity* passed over Alice's face, the first time she had *betrayed* emotion during their talk.

" No," she said, " no, *indeed*. There's a horrible implication in that." Then, *more* calmly, " After all, when he saw Nita, he would only hear *her* point of view. He hadn't seen Jimmy or me yet. He *could* have no basis for forming a judgment about our *marriage*— whether it was ' worth preserving.' "

" You hadn't written to him about it ? "

" No, not for a long time. He was supposed to be dead, you remember."

" How well did you know Merrion Squires ? "

The sudden change of front did not seem to disconcert Alice Lake. Indeed, Nigel thought she showed relief at it. She said she had gone about with Merrion a little, during the first year of her husband's infidelity, and he had made some drawings of her.

" I suppose I had some vague, silly idea of ' paying Jimmy back in his own coin ' "—her voice put the phrase into satirical quotation marks—" but of course nothing came of it. I'm not really that sort of woman. Perhaps Jimmy would never have left me, if I had been," she added with a delicate shrug.

" I'm afraid my questions get more and more impertinent," said Nigel, smiling at her, " but an awful lot does depend on this—you used a phrase about your marriage being worth preserving—please forgive me, but do you honestly think it was ? Now ? "

Alice Lake turned her face away from him, towards the window, and the trees, the flower-beds, the lake upon which it opened. There was a long silence. Nigel believed she understood perfectly the implications of his question, and not least of the tenses he had used.

" You mean," she said at last, " you mean, did Nita
Prince die in vain ? No, that's a vulgar, hateful way to
put it. I'm sorry. Well, I can't really tell you. It's
bound to take time for Jimmy and me to get readjusted
to each other."

" And at present you're lost and miserable together ? "
Alice Lake's mouth began to tremble. She plunged
into her handbag and took out a handkerchief.

" I'm sorry," said Nigel, " but it really is very obvious.
I don't want to hurt you, but——"

" What on earth has this got to do with the murder,
with that girl's death ? " she burst out resentfully.

" I think," said Nigel, picking his words with infinite
care, " I think you suspect your—suspect someone you
love of having killed her ; and your suspicions make it
impossible for you to take up the threads again with
Jimmy. Am I right ? "

Holding her handkerchief over her mouth, she went to
the door and opened it. In a muffled voice, she said :
" You'd better go now."

Nigel Strangeways descended the stairs, wrapt in
thought. He did not leave the house, though, but entered
Jimmy Lake's study again.

" I'm afraid I've been upsetting your wife," he said
without preamble.

The Director looked up at him keenly, but made no
comment. He was still sitting in the chair where they
had left him.

" I had to ask her some rather intimate questions."

" Alice isn't a great one for intimacy," said the
Director, half to himself.

" Questions about you."

" About me ? "

" About you and her. And you and Nita."

" She wouldn't know a great deal about Nita and me.
She's—there are certain things she hasn't it in her nature

to be able to know, or to imagine," said Jimmy in a brooding voice.

" So I'm coming to you for them." Nigel fixed Jimmy Lake with an intent gaze of his pale blue eyes. " Did your wife realise how much you wanted to get free from Nita ? "

The question seemed to fall endlessly into the silent room, like a pebble falling down a well-shaft. At last Jimmy broke the silence.

" I shouldn't think so. After all, I didn't fully know that myself."

" Until you *were* free ? "

" Nigel, I could get justifiably angry about these questions. Still, I'll assume you mean well by them. Until I was free ? No. I—well, there was always a part of me trying to get back to Alice ; put it like that."

" You hoped, perhaps, that Charles Kennington's return would solve the problem for you ? Hoped he would hold her to her engagement ? "

" Ye-es. I must confess the thought crossed my mind."

" So you told Nita that this was her last chance ? "

" Last chance ? " repeated Jimmy rather stupidly.

" Her last chance to release you, to regularise her life, to have the marriage, the security she'd always wanted, with Charles ? "

Jimmy Lake moved his tongue against the inside of his lips in that habitual, meditative way of his.

" I did certainly sound her, discuss with her what should be done now Charles had come back. But I didn't talk about giving her a last chance. Why, that sounds like a threat."

" Are you sure you didn't—how shall I put it ?— didn't urge her to go back to Charles ? "

" I wish you'd say straight out what you mean. Surely we know one another well enough for that ? "

" I mean exactly what I say."

The Director shrugged his shoulders impatiently.

" I used no threats to her. You're talking about the night before her death, I take it. Neither then nor on any other occasion." He seemed to become aware that this was rather a stilted utterance, and grinned at Nigel. " And if I had threatened her, you could hardly expect me to admit it even to you."

" I can't encourage you to say anything incriminating to me," replied Nigel, attentively studying Jimmy's pale, fine-bred face. " I'm the Gestapo just at present, and there it is. The trouble is that Blount's new theory of how the crime was committed simply torpedoes all one's previous assumptions about it. I'm bound to tell you that things are now very awkward for any one who possessed another supply of cyanide, particularly if he's unable to produce it."

" Meaning myself. And Alice. And Charles, I suppose. And old Hark'ee—he can't *prove* he got rid of his pill."

" But Hark'ee had no conceivable motive for killing Nita."

" So it boils down to us three ? Quite a family party."

" I'm afraid it does seem to. And each of you had a very strong motive for murdering Nita."

The Director settled his wounded shoulder more comfortably.

" Oh, come, Nigel. Not Alice, surely. She'd put up with my behaviour for five years."

" She'd put up with it, because she felt certain you'd come back to her in the end. But suppose something had recently happened which made her realise it wasn't by any means certain. Suppose she was afraid that Nita was on the point of winning, after all."

" My dear chap, that's nonsense. Alice—well, you've seen her and me together now ; you must have seen that the returning prodigal hasn't been welcomed with a fatted calf."

" I've realised, after talking to your wife, that she's as much distressed about this as you are. She may be very much in love with you still."

" Do you really think that ? " asked Jimmy, leaning forward to Nigel with an eager, boyish look which seemed to take twenty years off his face. Then, at once, his expression grew strained again. " Oh, I see. Loves me enough to have killed Nita to get me back ? "

" That's one possibility the police will have in mind," Nigel followed up smoothly. " And then there's Charles. And a third possibility."

The Director cocked his eye at Nigel interrogatively.

" That it was done in collusion between two of you three. What about Charles now ? You must have seen quite a lot of him lately. Does he strike you as very upset by Nita's death ? "

" This is quite a new side of you," said Jimmy Lake. " Positively ghoulish. And I *will not* provide putrid titbits of gossip about my family for you. So let that be an end of it." Jimmy was smiling quite good-temperedly, but his voice had the finality of a slammed door.

" Well, then, I won't bother you any more. Except just one question. That copy of Clough you gave Nita— why did she mark one passage in *Amours de Voyage* ? "

" Did she ? Which passage ? "

Nigel recited the first few lines of it.

" Oh, yes. To be sure. You mean the capital A in the margin ? "

Nigel nodded. The Director looked confused, embarrassed almost.

" It's the sort of silly thing one does—we did. She thought the character was like me, and wrote a J against it. She was teasing me about it. And I said the woman described in the passage sounded rather like Alice, so I turned the J into an A. Poor Nita—she wasn't really pleased about it ; she couldn't bear the thought of Alice existing, even as an initial in a book."

"But she didn't rub it out, for all that."

"The whole thing is perfectly trivial," said Jimmy. "You surely haven't found a clue *there*, have you ? "

"You've explained it," replied Nigel. "There was the possibility that you might have altered the letter J because you didn't want the police to get a hint of your real character."

"Good lord ! What misguided subtlety ! "

"Well, I'll be off now. Many thanks. Is Charles about ?—he's lunching with me."

"No. He went for a walk in the Park."

Riding back on the top of a bus, Nigel was glad of the respite. The interviews had been exhausting, and he needed to revive his wits before the third, and perhaps the crucial and most difficult interview. He had to admit that he'd got very little further. Both Alice and Jimmy had given the impression of an almost pedantic adherence to the truth, as they saw it : Alice especially. There had been an under-current of uneasiness, certainly ; but no greater than one might expect in a couple still rather at odds with one another, each perhaps unable to throw off the fear that the other was responsible for Nita Prince's death. If one of these two was indeed the culprit, then Nigel could only salute the formidable skill with which the culprit had played his hand, everything apparently so natural and above-board, yet refusing to be driven or enticed into the open. Nevertheless, Nigel believed that, while one of them had sincerely told the truth, the other had concentrated only on giving the impression of truthfulness.

Nigel had been at the Club for ten minutes when Major Kennington arrived, in uniform and tearing high spirits.

"I thought you would like me to come in full regi-

mentals, my dear," was his first remark, delivered with
much *empressement* in the full face of Nigel's fellow-
members lining up at the bar for their pre-prandial
drinks.

"Sherry? Gin? Or what?" asked Nigel hurriedly.

"Dubonnet, please, if they have it. Full regimentals,"
continued Charles, "for I know it's going to be a court-
martial. I should have brought my sword, but I've mis-
laid it. Now what can I have done with that sword?
It's too vexing. I distinctly remember brandishing it as
I led my men in our famous charge across the Rhine.
But afterwards? No, it's no good, my mind is a blank.
Well, cheers, ducky."

Charles Kennington took a gulp of his Dubonnet,
oblivious to the murmurs of the serried clubmen.

"And how is the murder going?" he asked. "Any
spicy revelations to dish up? Who's making the running
for the gallows-tree?"

"Jimmy, Alice and yourself seem to have drawn clear
of the field," answered Nigel amiably. "But let's not
talk about it till after lunch."

"Whatever you say. But not Alice. I can't have that.
My sister must be above reproach. And how are things
at the dear old Min.? Shocking goings on the other night,
I hear. The Reverend Billson caught *in flagrante delicto*,
touching off incendiaries all over the place. Archdeacon
Fortescue up to some dirty work *in camera*. I seem to
miss all the fun. In my day the Min. was a very different
sort of place."

A crusted and vinous-looking clubman muttered
audibly to his companion, "Disgraceful. An office-
wallah, of course. Can't think where he got all those
medal ribbons. Looks damn fishy to me."

"Bought them, my dear sir," said Charles brightly to
him. "In the Caledonian Market. A very fine range they
have there, I can assure you, if you're looking for a good

buy. And quite reasonable. This little white and purple one I can particularly recommend—so *amusing*, don't you think ? Just like a pansy."

The crusted clubman glared and snorted, struggling for speech.

" I think we'd better go up to lunch," said Charles to Nigel, " before the *mot juste* dawns upon our gallant friend."

Nigel was fortunate enough to secure a separate table for his guest and himself, out of earshot of his fellow-members. At lunch they talked on indifferent subjects, and it was not till they were sitting in Nigel's room that the " court-martial," as Charles had called it, began. Nigel told him that suspicion was now narrowed down to Jimmy, his wife and Charles himself, and that Blount's new theory invalidated Mrs. Lake's evidence of having noticed the container on Jimmy's desk, intact, only a minute before the murder.

" Meaning that it was not used for the murder ? "

Nigel nodded.

" Somehow I never thought it was."

" Oh ? Why ? " asked Nigel, rather surprised.

" Well, for one thing, if I'd used it, I'd have taken jolly good care to drop it quietly on the floor when no one was looking ; and then it'd have been found."

" I see," said Nigel, who had received a clear impression that Charles was telling the truth but not the whole truth. " Well, then, suppose you *had* poisoned Nita— with some other supply of poison, I mean—why would you want to remove Stultz's thing from the room ? Why would you take the enormous risk of having it discovered on your person, in order to remove it ? "

Major Kennington answered quite readily.

" In order to keep the eyes of the police fixed on it : to make sure they wouldn't go sniffing around after some other source of poison."

" Exactly. So when the police do find another source —Jimmy's cyanide capsule, to which you three had access, and nobody else—and find this capsule is missing——"

" Then things look black for the old firm of Lake and Kennington," said Charles, grinning cheerfully.

" But don't you think it rather odd that, if Jimmy did use this pill of his, he should have no story prepared, to account for its disappearance ? "

" I see your Socratic method is going to have me cornered in a minute. However, my dear Socrates, I will admit that indeed of a truth it does appear to me rather odd."

" You yourself did not go to the Lake's house till the morning of the crime. You only stayed there ten minutes. And, apart from your sister's evidence that you were with her all that time, it doesn't seem possible you could have taken Jimmy's capsule out of a locked drawer and left no signs of breaking into it."

" It wasn't possible for a better reason," said Charles, a little pettishly. " I didn't know the thing was there at all."

" You mean, this is the first you've heard of the capsule ? "

Charles Kennington wagged his forefinger coyly at Nigel.

" Now, now ! You'll not catch out a hardened old poisoner like myself as easily as that. I knew years ago that Jimmy had bought himself a pill. I didn't know till a couple of days after the murder that he still had it —was supposed to have it still—and where it was kept."

" Did Jimmy tell you ? "

" No, Alice did, as a matter of fact. It just came out, *en passant*."

" She didn't tell *me* she'd told you. Still, the point is this. You did not know of the whereabouts of this capsule till after the murder. Jimmy has attempted no explanation for its disappearance, as he surely would have if he'd used it himself. Which leaves Alice."

Charles Kennington's hands clasped over his breast in that strange little dramatic gesture of his, then went out to Nigel; but there was nothing of the *poseur* in him now.

" Look, Nigel, fun's fun, but——"

" And the Superintendent told me that your sister was distinctly rattled when he asked about the capsule. I don't think this is fun at all. Of course, the police might well consider a third possibility—that you and she were in collusion over it. That might explain a lot."

" I must say, this is the most cold-blooded conversation I've ever taken part in."

" The trouble with you three is that none of you ever tells an unnecessary lie."

Charles Kennington's eyes were veiled a moment by their long girlish lashes.

" Alice never tells a lie of any sort," he replied. " She's a regular old Bloomsbury blue-stocking; a positive glutton for truth."

" She was telling the truth, then, when she told me that you and she had discussed the question of divorce, that morning you came to fetch her ? "

" Perfectly true."

" And that *you* had discussed it with Nita the night before ? "

Major Kennington did not reply to this. Nigel persisted.

" You see, when you and your sister came to Nita's flat the day after the murder, you categorically stated that you had *not* discussed the question of divorce with Nita. It surprised me at the time : you were so very forthcoming about everything else, but so very monosyllabic about that."

" What a memory you have ! It's *too* unnerving."

" Yes. And I remember you also said ' I think I put her mind at rest, poor sweet.' And yet, the next morning, the morning she was murdered, the poor sweet was in a terrible state : she'd been crying ; she told Brian Ingle she was frightened, and said she had been given ' one last chance ' to release Jimmy."

" What ho, what ho ! " exclaimed Charles. " This is turning on the heat all right ! "

" The police," continued Nigel, gazing non-committally at the end of his cigarette, " could make a good case, out of all this, for collusion between Alice and yourself. Supposing you'd got in touch with her as soon as you returned to England—she tells you about Jimmy and Nita. You go and see Nita that night : you tell Nita she must give up Jimmy, or—— Nita refuses. You return to Claridge's and ring Alice, who is alone in the house. Nita won't play, you say. You concoct your plan together. Or perhaps you just ask Alice to take that poison capsule of Jimmy's and be ready to hand it over to you next morning. You are devoted to your sister ; you'd do anything to advance, or restore, her happiness. And of course, if the police do by any chance tumble to the real murder method, you've got a personal line of defence to fall back upon—it's Jimmy's poison pill that's missing, and suspicion inevitably falls upon Jimmy himself."

" My golly ! " said Charles Kennington, " I do seem to be in the toils ! Now if only I'd brought my sword I could fall upon it in the noble Roman way."

" I hope that's not necessary," said Nigel. " If only you'd tell me what really passed between you and Nita that night. There can be only two reasons why you don't —either to protect yourself or to protect someone you love. And——"

" Jolly good reasons too, both of them. You can hardly expect me to help you adjust the noose with my own delicate fingers. Look here, Nigel——" Charles had risen, and was pacing restlessly across the room. " I say, this Bonnard of yours is a bit of all right. I wish—no, I can't : not yet. Have you read any of Alice's novels ? "

" No, I'm afraid not."

" That's a pity. It'd enable you to see what she's really like. How shall I put it ? Can you imagine Jane Austen poisoning any one ? "

" No," Nigel answered, smiling.

" You see ? You can't help smiling at the idea. The Brontë girls, now—they'd poison your teacup as soon as look at you : at least, Emily or Charlotte would have. And why ? Because they were passionate, banked-up, inverted, all-or-nothing girls. All for love. Now Alice simply wouldn't understand the feeling of all-for-love. She's madly civilised. And she's under-sexed. She loves Jimmy, of course. But her passion is evenly distributed between him and her work. Always has been. She's a *genuine* artist : it's in her blood. Suppose she did lose Jimmy—well, she's got her other love, which is just as much in her blood as he is. Her life wouldn't be empty, just because Jimmy left her. You read any of her books —see how objective she is, and dispassionate : the excesses of love, the divine or satanic frenzy—she skirts them by, just as Jane Austen did, not because she disapproves of them or wants to ignore their existence, but because they don't come within her own experience ; and she's too conscientious, too meticulous an artist—too narrow, if you like—to have a dash at them imaginatively. And another thing. Her equilibrium is a very fine one. She's aware that, if it were violently assaulted, it might well mean the end of her as an artist. She's always avoided, instinctively, violence and excess, and getting too much involved with other people's feelings. There's a natural fastidiousness—how shall I describe it ?—well, she cultivates her own garden ; she diverts just enough of the stream of life to run through it, fertilise it, without making a mess of it: a sort of ornamental stream it becomes, with miniature bridges and little tinkling artificial falls, and tame fish in it—all very decorative and un-strenuous. She's a profoundly selfish woman: self-centred, anyway. Her defence against feelings and people that would trample over her little *hortus conclusus* is to be amused by them, to poke fun at them. You see, in so far as she had it in her to hate Nita, she could get it off her chest by making a neat little image of her and running it through with red-hot needles, in a book. She wouldn't have to murder Nita. She'd get far more satisfaction from murdering her in fantasy. And that's what she *was* doing, Nigel. She showed me some of her new novel the other day: and—well, it just takes poor Nita to pieces, undresses her—it reminds me of a certain female collaborator I saw after the Maquis had dealt with her; you can't imagine anything more—more sexually deflated—than the spectacle of a bald, naked female walking away down a *rue nationale* into the middle distance, in high-heeled shoes. Believe it or not, Alice is in quite a state because, now that poor Nita's dead, her novel seems to have lost its impetus."

Nigel had listened to all this most attentively, watching the vivacious, triangular face of Charles Kennington while, his affectations and flippancy laid aside, he made what amounted to a speech for the defence. One seemed to be alternatively warmed and chilled by him, attracted by his taking up of the cudgels for his sister so loyally, repelled by the way he used them.

" And what about yourself? " asked Nigel, after a minute's silence. " Do you revel in the downfall of Nita, as you picture your sister doing? "

Major Kennington looked a little resentful.

" ' Revel ' ? That's an angry word. You are on Nita's side, I see."

"Yes, I suppose I am. I really prefer the people who bite off more than they can chew, the people who don't make reservations about love. But that's neither here nor there. What I'm asking is, how far your picture of Alice could be taken as a fair likeness of her twin-brother?"

Charles' face broke into its ugly, intelligent grin: one could almost see him putting on the mask again.

"Oh, I'm not an artist like Alice. No sublimation for me: not that I usedn't to make some of my sitters look rather foolish, in my photographer days. But, by and large, I'm a vindictive little chap, you know: a whirlpool of seething repressions; not really a very nice character. On the other hand, I do sometimes bite off more than I can chew—I did get engaged to Nita, after all."

"But you still won't tell me what you and she talked about, that night?"

"The situation. I can't tell you more than that. Not yet. You see, I don't trust any one, not even you."

"What, to interpret the evidence correctly?"

"You're an astute old thing. Yes. And I'm rather hemmed in just now by—you know, can't see the grass for the snakes."

There was a knock at the door. A Club servant entered, and handed Nigel a note on a tray. The Superintendent's writing. He tore open the envelope.

"Object A," he read, "found amongst Major Kennington's belongings. Object B, possible remains of found in ash-bucket, taken for analysis.

"Ring me at once.

"D. BLOUNT (Superintendent, C.I.D.)."

"And talking of snakes in the grass," said Charles, "you look as if you'd found a viper in your bosom."

"It's not what I have found. The Superintendent has

o

been searching the Lakes' house. He has found a poison container, identical with the one you took off Stultz."

Major Kennington's eyes blazed. His voice was suddenly very cold and dangerous indeed.

" So you had me along here to get me out of the way while the police searched——"

" Yes," Nigel broke in, " it was found amongst *your* belongings."

Charles Kennington was out of his chair and at the door, moving with the fluency of a cat. Nigel made no attempt to stop him. At the door Charles paused for a moment.

" Now you've done it," he said. " Now you *have* done it."

Then he was gone.

CHAPTER X

NIGEL was thinking of those last words of Charles Kennington's a couple of hours later. Charles was speaking truer than he knew when he said, " Now you've done it." Nigel felt the exasperation of a man who has put together a whole jig-saw puzzle but for one piece, only to find that the one piece left does not fit the remaining gap.

He had got in touch with Blount immediately after Charles's departure, to be told that the poison container had been discovered in a locked suitcase of Charles', and the lock showed no signs of having been tampered with. Blount was still at the Lakes' house, awaiting Major Kennington's return and explanation. He had said nothing to the other members of the household about his find, and agreed to keep silent about it for the present. What he and Nigel knew as " Object B " was the PHQ file which had disappeared on the day of the murder. Certain remains had been discovered in an ash-bucket and were now under analysis at New Scotland Yard : the stove had been cleaned out by Alice Lake two days before, since Jimmy's injury prevented his doing this customary chore of his, but the ash-bucket had not yet been called for by the dustman.

An hour later, Blount had rung up again. Major Kennington, he said, had recognised the poison container as the one he had taken from Stultz, but would give no explanation of how it came to be in his suitcase. The key of the suitcase, he admitted, had never left his possession. He insisted most firmly that the container could not have been planted there by someone else. Though Blount had threatened him with a charge of obstructing the police in their investigations, and had made clear to him that his possession of the container put him in a very awkward situation, Kennington had remained adamant.   Blount could, in fact, carry things no further at the moment.   For a signal had come back from Major Kennington's Headquarters in Germany to say that he had handed in his own cyanide capsule, with which he was provided for his dangerous counter-Nazi work, before leaving the country : and at the same time Alice Lake's evidence seemed to make it impossible that Charles could have taken Jimmy's capsule out of the drawer in his dressing-room before the murder.

Leaving motive out of the reckoning altogether, Blount was faced by two questions to which he had no answers at the moment at all.   If Kennington poisoned the girl, where did the poison come from ?   If he did not, what was Stultz's poison container doing in his suitcase, and why does he refuse to give any explanation of it ?   For Nigel's theory of the murder method, provisionally accepted by Blount, involved the murderer's having removed " Stultz's thing " from the room in the Ministry where Nita had died.

Since receiving Blount's second call, Nigel had been scribbling on a number of pieces of paper.   It was as though, the jig-saw puzzle having failed at the very last moment to work out, he was dispersing the pieces and starting again from the beginning.   He arranged his bits of paper on the floor in four groups, A, B, C and D, lay down on his stomach, and began to pore over them, from time to time shifting one into another column and studying the effect.   Here are the groups with which he started :

A 1 : Nita's dismay at seeing letter in Charles's handwriting, the day before the murder.   Nita's insistence (evidence : C.K.) that his visit to her that night should be secret.

A 2 : Nita's words to Jimmy, afternoon before murder (evidence : M.S.), " It's too late to back out now. You can't do it. Everyone knows, or guesses. There's no use trying to pretend you're not in love with me." Nita doesn't wish to be at J.'s party for C.K. next morning (evidence : M.S.) J. says she must. Nita's general flap over C.'s return.

A 3 : Both C. and J. visit Nita night before murder.

A 4 : Nita upset next morning. " The last chance " (evidence : B.I.) Who gave it to her ? Last chance to do what ?

A 5 : Nita's words that morning, " Jimmy is practis-ing being hard-hearted. But it doesn't work " (evidence: self and M.S.).

A 6 : Nita's playing-up to Charles when he arrived in J.'s room : ? directed at Jimmy. Why ?

A 7 : Nita's apparent determination not to give up Jimmy (evidence : Miss Sproule, Brian and others).

A 8 : Brian's analysis of Nita's temperament and state of mind. Extremely convincing.

A 9 : Nita's words to B.I. " It startled me so when I saw him. I knew he'd be like that. But it was horrible, Brian. You wouldn't understand, though." " He " presumably Charles K. Was it this " he " who gave her the " last chance " to give up Jimmy ?

B 1 : Jimmy's general losing of grip, irritability, etc., during last few weeks. His behaviour to Nita day before murder : his refusal to give her the morning off on the next day.

B 2 : Jimmy's outburst against Merrion, morning of murder.

B 3 : Jimmy's consternation (?) when C. brought Alice to the party.

B 4 : Jimmy's behaviour after being searched by Sergeant Messer.

B 5 : Slight discrepancy of evidence between J. and

C. as to whose plan it was that C. should bring "Stultz's thing" to the party.

B 6 : Jimmy's preoccupation with PHQ file afternoon after murder.

B 7 : Jimmy's line about divorce (evidence : Alice L. " I'd say he dashed straight along here and told her he couldn't press a divorce on me, it would break my heart." ? Sound psychological comment).

B 8 : Jimmy's remark on recovering consciousness after being stabbed. " Alice. She won't let me go, darling." His determination not to be taken off to hospital.

B 9 : Merrion's remark on Jimmy. " It's Alice his emotional capital has always been sunk in." M.'s analysis of the Jimmy-Nita-Alice relationships : probably sound as far as J.'s share in them is concerned. (See also A 8.)

B 10 : The initial A in the Clough poems, and Jimmy's explanation of it.

B 11 : J.'s volunteering information about his own poison capsule.

B 12 : Alice to Jimmy. " You've taken the poor girl's death so calmly," etc. Jimmy on Alice. " There are certain things she hasn't it in her nature to be able to know, or to imagine."

B 13 : J. to me. " There was always a part of me trying to get back to Alice."

C 1 : Alice's evidence about " Stultz's thing " being on the desk a minute before the murder.

C 2 : Alice—a last-minute addition to the party in J.'s room (but of course she might have been intending to come all along, uninvited). See also B 3.

C 3 : The search of Alice by the woman policeman was thorough. She could not have had the poison container then. *But* . . .

C 4 : See B 10 : the remote possibility that initial J.

was turned into A by Nita and/or Jimmy as ironic comment on Alice's character, she having been in reality extremely jealous.

But C 5 : Charles's analysis of A. this morning : even if not disinterested (wish to protect her), still rings true.

C 6 : See B 8 and B 12.

C 7 : Alice and Merrion. A damp squib.

C 8 : Alice evidently wounded because J. had not acquired a cyanide pill for her in case of Nazi occupation.

C 9 : The whole situation between Alice and J. *now*. A.'s genuine sorrow that she and J. unadjusted : my sense of the gulf between them.

C 10 : A.'s evidence about J.'s capsule. Her being rattled when Blount first inquired about it.

C 11 : Alice either suspects, or is pretending to suspect her husband of having poisoned N. Which ?

D 1 : Charles Kennington bringing " Stultz's thing " to the party : either criminal, or criminally careless. His odd little phrase about it, in Nita's flat. " How was I to know that *publicising* it would lead to——" His look of amazement when Nita fell dead (or could I have misinterpreted that look ?).

D 2 : See B 5. C. and J. the only ones who could have known the day before that there would be poison on tap at J.'s party for C.

D 3 : Charles's interview with Nita the previous night : his refusal to say more about it or explain why he originally told us he had *not* discussed the question of J.-A. divorce with N. " I think I put her mind at rest, poor sweet "—very queer, and he hadn't—see A 4.

D 4 : " There are other causes than jealousy Superintendent, for *crimes passionels* "—was C. shooting in the dark when he said this ? cf. Hark'ee's remarks to me in the canteen just before attack on Jimmy.

D 5 : Charles took away his letters to N. but left the ribbon behind, because magenta would be " death to my complexion " : well, perhaps.

D 6 : Charles's dramatic instinct. But it was not he who laid out the photographs on the floor and propped Merrion's cover-designs on the bookcase.

D 7 : See A 9. N.B. that Nita also said to Brian, " I wish I could trust him. There's no one I can trust now."

D 8 : Alice's statement, " I thought he (C.) was sounding me about the divorce, for his own interest." Her statement that C. would do anything to preserve her marriage, if he thought it worth preserving. Her great discomposure at my asking if C. had told her he'd given Nita a last chance to release Jimmy.

D 9 : *But*, unless A. was lying, Charles could not have got possession of J.'s poison capsule before the murder (? or after). *But* Stultz's thing has been found in Charles's luggage.

D 10 : Charles's extraordinary alternation of frankness and evasiveness during our talk this afternoon. His insistence that Alice always tells the truth. His parting remark, " Now you *have* done it " : curious : why " you " ?

Nigel was still sorting these pieces, fitting them into place, and still finding the same one left over at the end, obstinately refusing to complete the pattern, when he was called to the telephone. It was Jimmy Lake, inviting him to supper. Yes, Charles would be there, but not Alice—Alice was taking the evening off, as Jimmy put it.

Nigel's first feeling was of positive apprehension. This, he felt in the pit of his stomach, this is it. Not that Jimmy's invitation was unexpected : after all the poking and prodding he had done to-day, it would be surprising

if the criminal were not, somehow or other, forced out
into the open. But Nigel could hardly look forward with
any pleasure to the last act of what seemed to him a
lamentable and a wasted tragedy. Nor could he be
certain yet, with that last obstinate piece refusing to fit
his pattern, how the tragedy would turn out.

As he sipped his sherry in Jimmy's study a couple of
hours later, Nigel became aware of two things : first, that
Charles Kennington was in a state of extreme nervous
tension, and second, that there was a strained atmosphere
between him and his brother-in-law—an air of antagonism
little the less perceptible for being at present subdued to
the polite conventions. Major Kennington was drinking
heavily. Nigel had noticed at lunch that he was greedy,
gobbling his food and gulping his wine unashamedly.
The whisky decanter at his elbow, he knocked back three
stiff glasses in ten minutes. One might almost have
thought he was nerving himself for some ordeal, or some
dangerous enterprise ; yet it was not to be supposed that
there could be much wrong with the nerves of the man
who had captured Stultz. Nigel had not seen Charles
and Jimmy together since the fatal party in the Director's
room. How much the two had discussed the crime with
one another, he did not know. But he could not fail to
notice that each of them now addressed his conversation
to Nigel alone and that they avoided each other's eyes,
like two men who have recently had a quarrel and not
yet made it up. It was impossible for Jimmy Lake to be
discourteous—his good manners were bred in the bone,
as it were, a kind of innate and natural grace : but the
strain upon them just now was evident from his distrait
air, from the rather forced attention he gave to Nigel's
remarks. As for Charles Kennington, one could only say
that he was impudent. The usual charm and *brio* of his
conversation, which took the edge off its impropriety, was

lacking : he was now, as he gave Nigel a wildly satirical account of Jimmy in his pre-war Public Relations job, outrageous ; he could not have been more savagely offensive if he had been trying to provoke Jimmy into some physical retaliation.

" I can't think how Alice hasn't brought Jimmy into a novel yet," he concluded. " He's *absurdly* down her street—the champion window-dresser—he could dress windows for England ; Test Match standard."

" I did," said Jimmy, softly and coldly. " That was my job."

" And now he's spent the war holding up his distorting mirror to the nation's morale—or whatever kind of mirror it is that makes the crooked seem straight—telling them how wonderful they all have been, how brave, how industrious, how democratic, how——"

" Well, I think on the whole they *have* been wonderful. Even Charles has behaved rather well."

" A good conduct medal from *you* ! That's too dishonouring ! "

" Let's go in and have some supper," said Jimmy firmly.

There was cold chicken, salad, a trifle and a tray of drinks on the sideboard in the exquisite, white-panelled dining-room.

" Do you mind ? " said Jimmy to Charles, indicating the chicken. " I can't carve yet. My shoulder. And Nigel can cut it up for me. It's an agreeable sensation, being quite helpless like this. Back to the nursery."

When they were all served and had started eating, Charles Kennington remarked :

" Well, Nigel, we're both *dying* to hear the latest about the crime. That's why you were invited, I hope you realise that. Come along, my dear, don't be bashful, put us out of our misery. Or have you got that forbidding Superintendent of yours hidden under the table waiting to pounce on the bricks we drop ? If so, I shall definitely hold my peace."

" You *really* want to know ? " asked Nigel, scrutinising him intently.

" Really. I can't answer for our host, of course."

" I dare say I can manage to answer for myself, Charles. Nigel must tell us as much as he sees fit to tell us."

" Well then," said Nigel, " I'd better tell you first what my theory of the crime is."

" Ah, it's *your* theory now," said the Director, smiling gently. " Or is this a different one from the theory you said the Superintendent had developed ? "

" The same. Mine. I'm sorry about the deception. It was necessary, at first."

" He really is a *monster* of duplicity, Jimmy—this blue-eyed, innocent-looking Temporary Civil Servant of yours. You ought to have sacked him long ago. He'll be the ruin of you yet."

" Oh, pipe down, Charles ! Gabble, gabble, gabble all day—let Nigel get a word in."

" It was like this," began Nigel. He described how, that afternoon in Nita's flat, he had wrestled with the two unyielding questions—how was the container hidden from the police and conveyed out of the room, and why was it necessary for the murderer to convey it out of the room ?

" I thought it might be possible to imagine a satisfactory answer to the second question. I found myself arguing like this : Why does a criminal remove the weapon from the scene of the crime ? Because, if it were discovered, it could be traced to him. But in this case we had all seen the weapon a few minutes before : therefore there was no point in the murderer's removing it, and at such a risk. But the murderer did remove it. I remember thinking—it's a vicious circle, absolutely unbroken. And suddenly the word " unbroken " put an image before my mind's eye—an image of the poison container *unbroken*, unused."

Charles and Jimmy were both leaning forward, following his words with the most concentrated attention, their food forgotten for the moment.

" Supposing Stultz's thing had not been used for the murder—not used, that is to say, except as a sort of decoy ? At once the question, why did the culprit have to remove it, was answered. He had to remove it simply *because* it had not been used. It was the only logical answer to that question. It was necessary for him to remove it in order to establish the belief in our minds that it *was* the instrument of murder. For, if it were found, *unused*, the police would at once investigate what other sources of cyanide had been available to the suspects."

" That's very bright, I must say," murmured Charles, who seemed to be cold sober again.

" And that answer, you see, also gave me an answer to the first question—*how* had the murderer concealed it. If Stultz's thing was used to poison Nita's coffee, it must have been broken. I found out that the Sergeant who searched you had been a trifle careless : he did not thoroughly search the mouths of the suspects. Logically, the only place any one could have hidden the container was in his back teeth. But, if the container had been broken, there'd have been a few drops of poison left in it, or at any rate fumes of cyanide, which would have caused at the very least a severe fit of choking. Obviously the murderer wouldn't dare risk this. And nobody did choke. But, if the container was unbroken, there'd be no such risk. Therefore the container must have been unbroken. Q.E.D. Mind you, there *was* the risk of having it found in his mouth. But no doubt he had some story prepared for that eventuality : he'd say he'd put the container absent-mindedly back in his pocket——"

" *Back* in his pocket ? " asked Major Kennington sharply.

" Well, *in* his pocket, if you like—before the death of Nita. And, when the search was announced, he'd lost his head and concealed the thing in his mouth. Some story, anyway. But, if it *was* found on him, it couldn't immediately incriminate him, simply because the poison would still be in it. No doubt the police would in consequence investigate what other access he had to cyanide, particularly carefully. But, either he was prepared to risky this, or he believed that no other source could be traced to him."

" Oh dear," said Jimmy : " my poison pill. Still, there was no difficulty in tracing that. I suppose the police were searching this house to-day in order to find Stultz's thing, then ? "

" Yes," said Nigel, aware of Charles Kennington's fingers tightly laced on the table opposite.

" But surely the—the murderer—well, the first thing he'd do would be to get rid of it. At any rate, as soon as he realised the police hadn't fallen for his little trick."

" You'd think so. Of course, he might have decided to keep it, you know—for his own use ; in case everything went wrong."

" Or to use on someone else," snapped Major Kennington.

" Or, as you say, to use on someone else."

" Well, presumably they haven't found it here," said Jimmy, " so we'd better all stop eating and drinking for the present."

Charles Kennington cut in quickly.

" This is all theoretical so far. What we want to know is, whom the police propose to pin it on. Always assuming," he added, with an acrid little grin across the table, " that we're to keep up the polite fiction that it's the police who are running the case, and not our Nigel."

He addressed himself to the remains of his chicken and salad. All three ate in silence for a little. Then Nigel said :

" Very well, I'll tell you exactly what's in our minds. Perhaps you'll tell me if you can find any flaw in this reconstruction of the crime. There were three people who had a strong motive for getting rid of Nita Prince— the three people at present living in this house. Two of them, Mrs. Lake and Jimmy, had access to the cyanide pill : Charles knew about it, but apparently did not have *direct* access to it. Agreed ? Very well. The murder takes place immediately after Charles's return to England. This seems to us extremely significant. You, Jimmy, had had the opportunity and the means to kill Nita weeks or years ago, if you'd wanted to. Why then, should you wait to stage a risky and elaborate murder, in full view of seven other people ? Does it seem reasonable ? No, let me finish," said Nigel, as Major Kennington began to protest. " The second piece of evidence pointing away from Jimmy is the use of Stultz's thing as a decoy. It was essential to the murderer that it should disappear, just before the murder. But it was being handed round for inspection then. So how on earth could Jimmy *rely* on getting it into his possession, without attracting notice ? Charles, on the other hand, had brought it along : it was his : it would be quite natural for him to take it quietly back from whoever had it, at the critical moment, and then *say* he'd put it down on the desk or somewhere. But that didn't prove necessary. For, in point of fact, who did have it at the critical moment ? "

" Nigel, this is——" began Jimmy Lake, in a broken voice.

" Alice had it. She was the last person to handle it that morning. Her evidence that it was lying on Jimmy's desk a minute before Nita died cleared Jimmy of the suspicion of having used it. *But it also cleared Charles.*

Now that is very important. And it became vitally important when we discovered that Mrs. Lake had access to the cyanide capsule with which the murder was really committed, and when she betrayed great confusion at this discovery of ours. Now we know there is a strong bond between Charles and his sister. It seems natural that his first act on returning to England would be to get in touch with her, and equally natural that she should at once tell him how her marriage was threatened. And indeed, she gave evidence herself that Charles did ring her up immediately after his arrival in London. Alice now knows that only the most drastic action will save her marriage. You, Charles, have been at great pains to impress me with the idea that your sister is not a jealous woman, that she wouldn't go far out of her way to keep her husband. But when Jimmy had been attacked by Billson, he muttered something—the doctor and the nurse heard it—he was semi-conscious: ' Alice. She won't let me go, darling.' Doesn't this suggest that Alice was more retentive than we've been assuming ? And she did, after all, more or less refuse to divorce Jimmy. She and Charles agree that he should see Nita and make a final appeal to her ; and, if she refuses to give up Jimmy, they will take that drastic action. Charles will do anything for his sister—that we know. Well, he visits Nita. He gives her this ' last chance ' to release Jimmy. She refuses, though she is badly frightened—Charles' ' appeal ' veiled what was pretty obvious to her as a threat. Next morning, Charles comes here to fetch Alice. He tells her that Nita won't play. They decide to put their plan into operation. Alice has got hold of Jimmy's cyanide capsule in readiness. They go together to the Ministry. One or the other finds an opportunity to drop the capsule into Nita's coffee. Alice quietly takes Stultz's thing off the desk at the last moment, while our attention is directed to those cover designs of Merrion's. She hands it, during

the general confusion after Nita's death, to Charles. This
again is most important. It would require extreme nerve
to conceal Stultz's thing, as it must have been concealed,
during the police examination. Extreme nerve, *and* the
sort of familiarity with such poison containers that would
breed contempt. The only one of our suspects who had
the familiarity as well as the nerve was Charles. And he
got away with it. Until the police found Stultz's thing
this afternoon in a locked suitcase of his. Which seems
just about to clinch this reconstruction, doesn't it,
Charles ? "

" Would you say that again ? " asked Jimmy, staring
at Nigel with ill-concealed amazement. Nigel said it
again. He went on :

" This is terribly painful for you, Jimmy, I'm afraid.
But—well, I couldn't help noticing, when I was here this
morning, your wife's behaviour to you—the sort of
invisible wall between you, which you were trying to
climb, and she—she was defeated by : as though there
was some terrible load on her mind that prevented her
climbing."

Jimmy Lake's right hand was over his face.

" Nigel," he said brokenly, " surely this is not true ?
I can't, I *will not* believe it. Not Alice." He looked up
and gazed into Charles Kennington's eyes. " Charles, is
this true ? For God's sake, tell me it isn't."

Major Kennington was staring back at him, an inde-
cipherable expression on his face. There was a moment's
silence in the room, the sultry, toppling stillness of banked
thunder-clouds before the first clap. Then he said very
quietly :

" You should know how true it is, Jimmy. You should
know." Then his whole mien altered in a flash. He was
transformed into the alert, intelligent, dangerous creature
Nigel had glimpsed but once before—just after the death
of Nita : the man who had lived for weeks in enemy

territory and hunted down Stultz with a remorseless skill as frightening as any of the cold-blooded acts of that execrable Nazi. He said :

" Now that Alice is to be arrested as an accessory before the fact, or a murderess, perhaps you will do something about it. Perhaps even *you* will do something about it."

" I ? My dear Charles, what can I do ? I'd do anything——"

" You don't have to do ' anything.' You just have to confess. That's all."

Jimmy Lake sat bolt upright, staring at his brother-in-law. The air between them seemed to crackle with wordless messages.

" I confess ? Have you taken leave of your senses ? "

" So you propose to bluff it out, and save your skin at Alice's expense ? Well, have it your own way." Charles Kennington turned contemptuously from Jimmy. " Now then, Nigel. That reconstruction of yours. It breaks down completely at one point. You say that, on the morning of Nita's death, I came round here and Alice had her husband's poison pill ' in readiness ' for me. Right ? "

" That's what I said."

" And this was the result of a conversation she and I had had the day before ? Part of a plan we'd prepared then ? "

Nigel nodded.

" Then how did she get hold of the capsule ? And when ? The drawer was locked. The police are satisfied there is only the one key to it—oh, yes, I took the trouble to ask Blount about that. And this key was on Jimmy's key-ring. And Jimmy's key-ring is always in his pocket, except when he undresses at night. *And that night Jimmy was sleeping at the Ministry.* So much for *your* reconstruction. Now, if you'll give me your attention, both of you, I'll tell you mine."

P

Major Kennington raised his forefinger, then lowered it slowly like a duelling pistol to point straight at Jimmy.

" That window-dresser there killed poor Nita.   I've kept quiet till now, because I love Alice, and as you say I'd do anything for her—I'd even refrain from telling all I know about Jimmy in order to protect her from the horror of knowing he's a murderer, and the murder trial and everything.   But I refuse to protect Jimmy when there's a danger of Alice herself being arrested."

Jimmy was gazing at him, in a measuring, contemplative way, a quirk of a smile at one corner of his mouth.

" Well, let's see what *your* case is.   I suppose the condemned man is allowed to eat his trifle," he said, and rising from the table, walked over to the sideboard and began to help himself.   " You chaps want some ?   One of Alice's specialities.   Nigel, you ought to try it.   Hallo, what's that ? "   Jimmy's voice fell to a whisper.   " Someone at the door."

Nigel went silently to the door and flung it open.   A superb marmalade cat walked in, taking its time, gliding and pausing with the studied movements of a mannequin. Jimmy laughed.

" Good old Marmalade.   I thought it must be the Superintendent at least."

Nigel wondered again at Jimmy's extraordinary knack for lowering the tension, for gently deflating a scene by disassociating himself from it : a champion spell-unbinder. Nigel went over and helped himself to trifle, feeling slightly ridiculous, as though he were responsible for the whole pack of accusations and counter-accusations— which indeed he was, and as though they had all been proved farcically wide of the mark—which was certainly not so. Charles Kennington was, it seemed, less impressed. He had refused the trifle.   He just sat patiently at the table, and when the other two were back in their seats, took up the scene where it had been broken off.

" If you're quite ready," he said, " I'll go on. We'll not discuss Jimmy's motive at any length. Nigel has a very fair idea of it. So have I. So, in spite of his prodigious powers of self-deception, has Jimmy. He murdered Nita because it was the only way he could get rid of her. Far be it from me to speak disrespectfully of the dead : but, if a bulldog gets a grip on your throat, there's no other way to dislodge it except to kill it."

" Pepper ? " murmured Jimmy, between mouthfuls of trifle.

" And Nita was, emotionally, a bulldog. She was absolutely determined to stick to Jimmy—though God knows why—and none of the ordinary methods would prise her off him. Jimmy had tried them all—every variation of the brush-off."

" What makes you think that ? " asked Jimmy gently.

" She told me. That evening I went to see her. She told me everything. Jimmy had just made his last attempt, an hour or so before I saw her. He had tried to persuade her that she ought to come back to me. Oh, yes, he put up a positively trumpet-tongued call to decency. She'd got to do the decent thing and fly back into the arms of her returning warrior. The sanctity of the engagement ring was touched on. Pity Jimmy had not thought of that some years before. I won't enlarge upon the disinterested appeal he made to her better feelings—I have a gorge which rises rather too easily. This, by the way, answers your point, Nigel, about why Jimmy waited so long before deciding to murder her. Of course one reason was that he had the normal man's distaste for imbruing his hands with the blood of a fellow-creature who loves and trusts him—I'll concede Jimmy that. But he also had waited because he was not certain I was dead, hoped for my return, hoped I would take Nita off his hands. I returned. But Nita wouldn't be taken. She made an appalling scene that night : she admitted it. The last of many. It tipped Jimmy over the edge. He got quite distraught, she said, and kept on muttering ' This is your last chance. I've given you your last chance.' Nita had realised, of course, that my return endangered her. She felt Jimmy would leap at any excuse for breaking it off—any excuse that would salve his conscience : that's why she was so insistent that my visit to her should be secret ; she felt Jimmy might even have his pretext if he knew a man had visited her late at night."

Charles Kennington broke off for a moment, took a gulp of whisky and lighted a cigarette. Nigel was fascinated and appalled : this duel in cold blood, between two antagonists so different in quality yet so equally matched, the one projecting his accusations like a series of venomous darts from a blow-pipe, the other maintaining a cold and unflinching silence, biding his time perhaps for the counter-attack—where would it end ? Nigel had set the ball rolling. He felt now like a man who, having dislodged a pebble, sees a whole mountainside rolling and tumbling down.

" Moral cowardice is an interesting thing," resumed Charles. " Here was a man who lacked the resolution to break away from a situation in which he was deeply involved. So outraged nature rose up and did it for him. Very macabre, really. He was in the position of a man with one foot on dry land and the other stuck fast in a bog, and he thought he wanted to get back on to the dry land. The Bible recommends you to cut off your foot if it offends you, and——"

" Could you spare us the religion and the morbid psychology, and get on to how I'm supposed to have committed the crime ? " asked Jimmy Lake, in a light, wary voice.

" Certainly. I suggest you'd been carrying that cyanide pill about with you for several days, unconsciously waiting

for a crisis which would compel you to use it. You saw
your opportunity when I returned. You gave Nita her
last chance to release you. She refused. From that
moment she was doomed. You arranged the set-up in
your room very cleverly—I always said you were a good
window-dresser : the photographs on the floor, the cover-
designs on the bookcase—they were all there for you to
focus our attention upon at the moment when you put
the capsule into Nita's cup, and the moment when you
pocketed Stultz's thing. You were considerably set back
because I brought Alice along—yes, I expect Nigel noticed
your consternation at that : for you'd always had a
feeling of guilt about Alice, and you didn't want her there
just then, and you were afraid that she might see through
your little deceptions—she always could see through you.
Well, anyway, you'd urged me to bring Stultz's thing
along to show the boys. You were determined that
Stultz's thing must be demonstrably the instrument of
murder, because you knew your possession of another
source of the poison would otherwise be discovered.
That's where, by a strange irony, Alice so nearly paralysed
your plan. You remember, Nigel, that Nita's cup was
half empty when she died, which meant she must have
drunk some of the coffee before the poison pill was put
into it. She drank that part of the coffee before putting
her cup down on Jimmy's desk. He then goes to his
desk, takes the cover-designs out of a drawer, and holding
them for an instant between us and Nita's cup, to screen
it, drops the pill into it. He intended to pick up the
container at the same moment and pocket it : but something prevents him—perhaps Alice looks round—I don't
know. Now at this point he was in great danger. At any
moment Nita might drink her coffee, poisoned now, and
the still unbroken container be found on the desk. On
the other hand, he realised that, *if* somebody noticed the
container on the desk after he'd moved away to prop up

the cover-designs on the bookcase, and *if* it were established that he himself had not been in reach of Nita's cup
after the container was so noticed, then it would be
proved that *he* hadn't poisoned the cup—poisoned it
with Stultz's thing, of course. So what he has to do is
to prevent Nita drinking the rest of her coffee till he has
found an opportunity to pocket the container. And that's
why he took her firmly by the elbow, and marched her
over to the bookcase, and held her by the elbow while
we admired the cover-designs—a rather unorthodox thing
to do with Alice in the room, and incidentally the first
sign of interest in Nita he'd shown since the party began.
When Nita's telephone rings, she goes to his desk to pick
up her cup before answering the call at her table. Jimmy
follows at once, takes his own cup and at the same
moment—while we are all vaguely looking at Nita, as one
does when a person begins to speak on the telephone, he
picks up the container and pockets it."

Charles Kennington paused again, to refill his glass.
Then he continued :

" So he'd brought it off. He goes to sit on Nita's table,
in full view of everyone, so we can all see him very
definitely not slipping anything into her cup. He gives
us good measure by beating the wretched girl on the
shoulders when she is choking with the poison, and telling
her to cough it up—a masterpiece of filthy improvisation,
that. And later Alice bears witness that she'd seen the
unbroken container on his desk, thereby cosily clearing
him of suspicion. All he has to do is to get rid of the
container now. But you, Nigel, warn him off when he
moves towards a window—I fancy he meant to flip it
out then. So he has to adopt Plan B and stick it in his
back teeth for the police search. You remember how
white and shaken he looked when he came out from behind
the screen ?—I don't wonder—and how he pulled out his
silk handkerchief to mop his face ?—no doubt he spat the

container out into the handkerchief then. It's really rather funny, that." A quirk of some cryptic amusement passed over Charles's face. "However, I think it quite possible that Jimmy had intended to rig the whole thing as suicide : in which case he'd have broken the container into Nita's cup, after she'd died, taking advantage of some moment when our attention was distracted, and dropping the empty container on the floor somewhere near her. But, if this was so, two things prevented it. Her cup being only half full implied that she could not have poisoned it till just before she took her last draught of the coffee. And therefore she could only have poisoned it after she'd gone to her table to answer the telephone. But Brian Ingle piped up to say he'd been looking at her all the time she was at her table, and she hadn't done it. So suicide was out." Charles Kennington sighed. " I'm sorry to be so tedious and long and dotting all the i's ; but I've thought about the business a good deal, in my dim-witted way, and I'm compelled to believe this is what happened. The facts won't bear any other interpretation."

" It's a pity," said Jimmy Lake at once, " that you shouldn't have remembered one rather important fact, as you are being so conscientious about the facts."

" Namely ? "

" That Stultz's thing has been found in your locked suitcase. Or is your theory that I—what's the word ?— ' planted ' it there ? "

" No, I don't suggest you did. We'll return to that presently : after you've had your say. Go on. I'm interested to know how our moral Houdini will try and wriggle out of it."

The positions were now reversed. Into Charles's eyes there had come a wary, calculating look : he seemed to be measuring up his antagonist, trying to anticipate the direction of Jimmy's first thrust. The Director, who had listened with a certain humouring contempt to Charles' attack, now visibly gathered force and indignation. His fine, pale face still showed a bitter distaste for these proceedings, but also a new resolution to carry them through to the bitter end. He smiled, rather sadly, at Nigel.

" I've been hamstrung, you see," he began. " I've known all along that it would kill Alice if—if the truth about Charles and Nita came out. She loves Charles, she's bound up with him, always has been, more deeply than with me. I suppose it's natural Charles should try to save his skin by making up a case against me : I dare say I might have done the same in his place——"

" This is rich ! " exclaimed Charles, his voice crackling with contempt. " This is the prime, peach-fed ham of hypocrisy ! Well, go on."

" Your mistake, Nigel, is to have assumed that Alice had anything to do with it. Your theory that she and Charles planned it together, because she couldn't get me back from Nita any other way—well, it's awfully weak, really : surely she would have asked Charles to have a talk with *me*, try and persuade me, first ? No, for some reason, old boy, you've entirely ignored Charles' own, personal motive. It's very odd you should—I suppose he's thrown too much dust in your eyes. Charles killed Nita, for the good and simple reason that she had been unfaithful to him. *I know this*. I'll tell you how I know it in a minute."

" We can hardly wait," murmured Charles Kennington.

" I haven't worked out Charles' method with such attention to detail as he showed in his rigmarole against me. But a liar has to be extremely plausible, and a murderer always protests too much when he's trying to incriminate someone else."

" Hear, hear ! " exclaimed Charles.

" You'll alter this schoolboyish attitude soon," replied Jimmy stiffly. " As far as I can see, it was perfectly practicable for Charles to have poisoned Nita's coffee in the way he ascribed to me. At any rate, he could have put poison into the cup while it was lying on my desk, couldn't he ? There was an opportunity ? "

Nigel nodded silently.

" But how did he get hold of the container—Stultz's thing ? I know that's a snag. Alice's evidence is supposed to have cleared him. Well, frankly, I don't know the answer. It's possible that Alice may have lied about the container's being on the desk a minute before Nita's death : lied to shield Charles : she may even have noticed him pocketing it. But I think not. Alice simply can't prevent herself telling the truth. I—oh, my God, what a fool I am ! " The Director's face lit up with intelligence. " I've been assuming that the container must have been removed from my desk *before* Nita died. We all assumed this at the time, simply because we assumed that it was this container which had been used to poison her coffee. But as it wasn't, then—yes, no doubt Charles quietly went and pocketed it during the confusion when she—when she was dying : or soon afterwards. Isn't that possible ? "

Once again Nigel silently nodded.

" That's a very ingenious thought of yours, Jimmy. I couldn't be more impressed," said Charles. " But the fact still remains that I was not in a position to pinch the poison capsule out of your dressing-table drawer. So you're stymied again."

" I presume you had some other source of poison."

" Oh, I had a little lethal tablet, for my private convenience, in Germany. But I handed it in at H.Q. there before I left. Didn't I, Nigel ? "

Nigel Strangeways nodded. He had nothing to do, at present, but to watch and to nod from time to time, and let things rip. Sooner or later, one of them would make a mistake.

" Well, I dare say Charles had other ways of getting hold of cyanide. Maybe he had other trophies of the chase, so to speak. It's not my job to do the police's work for them over that. I can only say that it was he who was so keen on bringing Stultz's thing to the party and show it off—which was rather like an Arms Instructor handing round a live Mills bomb to a number of civilians —careless, to say the least. And one more thing. I admit it doesn't seem likely that Charles could have used my poison pill for the murder. But he could easily have got hold of it, *after* the murder, when he'd come to stay with us here, *and removed it in order to incriminate me*. It's very interesting that the pill should have disappeared just when the police had changed their views about how the murder was done, just when they decided to look for another source of poison than the Stultz container."

" Have you any evidence to support this ? " asked Nigel.

" Charles had always known I possessed a poison pill. The other day he asked me if I still had it, asked me where I kept it."

" That's a damned lie, and you know it ! " Charles Kennington's voice almost broke. His small, triangular face seemed to have dwindled and wizened, like the face of a dead man.

" Oh, you made your inquiry in a very tactful way. But——"

" Did any one else hear this conversation ? Your wife ? " put in Nigel.

" No, Charles and I were alone."

Nigel relaxed again in his chair. " So it's your word against his once more."

" I'm afraid so. And my word against his over his threat to Nita."

" His threat to Nita ? "

" Yes. It's got to come out now. I dare say you noticed

that a certain amount of feeling crept into Charles's words just now when he was talking about his engagement to Nita. Oh, yes, Charles may pretend—he has pretended all along—that his feelings for Nita had evaporated, that he wasn't really interested in her any more. He even removed from Nita's flat the letters he'd written to her —yes, Alice told me about that—it would have been unpleasantly revealing if the police had read them, I dare say ; might have put ideas into their head. You'd hardly believe what virile passion burned behind that— that rather misleading exterior of his."

" This is most gratifying," said Charles. " I wouldn't have missed it for worlds."

" Nita *was* frightened, poor love, that morning. You see, Charles had cut up very rough when he visited her the night before. Oh, yes, he'd given her a last chance to honour her engagement : he *had* asked her to give me up ; but for his own sake, not for Alice's. He told her, ' If you don't leave my fascinating brother-in-law at once, if you don't announce to-morrow morning that you and I are to be married shortly, I shall make quite sure that he won't have the use of you any more.' Those were his very words."

" Did she tell you this herself ? "

" No. I heard him."

Charles Kennington said in a startled voice :

" You heard me ? What the devil do you mean ? "

" After I left Nita that night—yes, we did have a terrible scene—that's why I went back to the flat, I felt I couldn't leave it like that. I'd gone to the Ministry and tried to do some work. But I couldn't. So I rang her up and said I was sorry, said I'd come straight back. She seemed to get into a sort of panic at the idea. I couldn't understand why. But it made me suspicious. I began to wonder if—well, if I'd been deceived by her all along. Anyway, I told her I wouldn't return, but I made up

my mind that I would. I'm rather ashamed about all
this. Of course, Charles is right in a way: I would
probably have seized the chance of breaking with Nita ;
I'm afraid that was in my mind when I went back to the
flat—hoping to catch her with a man. Hoping to, and
fearing to. I let myself in with my own key, went quietly
up the stairs, crept into the hall and listened at the door
of her sitting-room. It was Charles's voice I heard. I didn't
know what to make of it at first. I listened for a bit. I
heard what I've just told you. And other things. He was
prepared to forgive her unfaithfulness, if——"

Jimmy broke off abruptly, closing his eyes as if trying
to shut out some imagined scene. His face was strained,
and full of anguish. When he spoke again, it was almost
a whisper.

"The next morning—oh, Christ ! I shall never forget
it. Nita was in a terrible state. She didn't dare tell me
that Charles had visited her. She felt she couldn't trust
me, I suppose—couldn't trust me now not to use Charles
as a pretext for ending our affair. ' Affair '—gah, what
a word ! I mean, if she told me that Charles insisted on
her marrying him, was threatening I don't know what if
she didn't, well, you can see what a graceful let-out it'd
be for me. She couldn't turn to me for protection any
longer : she'd no one to turn to. But if I'd had the
remotest idea that Charles's threat was serious "—Jimmy's
white knuckles ground into his forehead—" no, I *ought* to
have known, I ought never to have let—but it seemed
incredible that Charles should try and do anything with
all of us in the room there, after showing us all the poison
container itself."

He rose abruptly and began to pace the room. The
other two were silent. Nigel was thinking hard. Charles
Kennington, huddled in his chair, seemed to have shrunk
into himself, a figure almost as tiny as its own reflection
in the convex mirror at the end of the room. Jimmy

paused at the sideboard to pour himself out a liqueur.
" Sorry," he said.   " You like one, Nigel ?   Peach
brandy of some kind."

He moved back to the table, held out two glasses,
their stems between his fingers.   Nigel took one.   The
other, Jimmy put down beside Charles Kennington.
There was a feeling of intense embarrassment in the room
—the sort of social embarrassment that might be felt if
a member of a club were convicted before his fellow-
members of cheating at cards.

" I couldn't come out with this before," Jimmy spoke
to Charles as if they'd made a tacit agreement to ignore
Nigel's presence altogether.   " But you can't expect me
to sit here and do nothing about it.   Can you ? "   There
was almost a pleading note in his voice.   " I'm sorry.
Charles.   But you drove me to it."

Major Kennington's face looked small and sick.   He
said nothing at all.

" Nigel, I suppose it's no use asking you to forget
everything you've heard this evening ? " asked Jimmy.

Nigel shook his head.   He was still waiting.   It was not
all over yet, his instinct told him.

" I'll look after Alice.   I promise you.   She'll be all
right."   Jimmy was speaking to Charles again.   " Why
don't you say something ? "

From the figure of Major Kennington, sitting listlessly
as if foundered and saturated in defeat, words at last
came.

" I *was* very, very fond of Nita."

The words were spaced out : the intonation was high
and clear, almost a mimicry of Alice Lake's voice.

" There's only one thing to be done now, Charles,"
Jimmy Lake spoke with a kind of veiled urgency.

" Yes," said Charles, " only one thing to be done."
His fingers groped out, like an automaton's, towards his
liqueur glass.

" I think—oh, damn this sling! Nigel, could you loosen it a bit; it's hurting my shoulder: this knot here—I can't get at it properly."

Nigel rose and bent over Jimmy's left arm, wrestling with the knot. For a few moments his back was turned to Charles Kennington. Then he sat down again. Charles's fingers were still round the stem of his glass. He now raised it a little, peering into the apricot-coloured liqueur. He looked up, straight at Jimmy, his eyes blazing feverishly.

" Well, here's to the shade of Nita," he said. " May she rest in peace."

There was a queer little pause.

" Go on, Jimmy," he said, " you must pledge her too."

" Here's to Nita," muttered Jimmy Lake, his voice choked and hardly audible.

The two men drank, Jimmy sipping the liqueur, Charles taking one of his usual gulps.

The next instant, Charles Kennington was on his feet, his eyes glaring, his hands scrabbling at his throat.

" God! It burns!" His voice came in a difficult, scraping gasp. Nigel was on his feet too; but, as he started round the table towards Charles, he felt Jimmy Lake's right hand clamp down on his wrist with extraordinary strength.

" No, Nigel! It's better this way. For God's sake, let him——"

Charles Kennington swayed on his feet. He retched, and struggled for breath, his face becoming suffused, his eyes fixed wildly on nothing. Then he fell sideways over the chair, twisting like a worm, and slipped away from the chair on to the floor, where he lay face downwards and twitched a little, and then was quite still.

Jimmy's hand, still on Nigel's wrist, now relaxed. He shuddered violently, and sighed—a sound of pure exhaustion.

" Don't you see, Nigel ?—I couldn't let you—I had to give him the chance to—it would have been so appalling for Alice, the arrest, the trial, hanging, everything." He spoke jerkily, pleadingly. " It was my one hope, that he'd have my poison pill on him. I'm sorry I played you that little trick with my sling. I had to give him the chance to put the pill in his liqueur, if he had it, without you seeing."

Nigel looked at him steadily. He made no comment, but only asked if he might use the telephone to call a doctor and the police.

" In the recess there," said Jimmy, and rising from the table, led the way. The telephone was concealed behind one of the white panels. Jimmy slid the panel aside and pulled the instrument out.

" What's the number of your doctor ? " asked Nigel.

Jimmy Lake gave it to him. Nigel had just started to dial it when a voice behind them said :

" Don't trouble with the doctor, my dear. Just the police. That's all we want."

Nigel whipped round. Major Kennington was standing behind the table, on the very spot where he had fallen and died.

A dreadful sound, something like the miniature howl of a man in nightmare, broke from Jimmy Lake's lips. The sound broke off, as suddenly as it had begun, and Jimmy launched himself towards the door. But Nigel's hand shot out and caught him by the shoulder, his wounded shoulder, so that he was spun round and sent staggering towards the dinner table.

Charles put himself at the door.

" Nigel," he said, " will you search him. If it isn't in one of his pockets, it'll be on the floor, I expect. But the right-hand coat or trousers pocket is my bet."

" Stultz's thing ? " said Nigel.

" Yes. In a manner of speaking."

"All right, all right, all right," muttered the Director, his voice infinitely weary. He was slumped against the edge of the table. His hand went to his right-hand coat pocket. Nigel sprang at him. The end of taking risks had come. He seized the Director's wrist before his hand was out of his pocket again.

"All right," said Jimmy again. "You needn't be frightened. It's only this." And he gently raised his hand and opened it; and on the palm lay a tiny, broken poison container.

Jimmy's head moved stupidly from side to side. His face was dazed.

"I don't understand," he muttered, staring at Charles. "I don't understand."

"It's a dummy. There was nothing but water in it. Quite wholesome. I'd certainly not have drunk that liqueur you poured it into if I hadn't known it was pure water. Mirrors have some use, Jimmy. Oh, yes, I saw you break the container into the liqueur glass, when Marmalade created a diversion. I was watching you. In that mirror there. You bet I was watching you."

"Ah," said Nigel to himself. At last that last impossible piece of the jigsaw fitted into place.

"All right," said Jimmy Lake. "All right, all right." After the long duel of wits, after seeing victory and safety assured in his grasp, and then so uncannily whisked out of it, he had no fight left in him at all. He groped for his chair and sat down. His head bowed in his right hand, he said:

"All right then. I don't mind. I'd rather. It was the wrong woman I killed, the wrong woman I killed. I've realised it ever since, more and more. Oh, Nita, I——"

He began to weep, drearily and hopelessly. Avoiding Charles Kennington's eyes, Nigel went back to the telephone.

CHAPTER XI

PUT AWAY

" THE WRONG WOMAN ? " asked Blount. " Surely he
didn't poison Nita's coffee by mistake for his wife's ? "

" Oh, no. Nita was the intended victim all right. But
Jimmy Lake had realised, too late, after he'd killed Nita
in order to get back to Alice, that it was Nita, not Alice,
he really loved. That's *his* tragedy. You know, in spite
of everything, I pity him. He was torn in two. And no
doubt Nita's temperament spared him nothing : she
gave him hell, as well as heaven."

" It was an abominable thing, though, the way he
murdered her. If it had been in hot blood——"

" Oh, yes, I know. Still, I prefer that, of the two, to
the cold-blooded way Major Kennington finally trapped
him. Jimmy had a warmth about him : he didn't mind
jumping into life off the deep end : Charles and Alice
seem meagre spirits by comparison."

" Aye, they're a couple of cold fish all right. But I
doubt we'd not have got our man, by your account of it,
if Kennington hadn't bolted him out of his hole."

The pair were sitting in Nigel's room, the night after
Jimmy Lake's arrest. The glass of whisky by Nigel's side
was untouched. He had known for some time that
Jimmy's arrest was the only possible conclusion to the
dreadful and confused events of the previous week : yet,
now it had come, he felt sick at heart. One ought to have
no compunction for a man who had carried out so
atrocious a design. And yet . . .

" I dare say you're right, Blount. Even then, Jimmy
only had to sit tight. I'd absolutely failed to make him

Q

budge myself, in spite of the case I worked up against Charles and Alice over the dinner table. I expect he saw all its weakness. But then Charles attacked him. And Charles's accusations were plumb right all along the line: it was a bit too near the knuckle for Jimmy. He was fairly stung, so he decided to pin it all on Charles and clinch the case by an apparent suicide which would also account for the disappearance of his own poison capsule. It was a wonderfully bold piece of improvisation. And he might have got away with it, if only Stultz's thing had really been Stultz's thing. By the way, what is Charles's explanation of that ? "

" Simple enough. While he was chasing Stultz, he had one or two dummy poison containers made, of identically the same pattern as the Nazis', but filled with water. His idea was to have these handy in the event of his being able to find one of Stultz's girl-friends willing to betray him : he'd get her to substitute a dummy container for the poisoned one, so that Stultz wouldn't be able to commit suicide that way when he was arrested. Charles did, in fact, get at Stultz through a girl-friend in the end ; and she did the substitution. We ought to have realised that bit of his letter to Jimmy was just his nonsense."

" Yes, you aren't likely to dislodge a container wedged in a chap's teeth by slapping him on the back."

" So Kennington took the real poison container from the girl, and brought it home with the other dummy one as trophies. It was the dummy one he produced for your party at the Ministry, and the real one that we found in his luggage."

" I should have guessed that, somehow. We both thought it extraordinary that he should have been so careless over a cyanide container. And then there was the expression on his face when Nita died—I ought to have given more value to it—an expression of pure astonishment. A girl dying of cyanide poisoning, and the container disappeared, but there was only water in the container. No wonder he was astonished."

" A pity he didn't tell us about it at once."

" I think he was not sure then that it wasn't Alice who had poisoned Nita's cup. He knew that Jimmy had possessed a cyanide capsule of his own, and he soon discovered that Alice could have taken it. So he decided to work things out for himself : he didn't trust us to arrive at the right conclusions about that capsule."

" He behaved stupidly there," said Blount. " After we —after you'd produced your theory about Stultz's thing, it couldn't really have been any one but Jimmy Lake who'd done it. He had the strongest motive ; he had the means, and the opportunity. It was he who had done the scene-setting—the photographs and cover designs in the room. And then his refusal to go to hospital when he had been attacked by Billson. That gave him away. Why on earth should he fight like that against being taken to hospital if he wasn't afraid of blabbing out the truth there, in delirium or in his sleep ? At home, there'd only be Alice at his bedside—or so he hoped."

" She'd probably have trotted straight along to you with the information, the little truth-teller."

" Oh, now, Strangeways, you're a wee bit hard on Mrs. Lake."

" I don't like these cool-as-cucumber girls. Still. You know, Blount, you'd never have got the Public Prosecutor to sanction the case against Jimmy on the evidence you possessed. Much too thin. Just little straws showing which way the wind blew—and counsel for the defence could have blown them out of the window with one puff. All of them. That capital A, for instance."

" In the Clough book ? "

" Yes. Jimmy suspected the trap I was laying for him about that. He avoided it, as he avoided several others, by telling very nearly the truth. He admitted Nita had made the J part of it. He said she was teasing him ; and *in her presence* he'd altered the J to an A, teasing back. It made it all seem quite innocent. But, in fact, if it'd been a joke between them, he'd have made a much firmer letter, a bold exaggerated sort of A, wouldn't he ? Whereas the letter was so faint I hardly noticed it at first. Which suggested that Jimmy's explanation was false. Which implied that he *had* originally altered the letter in order to divert possible inquiry into his character, his predicament, and therefore his motive. But imagine Crown Counsel trying to make a brick out of that straw ! "

" You're right there. And those words he spoke after he'd been attacked—' Alice. She won't let me go, darling.' You could interpret them two ways. Either he imagined he was addressing Alice, and referring to Nita, or the other way round. The business of the PHQ file was very strange," continued Blount, after a ruminative pause. " He did burn it in the stove at his house. It's queer, because it's the only attempt he made, till the very end, to draw any red herrings across the trail."

" It always did seem odd to me that he should have turned the Ministry upside down looking for that file on the very day Nita was murdered—if he were innocent, I mean. Yet I'm sure he was telling the truth when he said he had no suspicion of the Billson-Fortescue transactions then. My own guess was that he simply wanted something to take his mind off the murder, and this file business was ready to hand."

" You're not far out. I asked him about it this morning. What apparently happened was this : while we were searching his room, he was working in Mr. Fortescue's. On his way to it, he took the In-tray from the ante-room and brought it along with him. On top of the pile in it was a file he decided to work on at home that evening. He put this in his brief-case straight away : but, in his

confused state of mind, he didn't notice that he'd taken up at the same time the envelope with the PHQ file in it. So this went into his brief-case too. He discovered it there when he got home. In the meantime, that afternoon, he started raising Cain about the file and the prints which Billson had been so slow in supplying. It was just to take his mind off what he'd done. He says that, on returning home, he had a moment of panic. He'd never intended to try to incriminate any one else. But, finding the Secret file in his brief-case, he thought he'd destroy it—simply in order to raise a dust and confuse the issue a bit more."

"It sounds so flat and natural, I expect it's true. But it seems to be the only moment of panic he did have."

"Until I started asking about other sources of cyanide."

"Yes," said Nigel. "Why do you suppose he didn't deny possession of a poison capsule."

"That's simple. First, Harker Fortescue knew that his Director *had* possessed a capsule. Second, Mrs. Lake was in the room when I asked her husband about it, and her agitation suggested either that she'd used it herself, or——"

"Or that she suspected her husband of having used it?"

"Well, at any rate, if she had known that the capsule had been destroyed or got rid of somehow, before the murder, she wouldn't have been upset by our questions about it. Therefore Jimmy Lake dared not pretend he'd destroyed it. And there would certainly be no way for him to prove he had—we'd only have his word for it."

"So, as usual, he·made no attempt to conceal the truth? That was his policy throughout, after the crime. He is a very clever man, and also something of a moral coward. His brain told him that criminals are often caught out by their own lies; unnecessary lies; particularly murderers. And the moral cowardice, which prevented him breaking cleanly away from Nita, also made him afraid to embark on any *positive* falsehoods to us. He lay doggo instead : he shammed dead, like a frightened animal : wouldn't commit himself. Yes, it was all in character. But of course it was a fatal inactivity over the poison pill. The pill wasn't there in the drawer, and that meant one of two things—he or Alice was the murderer."

" No doubt it was the damning fact of that capsule which determined him to come out into the open."

" Yes. And his repressed jealousy of Charles. The emotion was mutual, of course."

" Jealousy ? "

" I think so. The two of them stood in a queer sort of relationship with Alice. In a way, her twin brother was the great love of her life. I fancy this close relationship with him is really what was behind the failure of her marriage. If you'd seen them last night, Charles and Jimmy, you'd agree with me. The supper party turned into a pretty naked exhibition of mutual antipathy. The jealousy they'd repressed so long boiled over. It was pure jealousy that drove Charles to attack Jimmy so viciously : and I don't think Jimmy would have tried to make Charles the scapegoat if his instinct for self-preservation hadn't been directed by jealousy."

" You haven't told me yet exactly what happened at the supper party."

" I think Nita herself must have been aware of this jealousy, intuitively," pursued Nigel. " The way she played up to Charles in Jimmy's presence when he came to the Ministry that morning. And earlier, when she said ' Jimmy is practising being hard-hearted. But it doesn't work '—she was trying to convince herself that what had passed between Jimmy and herself the night before didn't really mean anything, that Jimmy would never be able

to harden his heart against her and give her back to
Charles. I'm sure she hoped that the effect of seeing her
play up to Charles would be to stir Jimmy's jealousy and
make him realise what he would lose if he threw her
away. It was *her* last throw."

"And the supper party?" asked Blount again.
"You're very reluctant to come to that." His eyes
sparkled frostily. "It got a bit out of hand, eh? You
lost your grip on it?"

"You're damned right I did. It took me out of my
depth, and—but I'd better start at the beginning. I'd
been up at their house in the morning, as you know, and
then Charles came to lunch with me. My plan was to
sow the seeds of discord. I was pretty sure then that
Jimmy was our man, and that Charles knew—or guessed
—a good deal more than he'd told us, and that Alice
suspected her husband of the crime. But Charles and
Jimmy, for different reasons, seemed determined to sit
tight. I had to shift them. With Alice herself I had tried
the line that you suspected Charles chiefly. I got a clear
impression from her that she had been worrying about
her husband, though, more than about Charles : she was
definitely on the defensive on his account—and it wasn't
only because Nita's death had failed to bring them any
closer together ; or rather, it was clear her suspicion that
Jimmy had killed Nita was widening the gulf between
them. I suggested this to her, and her reaction absolutely
dispersed any lingering possibility in my mind that she
might have killed Nita herself. I saw Jimmy immediately
after I'd seen Alice. I didn't get any change out of him
at the time. But I did make him uneasy. Both on his
own account and Alice's. I made it clear enough that
there was a strong case against him, against Alice, and
against Alice and Charles as accomplices. Then I left it
to simmer in his mind. He would be compelled to do
something, in self-defence or to defend Alice—that was

what I hoped : he wouldn't mind Charles taking the rap
for him, but Alice was another matter. Then it was
Charles' turn. The first thing I got from my interview
with him was that he'd tumbled to the poison method but
was still holding something back."

" His knowledge that the container he'd brought to the
Ministry was harmless."

" Exactly. I mean, I realise that now. At the time, in
spite of a broadish hint of his, I didn't grasp it : he said
he'd never thought it was used for the murder ; and,
when I asked him why, he said ' Well, *for one thing*,' if
he'd used it he'd not have bothered to take it out of the
room. After a bit, I turned the beam on Alice. Charles
then proceeded to give me a long and admirable character-
study of his sister, to prove she wasn't the murdering
type, and couldn't possibly have killed Nita either by
herself or in collusion with Charles. But he wouldn't be
drawn further than that. Not at the time. However, the
seed was sown. He knew he must act fast and decisively
if Jimmy, whom he had suspected almost from the start,
was to be caught out. Mind you, I hadn't yet altogether
dismissed the possibility that Charles himself might be
the culprit. But then your message came, about finding
Stultz's thing in his suitcase. It completely wrecked my
whole build-up of the crime, which depended upon the
murderer's having removed this container after the crime
and then presumably either destroyed it or hidden it
away. Charles' reaction to this discovery was very odd
indeed. He said, ' Now you've done it ' and tore out of
my room. It convinced me Charles was not the murderer :
no guilty person could have reacted like that. But unfor-
tunately it seemed to clear Jimmy too. Not immediately,
of course : I assumed he'd planted Stultz's thing in
Charles' suitcase ; I thought he'd been driven to act at
last. But then you rang up and told me Charles admitted
having the key of that suitcase in his pocket all the time,

and said it was impossible for any one else to have hidden the container in it."

" So when he said ' Now you've done it '——"

" I think he meant the end had come, for Jimmy, and therefore in a way for Alice. I believe Charles, up to this point, had kept dumb about the containers because he genuinely disliked the idea of Jimmy's being arrested, and he guessed that, if we knew about the containers, we'd have the missing piece of evidence which would lead to Jimmy's arrest. Not that he cared much what happened to Jimmy : but he did care for his sister's peace of mind—he didn't want to help us hang Alice's husband. But now he *had* to act, if only in self-defence. And at this point, I think, the other side of his personality took control—the Major Kennington who had hunted down Stultz. I think he suddenly realised he hated Jimmy— the man who had taken his sister from him, and then deserted her for another woman, and then involved her in a hideous crime. He was going to lay for Jimmy now. To reveal the truth about the containers might not clinch the case : Jimmy might wriggle out of it somehow ; and besides, Charles wanted a *personal* revenge."

" So you were asked to supper ? "

" So I was asked to supper. As soon as I got there, I sensed fire and brimstone in the air. Charles was drinking heavily—no doubt, to help work himself up to the big scene. The antipathy between the two of them—well, you could have cut it with a knife. Charles had obviously been taunting Jimmy, hinting at this and that, before I arrived. Deliberately getting on his nerves. In fact, he'd taken a leaf out of my own book : but of course he did it much more effectively, because he felt he hated Jimmy and despised him, and he positively enjoyed putting the screws on him, whereas I didn't—not one little bit. Jimmy was very cool and wary. He knew something was bound to happen ; but he didn't know what.

Well, we went in to supper. I decided to start the ball rolling, so I told them just how I'd arrived at my theory about the murder-method, and then I sketched out a case against Charles and Alice on the strength of it. That set them off, as it was intended to. Charles at once launched into his speech for the prosecution against Jimmy. It was a venomous performance, I can tell you. And it presented the true interpretation of all the facts at Charles's disposal."

" Just a minute," Blount interrupted. " Did Mr. Lake know at this stage that a poison container had been found in Kennington's suitcase ? "

" Yes, I brought that out as the climax of my case against Charles and Alice. Jimmy could not conceal his amazement. *Another* poison container ! For he had in his pocket the one which Charles had brought to the Ministry. Well, Charles told Jimmy he'd better confess. And Jimmy of course refused the offer. So Charles went to it. He first exploded, very neatly, my own ' case ' against Alice and himself. Then he accused Jimmy to his face of having murdered Nita. He said he'd refrained from ' telling all he knew ' about Jimmy, from a wish to protect Alice. That decided Jimmy. He didn't know how much Charles had to tell, but he could assume it would be deadly dangerous to him. So he at once put his plan into action."

" Plan ? To kill Charles Kennington ? "

" Yes. I imagine it was not all done on the spur of the moment. But I doubt if he would have put the plan into action, even though it might well seem to account satisfactorily for the disappearance of his poison pill, if Charles hadn't pressed him so hard and got his goat too. Anyway, he went to the sideboard to get his second course. Oh, it was very naturally done—he gave a wonderful performance last night, Blount : it had me foxed. But not Charles. Charles was watching him in the mirror ; he didn't trust Jimmy an inch. Jimmy pretended he heard something at the door. I went to open it. It was only his cat. Apparently his cat always comes to the door during meals, if it hasn't been let into the dining-room already. I didn't know that, of course. But Charles did. While I was opening the door, Jimmy broke the poison container into one of the tinted liqueur glasses. Charles saw him do it, in the mirror, but didn't say anything. He knew that container must be the dummy one he'd brought to the Ministry. Then Jimmy sat down again, and Charles resumed the attack. The poison, as Jimmy imagined it to be, was now all ready on the sideboard, invisible in a tinted glass, to be used or not used, depending on what Charles would now reveal. Well, Charles proceeded to state a damning case against Jimmy. You'll find it all in the full report of last night's proceedings I've written out for you. Amongst other things, Nita told him the night before the murder that Jimmy had made every sort of appeal to her to release him, and finished up by threatening her, telling her he'd given her the last chance. He went on to offer an extremely offensive character sketch of Jimmy and to describe the murder method in detail. Incidentally, he put forward the suggestion that Jimmy had originally intended to make Nita's death appear as a suicide."

" Yes," said Blount, " he has admitted that in his confession."

" Well, when Charles had finished, Jimmy first pointed out that the finding of Stultz's thing in Charles' suitcase seemed to make nonsense of Charles' recent accusations. Then he got down to business. It was a masterly piece of acting. He hadn't dared to bring out the truth before, he said, because he knew it would break Alice's heart if her brother was convicted of murder. But now, more in sorrow than in anger, he must speak."

"Masterly acting? Damned hypocrisy, you mean!"
growled Blount.

"Yes. I know. I can't get over my old affection and
admiration for Jimmy, though. And he put up such a
staggering fight. I *knew* he was the guilty man; yet I
had to pinch myself not to be lulled into a conviction
that he was innocent, that it was Charles who——
Anyway, the nub of Jimmy's accusation was that he'd
returned to Nita's flat that night and listened at the door
and heard Charles threaten to do her in if she didn't
leave Jimmy and come back to him. He presented a
picture of Charles as a crypto-jealous-he-man in fact."

"But he couldn't have——"

"No, of course he didn't really go back to her flat. It
was all one flaming but not unconvincing lie."

"The dog," began Blount.

"Exactly. The dog always barked when any one came
in, and the caretaker was quite definite that the dog had
only four paroxysms of barking that night—Jimmy's real
arrival and departure, and Charles's. Jimmy slipped up
there. I now knew for certain he was lying."

"But how did he account for Charles having Stultz's
thing in his possession?"

"Quite ingenious. He agreed Charles couldn't have
pocketed it before Nita died—the evidence had proved
that: he suggested Charles had done it during the confusion just after her death. Of course, he had to skate
pretty fast over that; and still faster over the question,
where had Charles got the cyanide with which her coffee
actually *was* poisoned. He couldn't suggest Charles had
used the poison pill out of his own drawer, because the
evidence proved that Charles could not have got this
pill, without Alice's help, before the murder. And anyway,
he needed the pill to be in existence still, so to speak,
because Charles had got to 'commit suicide' with it. So
he suggested vaguely that Charles must have had some

other source of poison ; and he accused Charles of taking
his poison pill, *after* the murder, to throw suspicion on
him. He even said that Charles had asked him where he
kept it. This was another lie, I imagine. Charles protested
it was, anyway. But Jimmy could afford to leave parts
of his accusation pretty vague and thin, because (*a*) this
gave it more verisimilitude, and (*b*) Charles's ' suicide'
was to vindicate it. And for the same reason Jimmy
could afford to admit now that he *would* have seized the
chance of breaking with Nita if Charles insisted on holding
her to her engagement. It was a brilliantly-timed admission. But he had realised all along how dangerous it
would be for him to conceal his motive for killing Nita."

Nigel paused. His hand went out automatically towards
his glass of whisky, but he put it down again untasted.

" Well, Jimmy then moved to the kill. Charles of
course knew just what was in Jimmy's mind, and played
up to him. He pretended to be floored by Jimmy's
accusation. Jimmy now had to get him before he made
his come-back, because he obviously couldn't expect
Charles to lie down indefinitely under what they both
knew to be a false accusation. So Jimmy went to the
sideboard, absently poured out some peach brandy for
himself, then apologised and offered some to me. The
other glass—the one into which he'd previously poured
the liquid from the container—he put beside Charles. He
did all this very openly. I should have been able to swear
to it afterwards that he hadn't done any monkey business
with Charles's glass then."

" Peach brandy, eh ? "

" Yes, same sort of smell as cyanide. He'd got it all
planned. Presently Jimmy said to Charles, ' There's
only one thing to be done now.' Charles still looked
rather stunned, and repeated the phrase dully. *He* was
acting up too, for all he was worth."

" I don't understand how Lake didn't suspect that,"

said Blount. " Surely he must have felt it was vairy queer for Kennington to be fitting in so neatly and tamely with his plan ? "

" You'd think so. But I suppose Jimmy was too preoccupied in putting over the suicide illusion on me to notice much how the victim was behaving. He'd ascribe Charles's behaviour to his being stunned by his own comeback ; and partly no doubt to his being drunk—Charles had been drinking heavily all the evening. At any rate, having given Charles the cue-line for suicide, Jimmy again distracted my attention : he asked me to adjust his sling, and he manœuvred it so that my back was turned to Charles for a minute. During that minute, Charles was supposed to have popped the cyanide pill into his liqueur."

" And you fell for all this ? "

" Well, yes and no. I was convinced that Jimmy was working up to something. He was obviously setting the scene for a suicide. But I admit I'd no idea it was to take place the next moment, in front of my own eyes."

" That's how Miss Prince was killed. In front of witnesses."

" Yes, I know," said Nigel. " I've no excuses. Jimmy'd got me hypnotised, I confess it. A very macabre thing happened next. Charles raised his glass and asked Jimmy to drink to the shade of Nita. Charles was enjoying his little act no end. Jimmy didn't like that at all. Well, Charles took a gulp—he's a greedy chap ; I'd noticed it before—fancy swigging a liqueur like beer ! Then he proceeded to give a revoltingly accurate imitation of a man who has just taken a gulp of cyanide. I was absolutely knocked cold. I hadn't expected anything so soon, as I told him. And Jimmy got a firm grip on me, to stop me running to Charles's help—I expect he had some bad moments then, wondering if Charles wouldn't gasp out an accusation against him of poisoning the liqueur. And he said, ' It's better this way,' to reinforce in my mind the impression that Charles had preferred to take that way out. And when Charles was ' dead,' Jimmy confessed he'd done the sling trick on me to give Charles that chance ' hoping that he'd still have my poison pill on him.' I then went to the telephone ; and I'd just asked Jimmy for his doctor's number—we'd both got our backs to the table—when we heard the voice of the man who had just died of cyanide poisoning calmly announce that it was only the police we needed. That broke Jimmy's nerve, as Charles had all along intended it to. We searched him and found the dummy poison container in his pocket, broken. It was absolutely damning evidence. Poor old Jimmy."

" I'm not wasting any of my pity on him," said Blount.

" You're right, I know. But I can't help it when I think of Jimmy's tragedy—the way Nemesis hit back at him through the very woman——"

" Aye, the vairy woman. It's Nita Prince you should be sorry for."

" Oh, I am. I'd never have got embroiled in this filthy case if I hadn't had a great feeling for her. But I don't mean Nita. Jimmy did it all for Alice : and it was Alice who quite unwittingly became the instrument of the Furies. It was Alice who wrecked his original plan to make Nita's death appear as a suicide, by preventing him from pocketing the poison container soon enough. It was Alice who, simply by turning up unexpectedly at the party that morning, shaped all the events to come : for her presence there, with the motive she had for hating Nita, was bound to put her under suspicion ; and if *she* hadn't been in danger, I doubt if Charles would ever have troubled to bring the murder home to Jimmy. It was Alice for whose sake Jimmy committed the murder ; only to find that Nita's death widened the gulf between them instead of bridging it. Jimmy had gradually built up a phantasy figure of Alice during the years when she was more or less estranged from him by the affair with Nita—a figure which seemed to offer the one thing Nita couldn't give him: peace of mind. But, when he'd released himself and gone back to Alice, he saw her again as she really was—a self-possessed, self-absorbed, thin-blooded creature ; an amusing companion, pleasant enough, to be sure; but fundamentally an un-loving, un-tender woman. And Jimmy had discovered in Nita what a really loving woman was like. Nita had been too much for him, I know—too loving, too exacting, too possessive. But, when she was dead, he found out that her sort of love, with all its scenes and torments, was what he really wanted. He'd destroyed it, destroyed her, because he hadn't been a strong enough character to sustain it. But it was still what he wanted. The mere memory of it turned Alice into a ghost for him."

" Aye," said Blount, " a classical case of Nemesis."

THE END